Also by Beth Kendrick

Put a Ring on It

New Uses for Old Boyfriends

Cure for the Common Breakup

The Week Before the Wedding

The Lucky Dog Matchmaking Service

The Bake-Off

Second Time Around

The Pre-nup

Nearlyweds

Fashionably Late

Exes and Ohs

My Favorite Mistake

Praise for Beth Kendrick's Novels

"A sharp, sassy, surprisingly emotional story that will make readers laugh out loud from page one and sigh from the heart at the end."

—Roxanne St. Claire, *New York Times* bestselling author of the Barefoot Bay Series

"Kendrick's impeccable sense of comic timing and flair for creating unforgettable characters make this effervescent novel a smart bet."

—*Booklist* (starred review)

"Kendrick manages to cook up a tender, touching, and very funny story." —Ellen Meister, author of *Dorothy Parker Drank Here*

"Kendrick deftly blends exceptionally clever writing, subtly nuanced characters, and a generous dash of romance . . . a flawlessly written story." —*Chicago Tribune*

"Kendrick perfectly captures the struggle between who we really are and who we want to be. . . . This novel balances humor and emotion in a way that begs it to be read in one sitting."

—*RT Book Reviews* (4½ stars)

"Kendrick not only shines in portraying the subtleties of female friendship, but also at rendering the unbreakable bond between man (or woman) and dog." —*Publishers Weekly*

"A charming tale about finding the perfect match . . . featuring a lot of laughs, love, and irresistible dogs." —SheKnows Book Lounge

"A warm, winning story about the complications of sisterhood—and the unexpected rewards."

—Sarah Pekkanen, international bestselling author of *Things You Won't Say*

continued . . .

"A funny, charming story about the power of female friendship."
—Kim Gruenenfelder, author of *Keep Calm and Carry a Big Drink*

"An astute and charming look at friendship, love, and self-discovery."
—*Kirkus Reviews*

"A delightful romp with depth." —Heroes and Heartbreakers

"Witty, juicy, and lots of fun."
—Susan Mallery, *New York Times* bestselling author of *The Girls of Mischief Bay*

"A smart, funny spin on happily ever after!"
—Beth Harbison, *New York Times* bestselling author of *If I Could Turn Back Time*

BETH KENDRICK

NAL
NEW AMERICAN LIBRARY

NEW AMERICAN LIBRARY
Published by New American Library,
an imprint of Penguin Random House LLC
375 Hudson Street, New York, New York 10014

This book is an original publication of New American Library.

First Printing, July 2016

For more information about Penguin Random House, visit penguin.com.

LIBRARY OF CONGRESS CATALOGING-IN-PUBLICATION DATA:

Names: Kendrick, Beth, author.
Title: Once upon a wine / Beth Kendrick.
Description: New York: New American Library, [2016]
Identifiers: LCCN 2016007194 (print) | LCCN 2016012686 (ebook) |
ISBN 9780451474193 (softcover) | ISBN 9780698188501 (ebook)
Subjects: LCSH: Man-woman relationships—Fiction. | Wine and wine making—Fiction. | Female friendship—Fiction. | Families—Fiction. |
BISAC: FICTION / Contemporary Women. | FICTION / Humorous. | GSAFD: Love stories.
Classification: LCC PS3611.E535 O53 2016 (print) | LCC PS3611.E535 (ebook) |
DDC 813/.6—dc23
LC record available at http://lccn.loc.gov/2016007194

Printed in the United States of America
10 9 8 7 6 5 4 3 2 1

PUBLISHER'S NOTE
This is a work of fiction. Names, characters, places, and incidents either are the product of the author's imagination or are used fictitiously, and any resemblance to actual persons, living or dead, business establishments, events, or locales is entirely coincidental.

For Marty.

Thank you for being a great friend and mentor.

(Even if it is against your will.)

acknowledgments

A thousand thank-yous to Peggy Raley-Ward and the team at Nassau Valley Vineyards in Lewes, Delaware. This book could not have been written without your generosity and expertise.

The Etchart family gave me lots of insight into farming life. Thank you to Marty, Miles, and Mike for answering my many questions and offering information I didn't even know I needed. I'll never look at the weather forecast the same way again.

Dylan Sheridan and Erin Connal helped me fine-tune the medical plot points, Diane and Phil Sheridan helped me fine-tune the tractor plot points, and Kathie Galotti and Brianne Butcher helped me fine-tune the dog plot points. I owe all of you a drink.

Jane Porter, Betsy Etchart, Chandra Years, Barbara Ankrum, Tai Burkholder, Bridget Lavin, Jenn McKinlay, Kresley Cole, and Gena Showalter—I'd be lost without you. You are the best friends a girl could ever have.

Mark Ruggiero, you are my rock, my inspiration, and my favorite drinking buddy. Thank you for all the brilliant ideas and home-cooked meals.

chapter 1

"Bold and bruising, but that's how I like it—almost aggressive." Cammie Breyer played with her hair and gazed down at a pair of handsome men wearing five-thousand-dollar suits and Italian silk ties. "No regrets. No apologies. It'll be a sensual roller coaster." She let that image sink in, then lowered her voice to a husky murmur. "But you have to be ready for it. Are you ready?"

The two titans of industry glanced at each other, neither wanting to show weakness. The older one cleared his throat.

Cammie leaned in. "Yes?"

He looked down, then back up at her. "It's really going to be that great?"

She leaned closer, knowing her skin looked smooth and supple in the candlelight. "Spine tingling."

The men exchanged another glance. "We'll go for it."

"You won't be sorry." She straightened, but not before batting her heavily mascaraed eyelashes. "I'll be right back."

Cammie suppressed a grin as she sashayed away from the corner table at Clover and Thorn, the hippest new restaurant in West Hollywood. The bottle of cabernet her customers had just ordered cost six hundred dollars.

Please, please, please tip twenty percent.

She felt her cell phone buzz in the pocket of the black skirt she wore as part of her uniform along with an off-the-shoulder red blouse and precariously high black pumps. Before she could sneak off to the kitchen to check her texts, her coworker pulled her aside.

"What did you do to those guys over there?" Pamela whispered, craning her neck to get a better look at the industry players in the power suits. "They looked like you were propositioning them."

"I was just hustling the Araujo cabernet."

"Yeah? What'd you say?"

Cammie started laughing. "I told them it was spine tingling."

"You did not."

"I sure did. Right after I told them it was bruising and aggressive."

Pamela started laughing, too. "You're going to win the pool this month, for sure." Clover and Thorn's employees contributed each week to a jackpot that was awarded to the server who used the most outrageous terminology when upselling customers on the wine list. Last month, the assistant manager had won by describing a Syrah as a "tattooed bodice ripper."

"Here's hoping." Cammie's smile faded. "You know why I'm hustling like the rent is due?"

Pamela tilted her head. "Because the rent *is* due?"

"It was due two weeks ago. I need four hundred dollars by the end of the night, or my landlord's going to kick me out."

"Well, that's the great thing about LA." Pamela, who had been trying to land a screenwriting agent for more than a year, looked determinedly cheerful. "You can always find another apartment or another waitressing job."

Cammie rubbed her forehead. "I don't want another waitressing job. I don't even want this one." Her phone buzzed in her skirt pocket again. She turned and headed for the wine cellar. On the way, even though it was against the rules, she glanced at the text from her cousin Kat on the screen:

Ginger snapped.

Cammie stopped in her tracks. A busboy barreled through the kitchen doors and cursed at her as he narrowly avoided knocking her over.

"Cammie."

She looked back up, flushing as she realized that Sergio, the restaurant's managing partner, had witnessed her cell phone transgression. He shot her a death glare from three tables away and lifted his chin toward the couple who had just been seated in her section.

Cammie tucked her phone back into her pocket and approached the guests with the wine list in hand. When the woman in the skin-tight black dress made eye contact, Cammie tried to read her expression. Diners in this part of town at this time of night wanted one of two attitudes: shameless fawning or brazen familiarity.

She had less than a second to make the determination, so she went with her gut and spun the wine list on the table with a flick of her wrist. "Looks like someone's ready for a drink."

The dining companions exchanged wry smiles. The man said, "Next time we buy a house, I'm bringing a flask to closing."

"You bought a house?" Cammie saw her opening. "Time to celebrate. May I suggest champagne? The Selosse blanc de blanc is exquisite."

"I don't know." The man with dazzling teeth and an action-figure jawline frowned. "Champagne is too sweet for my taste."

"Not this. You'll love this," Cammie assured him. And then,

because everybody wanted what they couldn't have, she added, "It's dry and, um, loquacious. And almost impossible to get. We have one bottle left, and our supplier says he doesn't think we'll ever get more."

"We'll take it," both diners chorused.

"Excellent choice." Cammie straightened as her phone buzzed yet again. "I'll give you a few minutes to look at the dinner menu, and I'll be back to answer any questions." She excused herself and took the long way to the kitchen, hoping that the dim lighting and crowded dining area would shield her from Sergio's eagle eyes.

Another text from her cousin Kat: I knew this day would come and now it has. CALL ME.

Across the room, she saw the guests who had just ordered the cabernet trying to signal her. She pretended not to notice and darted toward the kitchen.

"Cammie!" Sergio called after her as she dashed through the swinging doors and past the line cooks.

She ignored him. In the twenty seconds it took to make it through the kitchen, past the storage refrigerators, and out the back door to the dark, fetid alley, she received several more texts:

SOS

911

OMG

WTF

IWFTF

Wrinkling her nose against the stench from the Dumpster, Cammie dialed Kat's number and pressed the phone to her ear.

"Finally!" Kat yelled by way of greeting.

"What does 'IWFTF' mean?" Cammie shot back.

"It stands for 'I weep for the future.'" Her cousin sounded distraught. "Take a good long look at the world as you know it, because everything's about to go to hell."

Cammie glanced back over her shoulder at the smog, the traffic, the unattainable dreams, and the absurdly overpriced real estate—including the crappy apartment she couldn't afford anymore. "What did Ginger do now? And hurry up, because I'm at work and I kind of went AWOL."

"You're asking the wrong question," Kat said. "The question you should be asking is, *What didn't Ginger do?*"

Cammie clenched her teeth in frustration. "Okay, what *didn't* she do?"

"She didn't die, for starters."

"Hey." Sergio slammed open the door and glowered at Cammie. "Get back in here right now, or don't bother coming back at all."

Cammie pointed to the phone with a pleading expression and mouthed, "Emergency." To her cousin, she murmured, "Kat, you're going to have to get to the point."

Kat launched into a diatribe, starting with the words "the doctor" and ending with the words "nothing left."

"Wait, what? You cut out," Cammie said.

"Now," Sergio snapped. Cammie had never noticed the vein in his forehead. She knew this was her last chance to finish her shift and salvage any chance at making rent.

But she had always put family first. Maybe because she had hardly any family left.

"You're fired!" Sergio yelled.

"Oh shit," Kat said. "You're fired?"

"Apparently." Cammie turned her back on her boss and focused on her cousin. "Please tell me this conversation is worth it."

"You know I wouldn't say this if it weren't a dire emergency, but you need to book a flight to come out here. Right now."

"Why? Spit it out."

Kat's laugh sounded unhinged and unsettling. "You know a lot about wine, right?"

"Not really. I just throw out a bunch of SAT words and hope no one asks any questions." Cammie had to cover one ear as car horns honked.

"So you can sweet-talk a sour grape?"

Cammie was certain she'd misheard. "What?"

"You need to get on a plane, Cam. Tonight. This is not a drill."

chapter 2

"This is crazy. Who buys a *vineyard*?" Cammie hugged her cousin at the Baltimore airport baggage claim. "In *Delaware*, of all places?"

"My mother, that's who." Kat hugged back, her wiry arms surprisingly strong. With her petite frame, sparkling blue eyes, and choppy red hair, Kat was often mistaken for a delicate flower. Until people noticed the scar tissue and multiple piercings. "Someone needs to talk some sense into her."

"Well, I don't know why you called me." Cammie stepped back and regarded her cousin. Growing up, Kat had been a tomboy, her knees constantly scraped and her face perpetually smudged. While Cammie had preferred reading and crafts, Kat had been in motion from the moment she got up to the moment she finally crashed for the night. As she'd progressed from a daredevil child to a sarcastic adolescent to a strong, fearless woman, she'd managed to channel all that intensity and adrenaline into a career as a professional skateboarder. Kat had corporate sponsors, devoted fans, an agent, and a publicist—or at least she had, until six months ago. At thirty-three, Kat had officially retired from the sport because of a torn knee ligament and a spinal injury.

"Delaware vineyard." Cammie spotted her huge maroon suitcase and heaved it off the conveyor belt. "Is that a real thing? I've heard of wine from California, France, Italy, Spain, Argentina, Chile, Australia, New Zealand, Washington State, even Virginia. But not Delaware."

"There's at least one Delaware vineyard, and my mother is the proud owner."

Cammie still couldn't process this information. "I have so many questions. Like, how? When? And, most of all, why?"

Kat swatted Cammie aside so she could do the heavy lifting.

"Stop that." Cammie tried to wrestle the suitcase away from her cousin, to no avail. "You have a bad knee and a bad back."

"And I still strength train three days a week." Kat looked ready to bench-press the suitcase to prove her prowess.

"Really? Does your orthopedist know that?"

"No, and he never will." Kat started toward the exit, lugging the bag behind her.

Cammie hurried to keep pace, and forced herself to ask the question she'd been pondering for the duration of the five-hour flight. "Vineyards are kind of expensive, aren't they?"

Kat glanced back over her shoulder. "You can take the 'kind of' out of that sentence."

"Then how is this happening?" Cammie was hoping that perhaps there had been a misunderstanding somewhere along the way. "Did Ginger suddenly come into an inheritance or a lawsuit settlement or something?"

Kat's expression was grim. "Nope."

"Then how . . . ?"

"It's better if she explains the whole thing."

"Give me a hint," Cammie urged. "It's a long drive."

"Hint one: She cashed out her pension and her retirement accounts."

Cammie stopped walking so she could devote all her energy to freaking out. "Oh no."

"Hint two: She sold the house and most of the stuff inside it."

"But why?" Cammie just kept blinking. "The whole time I've known her, I've never heard a word about vineyards. I mean, I know she likes to drink wine, but you don't need a vineyard for that!"

As the sliding-glass doors to the sidewalk opened, Kat turned to face Cammie. "I wouldn't have called you and begged you to come out here if it wasn't an emergency."

"Well, I'm here."

"And I'm sorry I got you fired."

"You didn't get me fired." Cammie's shoulders slumped as exhaustion and despair settled in. "I did that all on my own. I was going to lose my apartment, anyway." She paused. "I can't afford the rent without Zach."

"Zach." Kat practically spit on the concrete. "I never liked that guy."

"I did." Cammie sighed, inhaling the exhaust fumes of a dozen idling cars. "And, it turns out, I'm nothing without him. I hate to think like that, but it's true. Everything fell apart when he left."

"You were too good for him," Kat declared. "And he's going to get what's coming to him. Trust and believe." Her expression suggested that she would be more than happy to mete out his karmic retribution with her own two hands.

Cammie thought about the rave review of Zach's new restaurant she'd just read in the *LA Times* but said nothing. This trip wasn't about her personal life. She was here to help her family.

"So, this vineyard Ginger bought. How big is it?"

Kat threw up a hand. "No idea."

"What kind of wine does it produce?"

"Your guess is as good as mine."

Cammie raised her fingertips to her throbbing temples. "Any chance she can still back out?"

"I doubt it. And even if she could legally get out of the contract, she'd refuse." Kat glowered. "She's being so stubborn."

Cammie had to smile. "You don't take after a stranger."

Kat's jaw dropped. "I have no idea what you're talking about. I'm not stubborn; I'm *tenacious*. Strong willed. Goal oriented."

"Uh-huh."

"I would never buy a winery on a whim."

"But you would get married on a Ferris wheel on a whim." Cammie followed Kat through the rows of cars in the parking garage. "Speaking of which, where's Josh?"

"At work." Kat quickened her pace. "He's used more than enough of his vacation days on my mom's craziness. Just last month, he spent two days dealing with a wasp's nest in her garage."

"He's such a good husband."

"He's the best." Kat's tone was flat. "Really nice, really smart, really nice."

"You said 'nice' twice," Cammie nearly stumbled as she tried to keep up.

"Because he's nice squared." Kat paused at the end of a row of cars.

Cammie studied her cousin's expression. "Then why does your face look like that?"

Kat dropped her chin, letting her auburn hair hide her face. "Like what?"

"Like there's more to this story."

"Let's get going." Kat located her sleek black coupe and popped the trunk. "We can talk in the car."

Cammie and Kat had to work together to wedge her suitcase

into the tiny trunk space. "This is ridiculous," Cammie said. "How do you fit any of your skateboarding gear in here?"

"I don't." Kat gave the suitcase a final shove. "I used to rent an SUV when I had to haul stuff to tournaments."

"Why didn't you just buy a minivan?"

Kat shuddered. "Minivans are for normal people. Settled, suburban people. Which I am not."

"Of course." Cammie noticed a shiny white line on Kat's biceps. "New scar?"

"Yeah." Kat paused to roll up her shirt sleeve. "Railslide gone terribly wrong. You like?"

"Very badass," Cammie assured her with an indulgent smile.

"There's no minivan that can hold me." Kat jingled her car keys. "Even though I do, technically, live in the suburbs. And I talked about the weather with the mailman yesterday. And I'm married to a philosophy professor."

"A very nice philosophy professor," Cammie reminded her.

"He really is." Kat's expression tightened as she slid into the driver's seat. "So very nice."

"Ugh." Cammie pulled her hair off her neck as Kat started the engine and cranked up the car's air-conditioning. "I forgot how humid it gets out here in the summer." She picked up a magazine from the floor mat and fanned her face.

Kat looked straight ahead as she said, "I'm glad you're here. It's great to see you."

"Even though I've basically come crawling back, totally broke and alone?"

"You came back to help, and I appreciate it." Kat, who hated any hint of sentimentality, donned her sunglasses to hide her eyes. "And you're not alone. You have me. You have *us*."

This is true, Cammie reflected. Kat and Ginger were all she had now that her mother had passed and her father's second marriage had pushed her out to the periphery. While Cammie had bonded with her mother's family, her father had distanced himself. His new wife was nice enough, but Cammie felt like an outsider whenever she visited.

She frowned as she noticed the title of the magazine in her hand. "Since when do you read *Wine Spectator*?"

"I don't." Kat took the turns in the parking garage at heart-stopping speeds. "That's for you. So are the other ones."

Cammie scooped up the other periodicals stacked by her feet. "*Wine Enthusiast*, *Wine & Spirits*, *The Wine Advocate*. What am I supposed to do with these?"

"Start reading," Kat commanded. "You're taking a crash course on wine."

"Why do *I* have to read them?" Cammie protested. "I know, like, ten percent more about wine than you do."

"Exactly—you have a huge head start." Kat tossed a few dollars at the parking-lot attendant and gunned it for the highway.

Cammie braced one hand against the dashboard. "There are speed limits and other cars. Just FYI."

Kat turned on the car's stereo system. "Noted."

Cammie flipped open the cover of *Wine Spectator*. "They make Malbecs in Chile?"

"What's a Malbec?" Kat rolled down the windows so they could feel the wind in their hair as they whizzed along under the clear blue sky.

Cammie closed the magazine and considered their situation for a long moment. "Your mom's a maniac."

"I'm well aware."

"None of us are qualified to run a vineyard. She's a retired school secretary, you're a skateboarder, and I'm a waitress."

"You're a restaurant owner," Kat corrected.

"I *was* a restaurant owner. Past tense."

"Past tense," Kat agreed. "And now we're all . . . What do you call people who make wine?"

"Vintners." Cammie flinched as the magazine pages fluttered into her face.

"We're vintners," Kat echoed. "Against our will."

"Vintners who don't actually know how to do anything but drink wine."

"What could possibly go wrong?"

chapter 3

Three hours later, the car was littered with empty water bottles and crumpled paper napkins. An open pastry box sat between Kat and Cammie on the front-seat console.

"This is the best thing about coming back to Delaware," Kat said through a mouthful of doughnut. "The food."

Cammie had to wait until she'd finished her bite of cruller before responding. "How I've missed Fractured Prune doughnuts. And Grotto Pizza."

"And boardwalk fries in those giant cardboard tubs."

"And the ice cream places on the boardwalk that have, like, two hundred flavors. Remember that time you ordered ghost-pepper ice cream?" Cammie laughed. "And you cried for an hour?"

"That was your fault," Kat said. "You forced me to eat it."

"What? I did not."

"Yeah, you did. You double-dared me. In front of a hot guy."

"Peter Moore." Cammie sighed at the memory. "I wonder if he's still dreamy."

"I doubt all those faux tribal tattoos aged well." Kat shook her head. "He tried so hard to be edgy, bless his heart."

"And yet you ate a double scoop of ghost-pepper ice cream to impress him."

"Because you dared me to!" Kat pounded the steering wheel.

"So? You could have said no."

"I can't say no to a dare. You know this."

Cammie did know it, and she had used it to her advantage many, many times throughout their adolescence.

"Anyway." Kat gestured to the stack of magazines. "Are you learning anything about wine over there?"

"I'm learning that most people who own a vineyard don't actually make their own wine. They hire winemakers who study wine making for years in France or northern California. Did you know that UC Davis offers viticulture and enology as a college major?"

"We should call the department chair." Kat changed lanes as the beach traffic slowed to a standstill. "See if they have anyone who wants to do an internship in Delaware. A last-minute, unpaid internship."

Cammie sucked in her breath as they narrowly avoided sideswiping a U-Haul van. "Could you please not kill us en route? Pretty please?"

Kat tapped the brakes. Barely. "Fun sucker."

"I'd just like to live to see tomorrow. Little quirk I have." Cammie sighed and stared down at the magazine. "Listen, wine making is not something you can learn in a week or two. It's an art and science. It's a whole lifestyle. You need years of training and a ton of money."

"Then you talk to my mom." Kat took a big, angry bite of doughnut. "Because she won't listen to me."

Cammie stopped fretting about the future for a few minutes and leaned toward the open window to breathe in the fresh air. She'd forgotten how green this area was. After just a few years of living in Los Angeles, she'd acclimated to palm trees and droughts, constant light and noise, and layers of smog so thick she couldn't see the mountains or the ocean on the other side of the city. Without really meaning to, she'd gotten into the habit of rationing everything: Water. Money. The cell phone battery that always seem to dip into the red zone while she was stuck in gridlock on the 405 freeway. She rationed other things, too—love and hope and faith in herself. As if lowering her expectations would protect her from getting hurt again.

Traffic got even heavier as they approached the shore. Cammie looked at all the drugstores and restaurants lining the highway, trying to get her bearings. Although she'd spent the entire month of July here throughout her childhood and adolescence, she hadn't been back since the summer she'd graduated college, and the landscape had definitely changed. Franchises and big-box stores had sprung up from the marshes and forests.

Then the car crested a hill, and the strip-mall ambiance gave way to a quaint, old-timey beach vibe. The ocean sparkled beyond the sprawling summer homes and hotels. And there, on the side of the road . . .

"It's the Turtles Crossing sign!" Kat and Cammie both bounced in their seats as they approached the weather-beaten wooden sign. "It's still here!"

"Pull over," Cammie urged. Kat complied with the precision of a NASCAR driver making a pit stop. They clambered out of the car and snapped several selfies in front of the parade of yellow-painted turtles.

As Cammie scrolled through the pictures she'd just taken, she succumbed to an unexpected wave of nostalgia. She and Kat had posed by this sign every summer for years. Her mother had taken this picture, too, first with a Polaroid and then a disposable Kodak.

When her mother died, everyone had assured her it would get easier. Cammie had hoped she would feel it less, think about it less, as time went by. But she actually missed her mother *more* now that she was an adult. Increasingly, she wanted to share questions and experiences with her mom now that life had gotten so complicated.

But her mother was gone. By the time Cammie reached adolescence, Aunt Ginger had taken over turtle-sign photographer duties with a digital camera. Ginger had done her very best to keep the family close; she'd treated Cammie like her own child over the past fifteen years. And now it was Cammie's turn to act like a real daughter. To love and care for her aunt, despite what seemed to be a disastrous mistake.

"What?" Kat had put down her phone. "You look sad."

"I'm not sad." Cammie gave herself a little shake. "I'm just thinking about our summers out here. A month used to seem like such a long time."

"I know." Kat started back toward the car. "And now we're old."

"We're not old. You're, what? Thirty-two?"

"Thirty-three," Kat corrected as she started the engine. "And my career is over."

"Your *first* career is over." Cammie opened a wine magazine at random, skimmed an article about unoaked chardonnays, and glanced out the window as the scenery grew ever more familiar: the white clapboard sign welcoming them to Black Dog Bay, the saltwater taffy shop, the gazebo and bronze dog statue in the town square. "Ooh, let's stop and get peppermint taffy."

But Kat was too busy cutting off several other cars as she veered across lanes and parallel parked with mere centimeters to spare on either end of the bumpers.

Over the blare of honking horns, Cammie yelled, "What are you doing?"

Kat pointed out the rickety wooden fruit stand across the square. "Look! Fresh strawberries."

Cammie sucked in her breath and grabbed her seat belt's shoulder strap with both hands. The sunlight filtering through the windshield suddenly seemed unbearably warm on her skin.

Kat frowned as she reached for the door handle. "What's that face about?"

Heat prickled all over Cammie's arms. "Um, nothing."

"You love fresh strawberries. In fact, didn't you once say that Delaware strawberries ruined you for all other strawberries? Remember that?"

"I remember." *That and so much more.*

Comprehension clicked as Kat studied her face. "Oh. This is about that guy."

Cammie tried to keep her expression neutral. "What guy?"

Kat raised one eyebrow. "You know what guy."

"Oh, you mean . . . Ian?" Cammie had to force the words out. "This isn't about him."

Kat smiled archly. "Uh-huh."

"That was ages ago."

"If you say so."

"And he didn't grow strawberries. He was all about the sweet corn." Sweat beaded on the nape of Cammie's neck. "I don't know if he even lives out here anymore."

This was another lie. She was certain of very little in life, but she knew with one hundred percent certainty that Ian was still in Black Dog Bay. Staying here was the one thing she couldn't live with and he couldn't live without.

Kat craned her neck, trying to scope out the strawberry stand. "It's just two little kids."

"All by themselves?"

Kat shrugged one shoulder. "It's Black Dog Bay. They don't have helicopter parents out here. Come on, let's go."

Before she got out of the car, Cammie made a cursory effort to straighten the wrinkles out of her sundress and wipe the powdered sugar from her lips. She tried to slow her racing pulse, reminding herself that what happened seven years ago no longer mattered. Ian had forgotten about her long ago. He probably wouldn't recognize her even if he saw her—which he wouldn't, because he wasn't here.

Two girls—maybe ten and twelve—sat behind the makeshift wooden stand, lining up boxes of berries and engaging in an epic battle of "No, it's *my* turn to sit on the good stool."

"Hey, guys!" Kat sauntered up and helped herself to a sample. "Mind if I try one?" she asked through a mouthful of strawberry.

The younger girl looked from Kat to Cammie and back again. "Um . . ."

"Oh my god. *Oh my god*. These are amazing." Kat reached for her wallet. "We'll take a pint. Two pints. Three pints."

The younger girl straightened her shoulders. "That'll be twenty-four dollars."

Kat looked scandalized. "Twenty-four dollars? That's ridiculous."

The older girl came to her sister's side, her eyes blazing with indignation. "Twenty-four bucks. Take it or leave it."

Cammie hid a smile and handed over a ten-dollar bill. "We'll take one, please and thank you."

The young girls glanced at each other. "We don't have change for a ten."

"I have change."

Cammie recognized the voice immediately, and once the man came into view, she recognized the face. The tall, lanky frame he'd had in adolescence had filled out a bit and his posture was steadier and more confident, but his brown eyes, the thick brown hair, the hint of sunburn on his cheeks looked just as she remembered.

For a moment, she was twenty-two again, full of hope and hormones, falling hard and fast, so sure that he would catch her.

And then Ian's eyes met hers. His expression hardened.

She couldn't tell what he was thinking, but she knew without touching him how it would feel to rest her hands on his soft gray cotton T-shirt. Her body remembered everything.

She forced herself to look away.

Kat took a step back and let Ian and Cammie have some space. The girls, oblivious to the tension, started clamoring for attention. "Money! Give us money!"

Ian reached into the pocket of his jeans and handed over a wad of singles without looking down. The girls squealed and jumped for joy.

Kat talked the girls through the process of giving change for the ten-dollar bill. Cammie and Ian stood, facing each other, staring over each other's shoulders.

Kat cleared her throat and broke the silence. "Hey, Ian. I'm not sure if you remember me. I'm Kat, Cammie's cous—"

"I remember you." He looked right into Cammie's eyes.

"Great! Anyway." Kat cleared her throat again. "Your daughters here—"

"Nieces," he said, still staring at Cammie. "I don't have kids."

"Got it. Well, your nieces here strike a hard bargain."

"Eight dollars a pint is a good deal," the older girl informed Kat with great authority.

Ian smiled as he reached out to ruffle the girl's hair. "Our farm uses environmentally responsible pesticides, and we give benefits to long-term employees. These go for twelve dollars a pint at the grocery store by the boardwalk."

Kat helped herself to another berry. "I guess it's not price gouging when it's this delicious. This is seriously the best strawberry I've ever tasted." She turned to Cammie. "You need to try one right now."

Cammie didn't need to try one; she remembered exactly how they tasted. She kept staring at Ian, fascinated by the mix of the familiar and unfamiliar. "You sell strawberries now?"

He paused for just a moment before answering. "I grow mostly strawberries now."

Then he smiled at her the same way he had on the day they first met. Her breath caught. The past two years had been so full of worry and disappointment, it was a relief to feel something else: Desire. Anticipation. Wild curiosity.

She didn't care that these feelings would never come to fruition. She'd gotten used to wanting things she couldn't have.

"What happened to the sweet corn?" she asked.

His expression shifted ever so slightly. "You don't like corn."

She had nothing to say to that.

"We still grow sweet corn; that's the big seller at the farmers' market on weekends. But strawberries take up less land and we make a better profit."

Cammie studied the lush red berries in Kat's hand. "Are these the same strawberries we . . ."

He gave a brusque nod.

"You *sell* them?" A note of betrayal crept into her voice. "To anyone with eight dollars?"

He waited until she met his gaze. "It's not like you were going to do anything else with them."

Before Cammie could come up with a reply, Ian continued. "If you like the strawberries, you should try the blueberries." He reached across the counter and took her hand. "Here." He placed a berry into her palm.

Cammie let her hand rest in his until he finally pulled away.

Then she tasted the blueberry, which was juicy and mellow, with just a trace of tartness. She didn't have to say anything—he looked at her face and he knew.

He finally relaxed a bit. "Yeah."

"Hey, don't be selfish." Kat elbowed her way into the conversation. "Share a blueberry with your beloved cousin."

"Here." Ian handed over a pint basket. "This one's on me."

Kat laughed. "First one's free?"

Cammie could still feel the warmth of his skin against hers. They regarded one another for a moment, but before Cammie could figure out her next move, Kat started hissing in her ear. "Ask him about grapes."

Cammie tried to hold her smile in place. "What are you talking about?"

"He's a farmer," Kat pointed out. "He knows about growing stuff in Delaware."

"I'm not having this conversation right now," Cammie muttered back.

Ian lifted one eyebrow. "What conversation?"

"Nothing." She shook her head, trying to clear her mind. "Nothing."

Kat kept widening her eyes and clearing her throat.

"We have to go." Cammie jabbed her elbow in the general direction of Kat's ribs. She missed, which sent her stumbling back toward the curb.

Ian stepped forward and caught her hand again. He held on a moment longer than necessary, his thumb brushing against the inside of her wrist.

Cammie squeezed his fingers, ready to pick up where they left off. Ready for anything and everything.

He let her go and stepped back. Then he turned and walked away.

Cammie blinked and tried to figure out what the hell had just happened. She could smell the sweet, ripe strawberries in the air.

"What was that?" Kat demanded.

"That was me almost falling on my face because you weren't where you were supposed to be."

"You were throwing elbows," Kat pointed out. "I'm not going to stand there and take that. Not when I have ninjalike reflexes."

Cammie pivoted on her heel. "You got what you came for. Let's go. Daylight's burning."

"Daylight's not the only thing burning." Kat gave her a knowing look. "Summer fling, my ass."

"It *was* a summer fling! I haven't seen that guy since the summer I turned twenty-two!"

Kat sighed and pressed the pints of strawberries to her bosom. "Star-crossed lovers, reunited at last."

"Oh my god, for the last time, we just—"

"This is like the start of a romantic comedy! Hot local farmer, cute city girl who's inherited a vineyard. Opposites attract. Lots of touching and glancing in the grapevines."

"I didn't inherit anything." Cammie rolled her eyes. "I'm just here because you told me to come."

"At the end, they whip up some fancy wine that's so good, everyone in Napa cries with shame."

"Despite the fact that the cute city girl has no clue about how to grow, harvest, or make wine?"

"Yes. It's a miracle. They make tons of money, move to France, and live happily ever after." Kat snapped her fingers. "We'll call it *Once Upon a Wine*."

"That's quite a tale," Cammie said drily.

"It could be your life."

Cammie shook her head. "Nope. Ian would never move to France."

"Fine, whatever. They can live happily ever after in Napa. I'm not picky."

"Ian won't live anywhere but Delaware." Cammie turned her face away as she ducked into the car. "And if we could live happily ever after, we would have done that when we first met." She took a breath. "He, um, he asked me to stay. At the end of that summer."

"You never told me that!" Kat exclaimed.

Because Cammie had never thought she'd see him again. She certainly never thought he'd want to see her, after the way they'd parted.

Then this is it, Cammie. I asked you once, and I'm never going to ask you again.

They got back into the car, but her cousin was not about to let this juicy tale go untold.

"I'm listening." Kat gestured to the open road stretching out before them. "Spill your guts."

"I'll tell you later," Cammie lied. "Shh. I'm trying to read about tannins."

For the next two miles, Kat continued to badger and Cammie continued to deflect. Then they came to an overgrown turnoff from the main road, marked with a little painted sign: LOST DOG VINEYARDS.

Kat hit the brakes and switched on her turn signal. "Ready?"

Cammie looked at the sign, looked at Kat, then back at sign. "No."

"Too bad. Here we go."

chapter 4

"Oh my god. It's the Chateau of Woe."

The pine trees and tall grass gave way to sloping hills lined with neat, orderly rows of staked plants that Cammie assumed must be grapevines. At the end of each row, there was a short, scraggly bush.

Across the field, she could see a weathered red barn with a crooked metal roof, and a small white clapboard house with green shutters and a sagging porch that looked as though it might collapse at any moment. Huge wooden barrels were stacked into pyramids alongside the barn. In the midst of all this quaintness, Aunt Ginger's gold sedan gleamed in the sunlight. Kat parked her car next to her mother's.

"This is . . . not what I was picturing." Cammie made no move to get out of the car. "This looks like an abandoned summer camp."

"A *haunted* abandoned summer camp," Kat added. "And the crazed killer is still hiding out in the hayloft in the barn."

"There's no central air, I'm guessing." Cammie gaped at the house's peeling paint and ancient windows. "How much did she pay for this?"

Kat gripped the steering wheel tightly. "A lot."

"Define 'a lot.' I'm going to need an actual number."

Kat shook her head. "You don't want to know the actual number."

"Yes, I do. Come on, I can take it."

Kat sat back and took both hands off the steering wheel.

"Just tell me," Cammie said. "I'm a grown woman."

"Fine. But remember, you asked for it." And then Kat named a figure so impossibly high that Cammie actually felt dizzy.

"Oh no," she murmured. "Oh no, no, no, no, no."

"See? I told you you didn't want to know."

"I had no idea she even had that much." Cammie covered her mouth with her hands.

"Me neither. Apparently, all those years she was brown-bagging lunch and using old jelly jars for water glasses, she was socking money away. Very *Millionaire Next Door*."

"The millionaire next door doesn't spend forty years hoarding money and then blow it all on a whim," Cammie said. "How could you have let her do this?"

"Me? How was I supposed to stop her?" Kat sputtered. "You know how she gets!"

"Couldn't you get power of attorney? A legal guardianship? *Something*?"

"On what grounds?" Kat demanded.

Cammie gazed at the dilapidated barn, the farmhouse, the rows and rows of grapevines that she had no idea how to care for. Then she glanced down at the wine magazine by her feet and started to laugh.

Kat scowled. "I'm glad this is amusing to someone."

Still laughing, Cammie tried to explain. "We are so far past *Wine & Spirits* magazine. It's time to pray for a meteor and a good insurance payout."

Kat bowed her head, clasped her hands, and prepared to lead them in prayer when the screen door of the house banged open.

"Girls! You made it! Welcome to paradise!"

Ginger had always been a bit eccentric. She felt it was more important to be true to herself than to follow trends, which resulted in wardrobe choices that could be best described as bohemian and hair colors that changed with the seasons. Today, she was wearing threadbare navy leggings and a billowy purple and turquoise caftan, and had honey-colored hair shot through with a bit of silver. Her neck, ears, and wrists were heaped with gold and silver jewelry, and she appeared to be almost vibrating with energy.

Cammie turned to Kat. "What's wrong with her?"

"Ask her." Kat glanced away. "I'm not allowed to say."

Ginger yanked opened Cammie's door and literally dragged her out into the sweltering inland humidity. "Let me give you a hug, sweetie! It's been too long since we were all together."

Cammie struggled to regain her footing in the loose gravel. "You bought a vineyard?"

"Yes. Isn't is fantastic?" Ginger spread out her arms to encompass the sky, the vines, the soil.

"Couldn't we have just rented our usual beach cottage for the summer?"

"I've passed the beach cottage stage of my life," Ginger decreed. "It's time to think bigger."

"But *why*? What's going on? Kat said—"

"Kat didn't say anything," Kat interjected with a quick glance at her mother.

"This isn't like you," Cammie finished.

"Oh, but it is." Ginger smiled serenely. "This is exactly who I am. This is what I've always wanted. I just didn't have the courage to go after it. And then when I saw the doctor—"

Cammie lifted her chin, dark suspicions mounting. "What kind of doctor?"

"Um." Ginger started up the fluffy white clouds. "An oncologist."

"Why did you see an oncologist?" Cammie's chest tightened.

Kat was staring down at her sneakers as fixedly as Ginger stared at the sky. "You have to tell her, Mom."

"Tell me what?" Cammie demanded.

"Just a little scare." Ginger's voice was almost frantic. "No big deal."

"You were sick? Why didn't you tell me?"

"I wasn't sick. They *thought* I was sick, but doctors don't know everything." Ginger sounded supremely smug.

"What?" Kat couldn't contain herself any longer. "You were totally sick. You had pancreatic cancer!"

Cammie clapped her hand to her heart.

"I barely had pancreatic cancer," Ginger insisted. "It hardly even qualified."

Kat, perhaps sensing that Cammie was on the verge of passing out, hastened to explain. "I know what you're thinking, and yes, pancreatic cancer is usually bad."

"Terrible." Ginger didn't sound quite so smug anymore. "A death sentence."

"But they caught it super early." Kat crossed her arms, her expression both exasperated and relieved. "Mom had surgery. They got it all out; she's fine now."

"I'm better than fine. I'm living the dream."

"You had surgery and you didn't tell me?" Cammie wrapped

her arms around herself. "You had *cancer* and you didn't tell me? How could you?"

"It all happened so suddenly, sweetie. I went in to urgent care one night because I had a stomachache that wouldn't go away—"

"They thought that might have been her appendix," Kat chimed in.

"And they ended up sending me to the emergency room for a CT scan. That's when they saw it." Ginger lowered her voice. "A little dark spot on my pancreas."

Cammie stopped breathing for a moment. Her aunt patted her arm.

"They weren't sure what it was, so they decided to take it out. And it did turn out to be cancer, but it's gone now. We caught it in the nick of time."

"You are so lucky you had that stomachache," Kat said.

"It's a miracle." Ginger tugged at the hem of her caftan. "Want to see the scar?"

"No," Kat said firmly.

"When did all this happen?" Cammie couldn't disguise the hurt in her voice. "Why didn't anybody call me?"

"It happened a few months ago. I didn't want to worry you until I knew what I was dealing with." Ginger squeezed Cammie's hand. "You've already been through so much with your mother."

"Everything I've been through with my mother is why I need to know the minute either of you even thinks you might have cancer!" She turned to Kat. "You knew about this? You knew and you didn't tell me?"

"She swore me to secrecy." Kat pointed at Ginger. "She made me promise."

Cammie blinked back the hot sting of tears.

"Please don't cry." Ginger looked as though she was on the verge of tears herself. "I just wanted to protect you. And see? It was a good thing I waited, because I would have upset you for nothing. I would have said 'pancreatic cancer,' and you would have worried."

"I would have flown out for the surgery," Cammie said.

"And it would have been a waste of your time and money. I don't have cancer."

"You actually did have cancer," Kat pointed out.

Ginger waved this away. "We've moved on."

"I haven't," Kat said.

"Me neither," Cammie said.

"The point is, I didn't die. I'm alive. I'm alive and I have a vineyard." Ginger beamed and threw out her arms. "Isn't it incredible?"

"It's . . . something," Cammie murmured.

"We didn't really know you wanted a vineyard," Kat said. "You never mentioned it the whole time we were growing up."

"I had more important things to focus on." Ginger eyed her daughter's collection of scars. "How could I possibly think about vineyards when I was trying to make sure Little Miss Adrenaline Junkie survived to adulthood?"

"Whatever. I was a great daughter." Kat ticked off her virtues on her fingers. "I never did drugs, I never got arrested, I never dropped out of high school—"

"You cut class to go to the skate park!" Ginger cried.

"Yeah, but I graduated."

"You dyed your hair blue," her mother countered. "The week before senior pictures."

"Only because you were going to make me wear pearls and that pink dress with the damn bow at the waist." Kat appealed to Cammie. "She can't force pearls and a pink bow on me and not expect retaliation."

Cammie nodded sagely, but she couldn't really relate to Kat's teenage-rebellion phase. She had devoted her own high school years to striving. She'd wanted to look and dress and behave just like her cute, carefree classmates. Classmates who had real families and normal lives. Cammie had felt like a field anthropologist studying the customs of an exotic and emotionally volatile tribe: Flirting. Shopping. Applying three hues of eyeshadow so it looked "natural." Bitching about your mother.

Except, of course, she hadn't had a mother to bitch about. The closest thing she had was her aunt. And who could ever complain about Ginger?

"You were trying to oppress me!" Kat yelled at her mother. "Why couldn't you just let me be who I was?"

"What are you talking about?" Ginger yelled back. "I never oppressed you! I spent thousands of dollars on skate gear! I drove you to all those competitions, not to mention the emergency-room visits afterward! I just wanted my seventeen-year-old daughter to have a nice senior picture!"

"It was nice!"

"Your hair was blue!"

Cammie stepped in and tried to speak soothingly. "You know, maybe we should just take a breath."

Kat was all but hopping up and down. "That's it! Cammie, we're dyeing our hair tonight. Purple for you; blue for me."

"Don't you dare!" Ginger narrowed her eyes. "You may be a legal adult, but you're still my daughter. And as long as you're under *my* roof, young lady—"

"Guys." Cammie clapped her hand like a grade-school teacher calling the class to order. "That was a long time ago. We've all changed a lot since then—"

"*Some* of us have," Kat muttered.

"—and it's so nice to be back together again. We're happy and healthy, and that's the important thing." She glanced at Ginger. "Right?"

"Right."

"Okay, then." Cammie opened her arms. "Group hug?"

Her cousin and aunt obliged. By the time they came out of the hug, Kat and Ginger had reconciled with each other and turned on Cammie.

"You know, Cammie, you're too afraid of conflict. There's nothing wrong with being assertive," Ginger said.

"Yeah, no one respects a pushover," Kat agreed.

"Sometimes you need to crack a few skulls," Ginger finished.

Cammie gawked at them. "Are you listening to yourselves? Really? 'Crack a few skulls?'"

"We're just saying, nice guys finish last." No one mentioned Zach's name. No one had to; they were clearly all thinking about him.

"Yes, crack a few skulls. She would know." Ginger nudged Kat. "Three concussions, four broken bones, and counting."

"Ah yes, multiple head injuries." Cammie raised her eyebrow at Kat. "That explains so much." She addressed her aunt. "Anyway. If you're interested in wine, might I suggest a trip to Napa? Perhaps a little jaunt to Bordeaux? You didn't have to buy a whole vineyard."

"Oh, I know I didn't *have* to. I *wanted* to. This vineyard is my gift to myself," Ginger said. "For surviving single motherhood. For cheating death, thanks to a stomachache. After the doctors saw that dark spot, I had to wait for surgery. And the whole time I was waiting, I thought about the things I hadn't done with my life. All the dreams I never chased, all the excuses I made. And I promised myself that if I didn't die, I would do things differently. So here I am."

Cammie couldn't argue with that. Her aunt had done more than her share, raising Kat by herself after her husband walked out, and raising Cammie after her sister died. Ginger had spent her entire adult life sacrificing for everyone else. Who the hell was Cammie to tell her she shouldn't buy a vineyard?

"It's also my gift to you girls." Ginger nodded at the house, the barn with the sloping roof, the weeds, the rows of delicate green vines. "One day, all of this will be yours."

Kat gave a strangled cough.

"This is your inheritance." Ginger rocked back on her heels and waited for applause and adulation.

Cammie chose her words very carefully. "We're happy that you're happy."

Ginger beamed. "You're sweet."

"But, and I'm just asking out of curiosity . . ." Cammie glanced over at Kat. "What happens if this doesn't work out?"

Ginger tilted her head. "What do you mean?"

"Well—and I'm just free-associating here—what if, by some chance, the whole wine thing doesn't work out?"

"Oh." Ginger waved one hand. "That."

"Yes. That. Because of the whole 'we don't know anything about making wine' thing."

"We'll figure it out." Ginger shrugged, her bracelets jangling. "It's glorified grape juice; how hard can it be?"

Cammie looked to Kat for help, but Kat had checked out of this conversation. Cammie could practically see the screensaver in her cousin's eyes.

"It'll be fine." Her aunt beamed. "I trust the universe."

"Um . . ."

"And, more importantly, I trust you, Cammie. You know all about wine."

"Um . . ."

Ginger leaned closer and whispered, "This is your second chance. I know things didn't work out in California, but you'll make it work this time. I have faith."

Cammie shut down. Her head ached; her stomach soured. She

didn't want Ginger to trust her. She didn't want to be responsible for yet another failure.

Ginger seemed oblivious to her anguish. "Besides, if this doesn't work out, I have a backup plan."

Kat snapped back to attention. "Oh yeah? What's that?"

"Worst-case scenario, I can always move in with one of you girls."

chapter 5

"Breathe," Cammie said, as much to herself as to Kat. "Breathe."

"If there was ever an appropriate time to hyperventilate, this is it!" Kat cried. "What are we going to do?"

"I don't know, but I'm going home." As soon as the word left her lips, Cammie realized that she had nowhere to go. Los Angeles was no longer an option. She'd given up her apartment and her job.

"What? You can't just quit!"

"Sure I can." Cammie tried to sound casual. "It's easy."

"No." Kat's eyes gleamed with determination. "Nobody's quitting. No one walks away until this place turns a profit."

"Kat, I know you're all gritty and hard-core, and that's great." Cammie took a deep breath, trying to quell the rising panic. "But do you have any idea how hard it is to make a profit here? Vineyards are a money pit. Unless you're a celebrity or a fifth-generation winemaker, it's not going to happen."

"You don't know that."

"Yes." Cammie looked at her. "I do."

"Okay, you do." But Kat seemed more determined by the moment. "So we have to bring our A game. Every competition of my life was just a warm-up for this."

Cammie leaned back against the side of the car and waited for reality to sink in.

Thirty seconds later, Kat frowned. "So, uh, where do we start?"

"We don't," Cammie said. "I'm telling you, we need to walk away. We'll put this place up for sale tomorrow and cut our losses."

Kat started to protest, but Cammie interrupted.

"No. I'm serious, Kat. I'm not doing this again. This is doomed to fail."

Kat joined her at the side of the car. "I hear you."

"Good."

They stood in silence, staring off into the clear blue sky and smelling the faint trace of grass and soil.

"Well, if you don't want to talk about the vineyard, let's talk about the hot farmer." Kat raised her voice and said, "Hey, Mom! Guess who we saw on our way into town?"

"Who?" Ginger hurried to join them.

"Remember that guy Cammie dated the summer after she graduated college? Well, he's still here and he—"

"Let's talk about the vineyard." Cammie silenced Kat with her palm and shifted her brain into business mode. "The first priority is cash flow. We need to pay for water, labor, and equipment."

Kat pulled out her phone and started taking notes.

"How much do we have coming in per month right now?" She looked at her aunt.

Ginger stared back blankly. "Well, nothing yet, dear."

"But we have to make and package the product before we'll see any profit." Cammie glanced around at the rows of vines. "We're going to be hemorrhaging money till harvest." She paused. "Which brings up another important question: How are we going to make the wine when harvest time gets here?"

Ginger patted her hair. "We have some time to figure that out."

"You're forgetting the biggest issue," Kat pointed out. "What the hell are we supposed to do with these grapes today? Right now?"

They all looked at one another.

Cammie crossed her arms. "What did the previous owners say about all this when you bought it?"

"They said that this was a hobby and they spent only two weeks a year at the property," Ginger reported, her confidence faltering. "The husband was a fancy Wall Street banker who used to hand out bottles of his wine to his friends at Christmas."

Kat shifted her weight and leaned toward Cammie. "Gee. If only we knew someone who knew something about growing grapes. Someone like, oh, I don't know—*a farmer*."

Ginger's face lit up. "That's a great idea!"

"No." Cammie shook her head. "Just no."

"Why not?" Ginger and Kat demanded together.

Cammie sidestepped the issue. "The grapes aren't going to matter if we can't make it to fall without going bankrupt."

"I can stake us some cash." Kat tucked a strand of hair behind her ear. "Josh found a great financial manager and invested most of my earnings. We were going to save it for . . . Well, never mind. I can have a check in about a week."

"Josh takes such good care of you." Ginger shaded her eyes with her hand and studied Kat's expression. "Where is he, anyway?"

"In Maryland," Kat replied ever so casually.

"Is he teaching over the summer? I thought he'd be here with you."

Kat mumbled something incomprehensible.

"He'll come out and join us, won't he?" Ginger pressed.

"Mom." Kat's tone made Cammie flinch. "Drop it."

Ginger clutched her daughter's arm. "Oh dear. Is there something wrong between you two? Tell me everything."

Kat wrenched her arm away. "This summer is about your crisis, not mine."

Ginger gasped. "So you admit there's a crisis."

Cammie stepped in between them. "If we're going to fight all day, can we at least do it in the house? It's hot out here."

Everyone could agree on this, at least. Kat strode toward the house with Cammie and Ginger on her heels.

"You know how I adore Josh," Ginger started. "Whatever is going on with you two—"

"Don't try to make this about me, Mother."

Cammie sucked in her breath and hung back. When Kat started referring to her mom as "Mother," it was time to duck and cover.

"The only reason I'm here instead of back in Maryland with Josh is that you decided to throw away your life's savings after you watched the Travel Channel in a hospital waiting room."

Ginger's mouth dropped open as they climbed the creaky steps up to the porch. "Is that what you think this is about? A few minutes of watching the Travel Channel? For your information, I've wanted to buy a vineyard ever since your father and I honeymooned in Europe forty years ago."

At the mention of her father, Kat looked a bit sheepish.

"We went to Italy," Ginger informed them as they reached the front door. "We toured lots of vineyards." She turned to Cammie. "Red super Tuscans like you wouldn't believe." Back to Kat. "The sun and soil and fruit. It seemed like such a wholesome, simple life. We agreed that when we retired, we'd buy our own vineyard. But then, of course, he left, and I had to get practical."

Kat mumbled an apology.

"I've been thinking about this for decades," Ginger continued.

"I did my job, I raised my child, and now I can do anything I please." She held open the screen door. "Now stop talking back and make yourselves at home."

From Ginger's description of the vineyard's previous owners, Cammie expected the farmhouse's interior to look cozy and rustic but luxurious—lots of exposed beams and exposed brick. Instead, she found wide wooden floor planks, fading floral wallpaper, and dust. So much dust. What had once been the front parlor had been converted into a tasting room, complete with a bar and several empty wine barrels that were, presumably, intended to serve as tables. The curtains were lacy, the windowpanes were smudged, and the old-fashioned wallpaper looked out of place with Ginger's furniture, most of which was midcentury modern.

"It's . . ." Kat trailed off.

"A work in progress," Ginger finished. "We'll redecorate later."

Cammie walked past the parlor and checked out the rest of the first floor, which included a large, sunny kitchen; a refurbished bathroom; and a pantry as big as the closet in her LA apartment. She was reaching for the basement door when she heard Kat's voice sharpen in the parlor.

"Hey! Put down my phone."

"In a moment, dear." Ginger sounded sweet but implacable. "I just want to check something."

"Who are you calling?" Kat demanded. Cammie returned to the tasting area in time to see Ginger fending off Kat and greeting someone on the other end of the line. "Hello? Josh?"

Kat snatched the phone away and hung up.

"Katherine Elizabeth Milner." Ginger pressed her palm to her heart. "You just hung up on your husband."

"Technically, *you* did." The phone started ringing, and Kat dropped it onto the table as if she'd been scorched.

"Would you two stop?" Cammie put her hands on her hips.

"We are dealing with a situation here." She ignored the still-ringing phone. "This is not the time to turn on each other. We're a team, and we need to start acting like it."

"Fine." Kat took a seat on one of the wine barrels. "I say our first team decision should be drinking heavily."

"I second that." Ginger clicked the phone to "silent."

Cammie nodded. "Motion carried. We're in a damn vineyard. Where's the wine?"

"The previous owner left a few bottles in the kitchen," Ginger said.

Cammie frowned. "Like, in the refrigerator or in the cabinets?"

"Right on the counter, next to the stove." Ginger started toward the back of the house. "I'll go get a bottle right now."

"Great." Cammie sighed. "This place was owned by some rich guy who doesn't know that the number-one rule of wine is to keep it away from sunlight and heat."

Kat looked heartened. "See? We're kicking that guy's ass already."

Ginger returned with a dusty bottle of wine, a corkscrew, and a few water-spotted drinking glasses. As Cammie dug the sharp tip of the corkscrew in, the cork started to crumble. She made a conscious decision not to interpret this as a bad omen and kept going.

"This actually looks better than I hoped for." When Cammie poured, the red wine was dark but not cloudy. She leaned over the rim of the glass and took a few tentative sniffs. "Smells okay, too."

Kat sniffed her glass. "What are you smelling? Because I just smell wine."

"That's good." Cammie straightened up. "If the bottle had been corked—that's what they call it when it gets contaminated with cork taint—it smells . . . not good."

As Kat and Ginger looked on with wide eyes, Cammie took a tiny sip of wine. She swirled it around her palate. She swallowed. And then she went to the sink to get a glass of water.

"Well?" Ginger demanded.

Cammie busied herself with the faucet handles. "Um, what kind of wine is that? Merlot? Pinot noir?"

"You tell me," Ginger said. "You're the wine expert."

"Answer the question," Kat said. "How was it?"

"Don't keep us in suspense." Ginger stepped closer, her eyes wide.

Cammie considered this for a moment. "Better than vinegar; worse than Franzia."

Kat groaned.

Ginger looked around, confused. "What's Franzia?"

"The lofty heights to which we aspire," Cammie said.

"It's wine in a box," Kat informed her mother. "We used to drink it at college parties."

"So there's a market for it, is what you're saying?"

Cammie turned around and leaned back against the sink. "My opinion doesn't count. At the end of the day, I have no clue what I'm talking about. We need to take this to an expert."

"Something every buyer should do *before* finalizing their vineyard purchase," Kat added pointedly.

"I had cancer!" Ginger retorted. "Think about that!"

"How can I not, what with you reminding me every fifteen minutes?"

Ginger stood up, wedged the cork back into the wine bottle, and appealed to Cammie. "You're the only one of us with any related experience. It's your call, Cammie. If you say this is hopeless, if you say we should give up now, I'll listen."

"What?" Kat cried. "You'll listen to her but you won't listen to me?"

"That's right. You're a skateboarder, not a restaurateur," Ginger said.

"Not anymore," Kat muttered.

And Cammie wasn't a restaurateur anymore. None of them had turned out to be the woman she'd thought she'd be. But at least

Ginger was trying. Ginger would rather try her damnedest and fail than listen to all the voices in her head that told her to give up.

So Cammie didn't tell the truth. She told her aunt what she wished was the truth: "It's not hopeless. We've come this far. Let's give it a shot."

Lots of hugs and high fives, which dwindled into awkward standing around. Kat and Ginger both regarded Cammie expectantly. "What now?"

Cammie pulled out her phone and did a quick search. "Google tells me there's a wine bar on Main Street. Someone there must know something about wine. Let's go."

chapter 6

Despite their bravado, all three women breathed sighs of relief as they piled into Ginger's car and sped away from the vineyard. After circling the town square for ten minutes, stalking beachgoers heading to their cars, Ginger finally found a parking spot.

"How long has this place been here, and why didn't it exist when we spent weeks at a time here?" Kat marveled as they entered the Whinery.

The barroom looked like a grown-up version of a princess-themed tea party. Pink, black, and silver were everywhere, accented with toile wallpaper and crystal chandeliers. Instead of mixed nuts or pretzels, the bar featured silver candy dishes filled with M&M's, Hershey's Kisses, and miniature peanut butter cups. The overall effect was unapologetically feminine, right down to the Annie Lennox song playing on the stereo.

Cammie parked herself on the stool nearest the bartender, a

curly-haired brunette in a snug black T-shirt. "Hi. Can I just lease this stool for the summer? Because I'm never leaving."

The bartender smiled, but she looked tired. There were dark smudges under her eyes. "Leasing out stools for the season? That's not a bad idea, actually. I could make little engraved plaques for each one."

"She's full of good ideas." Ginger placed her hands on Cammie's shoulders. "She owned a restaurant, you know."

"Oh yeah?" The bartender looked interested.

Cammie flushed and stared down at the glossy black bar top. "I'm just a waitress now."

"She's being too modest. She dropped everything to fly out here and help me." Ginger fluffed her hair. "I just bought the vineyard at the north end of town."

The bartender looked confused. "Which town?"

"Right here." Ginger tapped the bar. "Black Dog Bay."

"There's a vineyard in Black Dog Bay?"

"That's exactly what I said." Kat sat down next to Cammie.

The bartender's confusion turned to skepticism. "You're sure?"

"We're sure," Cammie said. "Because we're currently living there."

"Huh." The bartender leaned back, nodding. "I feel like if there was a vineyard in town, I would have heard about it by now."

"We think the previous owners were there only a few weeks a year," Ginger said. "They lived in New York."

The bartender nodded. "We have some pretty, um, eccentric summer residents, all right. So what varietals do you grow?"

Ginger looked at Cammie. "Um . . ."

"What's the terroir like?"

Cammie fidgeted in her seat. "Well . . ."

"Is the wine any good?"

"We're hoping you can tell us." Ginger produced a metal thermos with great éclat. "You're the local wine expert."

The bartender grinned. "Not to brag, but I do have an amazing palate."

"So, maybe you can start stocking our wine?" Ginger all but poured the wine down the bartender's throat. "Local businesses supporting each other and all that."

"The soft sell," Kat murmured. "Look into it."

"If you don't ask, you don't get," Ginger countered. "Look into *that*."

"I'm always happy to support local business owners." The bartender extended her right hand. "I'm Jenna, by the way."

The women all introduced themselves while Jenna located a wineglass. Cammie held her breath as Jenna took a small sip.

"Well?" Ginger couldn't contain herself. "How is it?"

Jenna spat the wine back into the glass. "It's . . ."

"Yes? Yes?"

"It's . . . interesting."

Cammie dropped her head into her hands. "I knew it."

Ginger sank onto the barstool next to Cammie's. "Well, I mean, we know it's not *good*, but it's not *awful*. Right?"

Jenna's gaze slid sideways.

"Let me taste that," called a willowy blonde at the end of the bar. "My palate is cheap and easy."

"Be my guest." Jenna poured another glass and slid it across the bar in a practiced, Old West–saloon move.

"Thank you." The blonde lifted her glass in a salute to Cammie, Ginger, and Kat. "Cheers."

She sipped. Everyone else leaned forward, waiting.

Finally, Ginger could stand it no longer. "Well? *Well*?"

Unlike Jenna, the blonde managed to force the wine down with what appeared to be Herculean effort. She raised her gaze to the ceiling, searching for an apt comparison. "It kind of reminds me of this wine I had at a restaurant in France."

"France!" Ginger nudged Cammie. "France is good, right?"

"After we finished dinner, the restaurant told us that they'd just served us the crappiest wine they'd ever come across to prove that ignorant Americans will drink anything." The woman got up and left her glass, still full, on the bar.

"Summer, did you know there's a vineyard in town?" Jenna asked the newcomer.

The other woman shook her head. "No. And I know everything that goes on around here." She offered a handshake to Ginger. "Hi, by the way. I'm Summer Benson."

"Ginger Sheridan, proud vineyard owner. It's inland, over by Lewes."

"Huh." Summer looked back at the abandoned wineglass. "Well, I'm sure it's going to be great."

"She's humoring us," Kat informed Cammie and Ginger.

Ginger responded by clasping her hands together and begging Jenna. "But you'll put it on your menu, right? You'll give it a chance?"

Jenna ducked down and started rummaging through a supply cabinet. "Um . . ."

"We have a white wine, too." Ginger looked prepared to kneel on the floor and grovel. "Maybe that one's better."

Jenna ran a hand through her hair and managed to avoid replying to Ginger by focusing on a new arrival. "Hey!" She sounded almost accusatory to the man who walked through the bar's front door. "What are you doing here? Again?"

The tension in Jenna's tone made Cammie frown. She turned to Summer and muttered, "Ex-boyfriend?"

"Worse," Summer whispered back. "Health inspector."

"Good afternoon, ladies." The health inspector, a dour middle-aged man with a cheap sport coat and an air of superiority, gave them a smile. "Taking time out of your busy day for a little girl talk at"—he glanced at his watch—"three o'clock? Must be nice not to have to work."

Summer opened her mouth and took a deep breath, but before she could launch into a tirade, Jenna said, "I assume you're here about the cooler?"

"I am." The inspector gave a curt nod. "You've replaced it?"

"Well, no." Jenna's smile was placating. "But I found a solution that should keep everybody happy."

The man's expression darkened. "I expressly told you to replace it."

"I know, but . . ." Jenna couldn't suppress a little eye roll. "Just come back and see, okay?"

The two of them adjourned to the bar's back room. Two minutes later, the health inspector strode back into the bar with a smirk on his lips. Jenna followed, sputtering and stammering.

"You're kidding!" she cried. "I paid five hundred dollars for that!"

"Then you wasted your money." The inspector whipped out a little pad and pen. "Because you ignored my recommendations."

"This is ridiculous!" Jenna threw her hands up. "This is just . . ."

The inspector arched a brow. "Just what?"

Jenna wrestled with her temper for a few moments, then went stone-faced. "Nothing. Have a good day. Sir." Her tone said "go to hell," but her words were sufficiently polite.

"You, too." He brushed an imaginary speck off the sleeve of his jacket. "I trust that will be fixed before I come back."

Jenna just waved, a choppy gesture of dismissal.

As soon as the inspector left the premises, Jenna whirled to Summer. "I can't do this anymore! This is unfair! This is harassment!"

"He does seem a little uptight," Ginger said soothingly.

"Seriously. What's his problem?" Kat asked.

"He's a petty, petty man on a power trip—that's his problem." Jenna glowered. "I just spent twenty-six hundred dollars on a cooler, and he refuses to let me keep it in the restaurant because it has a beer logo painted on the side."

"So what? This is a bar," Cammie pointed out.

"I know!" Jenna looked ready to started throwing glasses. "And it's in the back! The customers can't even see it! I bought it at a used-equipment sale, and since I'd already spent the twenty-six hundred dollars, I decided it'd be cheaper to repaint than replace it."

Everyone nodded in sympathy.

"It cost five hundred dollars to get it repainted, and now that . . . that *evil man* is saying I still have to get rid of it."

Summer looked outraged. "Can he do that?"

"He can do anything he wants. He's the health inspector." Jenna turned to Cammie. "You were smart, getting out of the restaurant business. I swear to you, between the health inspector and the drunken debauchery and the constant threat of lawsuits—"

"There was only one lawsuit threat, and I took care of it," Summer said.

"—I've had it with the hospitality industry." Jenna brushed her palms against her crisp black apron. "I'm done. Hear me? Done."

"Stop talking crazy," Summer said. "The heartbreak tourists need you, and you know it."

Cammie and Kat glanced at each other, bewildered. "Heartbreak tourists?"

"Yeah. Black Dog Bay is the 'best place in America to bounce back from your breakup.'" Summer looked aggrieved that they hadn't heard this. "It's all over the media."

"It's pretty recent." Jenna pulled up some news stories on her phone. "But it was a big deal around here."

"That explains the business names," Kat mused. "The Jilted Café, the Rebound Salon, the Eat Your Heart Out bakery . . ."

Cammie peered at the store signs lining the streets. "What's the Naked Finger?"

"That's where you can sell your wedding rings after you divorce," Jenna said.

"Everyone here knows what it's like to start over," Summer said. "This is more than just another pretty beach town. We've got it all—magic dog included."

Cammie smiled, certain she'd misheard. "Magic dog?"

"You'll see."

Ginger appealed to Jenna. "So, about our wine . . . ?"

Jenna shook her head, regret evident in her brown eyes. "Sorry. Maybe next year."

Kat, Cammie, and Ginger spent the rest of the afternoon wandering around town, introducing themselves to other business owners and telling themselves they were networking. Laying the groundwork for success. Building an empire.

Really, of course, they were delaying their return to the vineyard. Prolonging their blissful denial. But as the sun sank into the sparkling blue Atlantic, Ginger sighed and announced, "We'd better go back."

They drove back to the Lost Dog Vineyards in silence, each woman thinking about her own plight. When they arrived at the long, uneven road that led to the main house, the grapevines looked even more fragile, the house even more ancient.

"Time for bed," Ginger announced in the same tone she'd used when Cammie and Kat were seven.

They obliged, hauling suitcases up the stairs to the small bedrooms. The sleek, modern Danish headboard and nightstands in Cammie's room were jarring juxtapositions to the faded rose wallpaper and worn, whitewashed floorboards.

The previous owners had never really understood this place, that was certain. Cammie didn't know if she'd ever understand it, either. She pulled on a threadbare, oversize T-shirt and rested atop the fluffy down comforter on the bed. Even with the windows open, the house was stifling. They were too far from the ocean to get a cool breeze.

She stared up at the ceiling and tried to fall asleep. Instead, she thought about Ian. Yes, the end had been awful. But the beginning had been so good.

She didn't want to think about the beginning. She didn't want to think about him at all. Yet somehow, impossibly, she could smell the strawberries he'd grown. The sweet, ripe scent drifted up from the kitchen.

Finally, an hour later, when the whole house had gone silent and still, she gave up on sleep and padded downstairs in her bare feet. If she had to face her past, she'd face it with a drink—courtesy of her mother's secret recipe.

chapter 7

Cammie flipped on the kitchen light and breathed in the scent of the berries heaped in a bowl on the counter. The summer she'd met Ian, she'd stumbled across her mother's recipe for strawberry wine, which she'd filed away in her digital archives and forgotten about until now.

Her mother and Ginger used to drink this on summer evenings by the shore. Cammie and Kat had begged for a taste, imagining it tasted like Kool-Aid, but their mothers had never relented. "When you're grown up," Cammie's mother had promised her.

Well, now she was grown up. And she wanted to share this tradition with her mother, if only in spirit. She found a large stainless-steel pot in a cabinet, filled it with water, and added several cups of sugar. While she waited for the water to boil, she washed the berries and hulled them with a paring knife.

By the time she'd finished with the berries, she had sweet pink juice on her fingers and total recall of the summer she'd been so determined to forget.

She'd just turned twenty-two and she had big dreams for the future. On her birthday, she'd legally gained access to the inheritance her mother had left, which her father had carefully invested for the previous ten years. The first thing she'd done was buy a car (used, but she'd splurged on the leather interior and sunroof; she figured her mother would approve). As she sped down the beach town's back roads, cruising past a cornfield in her little red coupe, she turned the music up and rolled down the window. Finally, real life was about to begin. Nothing could stop her.

The car slowed.

Frowning, Cammie stepped on the gas. The car slowed down even more. She steered onto the gravel shoulder as the car rolled to a stop.

She turned off the ignition, took her hands off the wheel, and started cursing. As she dug through the glove compartment for the user manual, she heard the crunch of gravel. A rusty blue pickup truck had pulled up in front of her.

"I don't need any help!" she yelled as she heard footsteps approaching.

"Flat tire?" a male voice asked.

Cammie glanced up to find a very cute, very tan guy standing by the driver's-side window. "No, I think it's engine trouble."

"Yeah? What makes you think that?"

She gave him a very quick, very insincere smile. "The fact that the engine stopped. One minute it was running; the next minute, nothing."

"Did you hear a banging noise? Rattling?" He leaned down, rested his forearms on the roof of the car, and positioned his face closer to hers. He had dark, kind eyes and a dusty blue baseball cap covering his brown hair.

She shrugged one shoulder. "I didn't hear anything because I had the music cranked up to eleven."

He nodded. "Can I take a look?"

She shifted in her seat. "I don't need some guy to bail me out. I can handle this."

"Let me help. I want you to owe me a favor." He grinned, and she had to smile back. A real smile this time.

"I bet you say that to every girl stranded by the side of the road." But she handed over her keys.

He opened her car door for her and offered his hand to help her out.

She placed her hand in his, and as she stood up to look him in the eye, she was acutely aware of the cobalt sky above them, the gritty gravel on the ground beneath them, and the endless rows of green corn stalks all around them. Life came into focus, sharp and clear and almost painfully vivid.

She pulled her hand away and let her hair fall over her face, trying to pretend that the moment hadn't happened, that he hadn't felt it, too.

He slid into the driver's seat of her car. After turning the key in the ignition, he immediately got out of the car. "I found the problem."

She took a deep breath, determined to steady herself. "That fast? Damn, you're like the car whisperer."

"You're out of gas."

"What? No, I'm not." She ducked down to peer at the dashboard.

He pointed out a glowing yellow symbol. "The little gas tank light's on."

She waved this away. "Yeah, but when it comes on, I still have thirty-three miles."

He looked at her. "How long has the light been on?"

She mentally calculated the distance between her aunt's cottage and the cornfield. "For about twenty miles? There's a gas station five miles thataway. I have an eight-mile cushion!"

He glanced at the dashboard vents. "Have you been running the A/C?"

"Um . . ."

"Because that's going to affect your mileage." Before she could reply, he assured her, "This happens to everyone out here. It's harder to fill up when the nearest gas station is clear across town."

"But I . . ." Cammie pressed one hand to her cheek, mortified. "I don't do stuff like this. I'm really smart, I swear. I just graduated magna cum laude."

"They're not going to take away your diploma for this." He settled back against the car, watching her. "I'm Ian McKinlay."

"Cammie. Cammie Breyer." She reached up and toyed with the silver pendant at her neck. "So, what are you doing out here in the cornfields, Ian?"

"Working. These are my family's fields."

She regarded him with renewed interest. "You're a farmer?"

He laughed, his smile easy and white. "Yes."

"Is that the right word?"

"Yeah. I'm a farmer."

"I've never met an actual farmer before." After growing up in the suburbs, the idea of farming seemed like something out of a fairy tale or a TV series. Not real life. Not something someone her age would do.

"It's your lucky day. Farmers are the best." He strode over to the nearest green stalk. "Here, take some with you. Best sweet corn you'll ever have."

"No, thanks."

"Take it," he insisted. "You'll thank me later."

"I don't like corn," Cammie confessed.

"What?" Ian looked almost offended. "Everybody likes sweet corn."

"Everybody except me."

"You'll like this. This is a whole different experience from the corn you've had before. Just try it." He handed her the corn, and she accepted without further protest. "So, what do you do?"

"Right now, I'm waitressing, but I'm starting graduate school in the fall."

Ian closed the car door and turned toward his truck. "Come on. I'll drive you into town, and you can get a few gallons at the gas station."

Cammie fell into step beside him, and they were halfway to his truck before her magna-cum-laude common sense kicked in. "How do I know you're not a serial killer?"

"How do I know *you're* not?" he countered.

She smiled sweetly. "You don't."

And that was the beginning. By the time they got to the gas station, it was like they'd known each other for years. By the time they drove back to the cornfield and refueled her car, she was wondering what it would be like to kiss him.

So she decided to find out. As he screwed the gas cap back into place, she got up on tiptoe and brushed her lips against his cheek. His skin was warm and he smelled wholesome, like sun and grass.

He turned to face her. "What was that for?"

"I owe you, remember?" She kissed him again, this time on the lips.

He slid his arms around her waist. They kissed and kissed under the bright summer sun, out in the middle of a dusty road surrounded by tall green fields.

"Let's go somewhere," he said when they finally broke apart.

"Where?" Even as she asked this, she knew what he would answer: *My room. Under the boardwalk. Backseat of the truck.*

"Let's count the rows."

She glanced at him, confused, and he laughed. "Come on, I'll give you the full farmer experience."

"Like a field trip?"

"Best field trip ever." He took her hand again and led her to the far end of the rows of corn.

"When you walk the field, what you're really doing is counting the rows," he explained. "Checking the spacing between plants, checking to see if everything's growing, checking to see if there's any damage from birds."

He started walking slowly. Cammie matched his pace, trying to see what he saw: creation in progress, life all around them.

But all she saw was corn.

"Aren't there the same number of rows as there were yesterday and the day before?" she asked.

He squeezed her hand. "Yeah. Isn't it great? Everything else changes every day. But the number of rows stays the same."

She had no idea what he was talking about, but she loved hearing him say it. After two hours of counting the rows, she was totally sunburned and halfway in love.

He called her the next morning. They got together the next day, and every day after that. They would meet in the cornfields in the late afternoon and walk the field, counting rows.

"Did you try the corn?" Ian asked when he leaned in to kiss her hello.

"Yes," Cammie said.

"And?" he prompted.

"And you were right—it was better than any corn I've ever had before." Also truthful.

Something in her voice made him laugh. "But?"

Cammie hung her head. "But I still don't like corn."

She spent the summer in a constant state of distraction and desire.

While her aunt whiled away the days learning to knit and Kat accumulated an ever-growing collection of scabs and bruises, Cammie thought about Ian.

"What else do you do all day?" she once asked him as they paced the perimeter of the fields. "Besides count the rows?"

"Lots." He kind of shrugged. "But most of it's done before noon."

"Like what?" she pressed.

"You really want to know?"

"I really do."

"Plants don't sleep," he told her. "They grow all night, so you want to check on them first thing, before it gets hot. Bugs get up early. If you get out there early, too, you can head off some of the damage."

She rested her hand on his back as they walked.

"The first thing I do when I get up is check the weather." He grinned sheepishly. "That's a farmer thing—we're obsessed with the weather. We can't change it or control it, but we have to know about it. All the time."

"So you'll know what's coming?"

"We're never sure what's coming. I took a course in meteorology in college, and what I learned is that no one really understands how all the different systems work together. The forecast is just a guess. But we all have our favorite weather websites." He paused. "And we all buy the *Farmers' Alamanac*, every year."

"The *Farmers' Almanac*?" Cammie was incredulous. "Is that thing accurate?"

"No." Ian lowered his voice. "Except it *might be*. You never know."

"You never know," Cammie echoed.

"What about you?" he asked. "What were you studying while I was reading up on barometric pressure in college?"

"Hospitality management. That's what I'm going to grad school for. There's a great program in California. It's really hard to get into; I was shocked when I got accepted." She couldn't hide the excitement in her voice. "My plan is to open a restaurant."

"Oh." His voice was flat.

"What?" she prompted.

"Nothing."

"What?" Cammie demanded.

He led her into the shade offered by a row of cornstalks. "Don't a lot of restaurants go out of business pretty early on?"

"Well, yeah."

"Like ninety percent?"

Cammie flipped her hair back. "I don't know the exact percentage, but that's why I'm going to grad school. To learn how not to go out of business."

"Okay."

"What are you saying?"

He held up his hands. "I'm not saying anything."

"You're saying my restaurant's going to go out of business," she accused.

He started walking again. "Ninety percent is pretty bad odds."

"Well, odds don't apply to me," she informed his back. "I'm going to be very successful. *Very* successful."

When Ian talked about his family's land, she could sense how much he loved it. The land, the growing cycle, the lifestyle. But no matter how much she wanted to, she couldn't feel the way he felt about it.

She tried to appreciate the smell of fresh fields when she turned the soil over in her hands. She tried to read the weather blogs he'd recommended. She tried to identify the moment that a plant "broke," just as the new green sprout appeared. She just couldn't seem to find any passion for corn.

But she had plenty of passion for Ian. She couldn't get enough of his time, his body, the sound of his voice. Their preferred activity was to park out in his family's farmland, under the stars, and make out.

"What's going to happen in September?" he asked her one sultry night in July as they stretched out, both topless, on a blanket in the bed of the truck.

"I have to go to California." The reality started to sink in as she said the words.

"You don't *have* to go to California." He pulled her closer against his chest.

She went still for a moment, thinking about that. *What if he's right? What if I stay here?*

"What kind of restaurant do you want to open?" he asked, breaking the silence.

This was one of things she liked best about him: He was always interested in what she had to say, even when she had her shirt off.

"I'm not sure." She shifted, rested her cheek against his warm bare skin. "In my mind, it's a fancy, upscale lounge. Like a really fancy bar. By the beach, maybe."

"That's really what you want to do?"

"Yeah. It's what I'm going to do." She pressed her lips over the steady thud of his heartbeat.

"But why do you want to?"

She lifted her face. "What do you mean?"

"Why do you want to open a restaurant?" He rested his hand on her lower back. "You could do anything you want."

Cammie hesitated for a moment before confessing the truth. "My mom always wanted to open a restaurant. She was a great cook; she would try anything. And she loved entertaining. She always said when my dad stopped traveling for work so much and I started high school, she'd open a little café."

"But she didn't?" Ian asked.

Cammie sighed. "She died when I was in sixth grade."

He didn't say anything, just held her close.

"Breast cancer," Cammie said, as if this told the whole story. She supposed that in a way, it did. "When she died, she left me a trust fund. I gained access to it when I turned twenty-one. I can't cook the way she did, but I love that feeling of getting people together. Dressing up. Escaping from reality a little bit. She and I were alike that way. That, and we have the same middle name."

Ian rubbed her bare skin, sending a delicious shiver through her. "What's your middle name?"

Cammie blew out a breath. "It's weird."

He waited.

"Really weird. It's a family thing."

"You get that the longer you put this off, the more I want to know?"

She turned her head so she didn't have to see his expression when she confessed, "It's October."

"Like the month?"

"Like the month," she confirmed. "That was my grandmother's middle name, too."

He let this sink in for a moment. "Were you born in October?"

Cammie laughed. "No. January twenty-ninth."

He laughed, too. "Hang on. You're initials are COB?"

"Yeah."

"And you don't like corn?"

"Oh, the irony." They laughed and kissed and laughed some more.

Finally, Ian pulled away. "You know, there are a lot of restaurants in Delaware. Graduate schools, too. You could do everything you want to do right here. Less risk of failure than in California."

"I'm not scared of failure. I told you—I've got this."

"Then stay here because I want you to." He hauled her up

across his chest. Her hair fell down across her face, blocking them both from the glow of the moon.

"You make a good case." But her tone was apologetic, reluctant.

"Stay," he urged her, pulling her closer against him.

She shivered as a cool breeze blew across her damp skin. "I can't."

"Why not?" He loosened his arms around her. "We can do whatever we want."

As he relaxed, she tensed. "Then come to California with me."

"I can't move to California." He said this without even a hint of hesitation.

"Why not?" she challenged. "You expect me to move across the country for you, but you wouldn't move across the country for me?"

"You wouldn't be moving across the country; you already live here."

"I don't live here. I spend the summer here in a rental house. Big difference."

"You could live here." He squeezed her hand in his. "You could move in with me. We could walk the fields every day."

He made it sound so easy. So tempting.

"It's not that simple." She drew back so she could study his face in the starlight.

"It is that simple," he insisted. "All you have to do is make up your mind."

"But that's what I'm trying to say: Why do *I* have to be the one to make up my mind?"

He kissed her again. "My mind is already made up."

"Then you take a chance. Come with me to California."

"I can't." His voice was so kind but so unyielding.

Cammie sat up and pulled on her shirt. "Because of the farm?"

"Yes." Not a trace of regret or apology.

"The farm doesn't own you. You can leave if you want to."

"No. I can't. I'm not hoping to start a business. My job is to keep this business going." He sat up, too, and she recognized her own stubborn determination in the set of his jaw, the fire in his eyes.

"What's the failure rate for farms?" she challenged.

"Doesn't matter; I'm already invested. And I don't want to leave."

"So you're saying that I have to rearrange my life because you'll never rearrange yours? You and your farm will always come first?"

He hesitated for a long moment. "I want you, Cammie, but I can't leave."

"Because a bunch of dirt and corn mean more to you than I do."

"It's not just dirt. It's not just corn." He looked around at the vast green acres around them. "All of this belonged to my grandparents and great-grandparents. It will belong to my children and grandchildren someday. It's part of me; I'm part of it." He rested his hand in hers. "Stay here with me."

He sounded so sure of himself. She tried to envision what he envisioned. "And do what? Be a farmer's wife?"

"Yeah." He cupped her cheek in his palm and smiled that slow, heart-melting smile. "Be a farmer's wife."

Cammie couldn't help herself. She started laughing. Ian surprised her by laughing, too.

"Come on," he coaxed. "A straw hat, a pitchfork, some overalls . . ."

"You forgot the little piece of straw between my teeth."

"Piece of straw?" He shook his head. "Go corncob pipe or go home."

This was why it was impossible to dismiss his entreaty to stay as an adolescent fantasy. He was funny and playful and sexy and smart. He was everything she wanted in a man. Even at twenty-two, she knew that this kind of connection was rare.

But she'd have to give up everything she wanted for herself to be with him.

He saw her expression changing, and his changed, too. They

got dressed and he drove her home in silence. When they pulled up in front of the rental cottage, he gave her a slow, gentle, thorough kiss that she knew would have to last her forever.

Because August was all they had left.

The next afternoon, when she drove to the farm to count the rows with Ian, he led her to a corner of earth on the far end of the cornfield.

The land had been cleared and cordoned off. Where yesterday there had been burgeoning stalks of corn, there were now tiny green sprouts, so new that Cammie couldn't guess what they were going to be. She knelt down to examine the tender leaves with jagged edges and the tiny white flowers with yellow centers.

"Strawberries," Ian said when she glanced up at him. "I know you like them better than corn."

She did love strawberries—in pies, ice cream, cocktails, and fresh off the vine—but she hadn't realized he'd noticed. She should have known better. Ian noticed everything, even if he didn't remark on it.

"I planted them this morning." He knelt down next to her in the freshly turned dirt. "I think I got the depth right. You can still see the crown here. Look." He pointed out the section of the plant where the leaves and stems met the roots. "That's the sweet spot."

Cammie reached out and brushed one of the green leaves with her finger. "So, now what?"

"Now we keep them alive."

Over the next few weeks, Cammie watered and weeded the berry plants before she went to work. She chased away birds and covered the plants with long strips of burlap when ladybugs threatened. Every day she checked for signs of progress.

"When will the berries show up?" she asked Ian as August drew to a close.

"Next year."

She blinked, confused. "What?"

"Right now, the plants have to put all their energy into growing." He produced a small, sharp knife. "We'll prune the flowers this year."

She threw herself between the blade and the berries. "But they're about to blossom!"

He rolled his eyes at her theatrics. "If we cut them now, the fruit will be better next year. The plants will spread and we'll have more. It's all about delayed gratification. We have to wait until next spring."

She sighed. "But I won't be here in the spring."

In the end, they compromised. Ian severed all the flowers on all the plants—except one. One plant was allowed to pursue its natural course, and at the end of the month, Cammie plucked a single red berry from the vine.

"Wow." She offered the half-eaten fruit to Ian. "Taste this. Is it really this good, or do I just *think* it's this good because I've been working on it every day for a month?"

He tasted it, deliberating. "Does it matter?"

She decided it didn't and plucked another berry. "These can't possibly get any better."

"Yeah, they can," he promised. "Just wait."

She hated to say these words because she knew it would ruin the moment. But she couldn't lie—not to him and not to herself. "I can't wait. I can't stay."

"You can—but you won't." He turned his whole body away from her.

"I have to go, Ian. I'll regret it for the rest of my life if I don't." She waited for the tension in his back to soften, and when it didn't, she rested her palm next to his shoulder blade. "You can visit me. Call me. Wait for me." Her voice was high and light, and she knew that she shouldn't try to appease him like this. She shouldn't explain or apologize, but she couldn't seem to stop herself.

He finally shifted his body so he was facing her. "How long do you expect me to wait?"

She forced herself to take a deep, calming breath. "Two years, maybe three. We can take turns flying cross-country. I'll have Christmas and spring break and summers. Long-distance relationships can work."

"Delaware to California is pretty damn far," he said.

She desperately hoped he would say that she was worth the wait, that he'd never met anybody else like her. But he didn't. He stared at her with that cool, assessing look in his eyes.

So often when she'd dated boys in college, she'd wished she could find a guy who knew what he wanted. A guy with confidence and unwavering conviction. Now that she'd finally found that in Ian, it had backfired. He knew what he wanted most, and it wasn't her.

She forced herself to meet his gaze without speaking. No more cajoling. No more hopeful propositions for long-distance relationships. They'd met only two months ago. What did she really know about him, other than what he'd told her? What made her think that they could be happy if they stayed together?

She got to her feet and dusted the dirt off her hands. "You know what? Don't worry about it. This was just a summer fling, anyway."

He followed her, took her hand. "Hey. This isn't just a fling." He paused. "Not for me. I asked you to stay here forever and I meant it."

She stared down at the rich, dark soil that kept him rooted forever to this life and this town.

"This is it." His voice hardened as he let go of her hand. "Stay, Cammie. I'm not going to ask again."

. . .

She hadn't stayed. She flew to California, and she didn't hear from Ian. She didn't contact him, either. She moved on with her life and assumed he'd moved on with his. But for years, she associated the smell and taste of strawberries with the summer they'd spent together. Every now and then, after a grueling night on the restaurant floor, she checked the weather blogs he'd recommended. Eventually she'd come to see their romance as sweet and poignant puppy love, a moment of her youth that could never be recaptured.

But now she was back in Black Dog Bay. And he was still here. The strawberries she'd been hulling brought back a flood of feelings.

While the sugar water cooled, Cammie found a lemon in the refrigerator, rolled it hard against the counter to make juicing easier, then squeezed the juice into a little glass dish. She added the strawberries, lemon juice, and grated lemon peel to the water.

"What are you doing?" came a sleepy voice from the doorway.

Cammie turned to find Kat, bleary-eyed and blinking against the overhead light.

"I'm making my mom's strawberry wine." Cammie glanced at the big metal pot. "Trying to, anyway."

"The strawberry wine they would never let us have?" Kat asked.

"Yeah." Cammie frowned down at the faded handwriting on the recipe card, which she was viewing via her phone screen. "It says to mash the strawberries and lemon juice gently. How do you mash gently?"

"Step aside." Ginger appeared next to Kat in the shadowed doorway. "Let an expert take over."

Cammie obliged. Ginger muttered to herself while she rummaged through the kitchen drawers.

"Why are you up?" Kat asked.

"How could I sleep with you girls yelling and carrying on down here?" Ginger retorted.

"We were barely whispering," Kat said.

Ginger harrumphed, and Cammie suspected that she wasn't the only one battling stress-induced insomnia. They were all freaking out but they refused to admit it. Everyone was putting on a good face, holding the line. And maybe that was the right thing to do. Maybe that would get them through to the grape harvest and beyond.

Speaking of which . . . "I have to get up really early and walk the fields tomorrow." Cammie stifled a yawn and sat down at the kitchen table. "Plants never sleep, you know."

"Worry about that tomorrow." Ginger located a potato masher. "Right now, watch and learn."

Cammie and Kat watched Ginger muddle the berries with warm water and sugar, then drape a dishcloth over the pot.

"Now what?" Kat eyed the faded red gingham.

"Now we wait for two days. In the meantime, don't touch." Ginger slid the pot on top of the refrigerator with Kat's help. "Cammie, what on earth possessed you to start making strawberry wine in the middle of the night?"

"You and Mom always said I could try it when I grew up." Cammie rested her bare feet on the edge of the chair and hugged her knees to her chest. "I think I finally qualify."

The three of them stayed up late into the night, chatting and snacking and playing a cutthroat game of Uno with a deck of cards Kat found in a kitchen drawer. Everyone straggled off to bed as the first light of dawn crept over the dark horizon.

"I'm only going to get like an hour of sleep," Cammie warned. "There's weeding and fertilizing and watering and pruning to be done."

"We're with you," Kat vowed. "Bright and early."

"Up and at 'em," Ginger agreed. "Just need a little catnap."

With the whole house smelling faintly of strawberries and lemon, they all went to bed.

The next thing Cammie knew, it was noon and someone was pounding on the front door.

chapter 8

Cammie startled awake, glanced at the clock, and tumbled out of bed. She felt disoriented and desperate for a shower and a cup of high-octane coffee.

The doorbell rang, followed by the rapping of knuckles against the window.

"Coming," Cammie yelled, her voice hoarse, as she threw on a robe and hustled downstairs. She smoothed back her hair and opened the door.

"Josh." She was shocked to see Kat's husband. "Hey. What are you doing here?"

Even in jeans and a baseball cap, Josh Milner looked like the philosophy professor that he was. Placid and thoughtful, he was the counterbalance to Kat's constant, frenetic adrenaline.

"I thought I'd have breakfast with my wife. Yesterday was the last day of classes." He shifted, revealing a small brown-and-white dog in the crook of his arm. "Is she here?"

Cammie rubbed the back of her hand across her eyes. She felt like she should hug him or something, but she wasn't wearing a bra and she hadn't brushed her teeth. They could hug later. "Hang on a second. I'll go wake her up."

"She's still asleep?" He looked surprised, which was understandable, considering Kat's energy level. "Was she out late last night?"

"We all hung out in the kitchen, making strawberry wine and playing Uno." Cammie smiled. "We're officially old."

"Yeah, that's what Kat keeps saying."

She invited him into the front room, where he took in the makeshift bar and upended barrels.

"I like what you've done with the place," he said.

"Yeah, we're kind of in transition." Cammie looked at the dog. "Who's this little guy?"

Josh shuffled his feet, clearly self-conscious. "This is Jacques. Listen, Cammie . . ."

Something in his tone made her snap to attention.

"I know we haven't talked much, but I have to ask: Does Kat seem different to you?"

Cammie edged toward the staircase. "Different how?"

"I don't know." He took off his cap. "Something's going on with her. She won't talk about it. She used to tell me everything, but then she moves out of the house and won't answer my texts."

"I'll . . . go see if she's up." Cammie put her foot on the bottom stair tread.

"And since when does she play Uno?" His dark brows snapped together. "She hates card games."

Cammie moseyed up to the landing, then sprinted the rest of the way to Kat's tiny room at the end of the hallway. Before she could knock, the door swung inward. Kat gripped the doorknob, her eyes wild. "Is that Josh down there?"

"Yes." Cammie pointed toward the stairs. "He wants to take you to breakfast."

"What the hell? What is he *doing* here?" Kat clutched the doorframe for support.

"I don't know. Maybe you should ask him."

Kat hugged the frame even closer. "What am I going to do?"

Ginger cleared her throat, startling both of them. "Are you aware that Josh is downstairs?"

"Yes," Cammie and Kat chorused.

"Then why are you up here, ignoring him?"

"I'm not ignoring him," Kat hissed.

"They're going to breakfast," Cammie said helpfully.

Kat panicked. She turned to Cammie and commanded, "Tell him I'm sick. Tell him I'm throwing up and supercontagious. Tell him—"

"Tell him nothing of the sort." Ginger pursed her lips. "Kat, you're a grown woman with a marriage and responsibilities. Whatever is going on between you and Josh, running away to the Delaware beach is not going to solve it."

"I ran here for you, Mother. And this is none of your business!" Kat went from panicked to enraged in a split second. "You have no idea what's going on with us."

"That's right." Ginger matched Kat's steely glare. "Because you won't tell me."

Josh *ahem*ed downstairs. Everyone jumped.

"He's waiting for you," Cammie whispered.

Kat closed her eyes. "What am I going to do?"

"I thought you were all about confrontation," Cammie said. "I thought it made you feel alive."

"Yeah, with you guys; not with my husband."

Cammie studied her cousin's expression. "You did something bad, didn't you?"

"What?" Kat's eyes snapped open. "Why would you say that?"

Ginger started nodding along with Cammie. "If Josh had done something wrong, you'd already be down there, ripping him apart. But the fact that you're still here, cowering in your room . . . You screwed up."

Kat pulled her giant Quartersnacks skateboarding T-shirt closer around her torso. "Nobody screwed up. That's not what's happening here."

"Then what is happening?" Ginger asked. "Enlighten us, please."

They all fell silent, casting looks of reproach and suspicion at one another. Then they heard a high-pitched yelp from the vicinity of the front door.

Kat furrowed her brow. "What was that?"

"I think it was Jacques," Cammie said.

"Who's Jacques?"

"Your dog?" Cammie described the brown-and-white dog Josh had been carrying.

Kat looked mystified. "We don't have a dog."

Another yelp.

Kat finally released her death grip on the doorjamb and started down the stairs. Ginger prepared to follow, but Cammie stopped her with a hand on her arm.

"We should probably give them their privacy."

"*You* give them their privacy." Ginger shook off her hand and crept toward the stairs. "*I* intend to find out what's going on."

"Eavesdropping is wrong." But Cammie tiptoed behind her aunt. "If Kat catches us, I'm blaming you."

"Go ahead," Ginger whispered over her shoulder. "I'll play the cancer card."

"For the last time—you don't have cancer."

"But I *did*."

They huddled on the landing. Cammie could hear Kat's voice, soft but strained:

"I wasn't expecting to see you. What . . . ?"

Josh answered, "Here, I brought you this."

There was a rustling of cloth and excited canine yips.

"Josh." Kat didn't sound excited. "What is this?"

"It's a French bulldog. His name is Jacques."

"But why?"

Josh started to sound a wee bit testy. "When we first met, you told me you always wanted a French bulldog."

"I did?"

"Yeah, on our first date."

Kat paused. "Huh. I don't remember that."

"Well, I do."

"Where did you get him?" Kat asked.

"The dean of students' sister is a breeder, it turns out. She trains them and shows them in those fancy dog shows. Jacques here was one of her champions."

"Then why is he here with you?"

"He's retired," Josh said. "She said he did great until he was about four years old, and he hasn't won anything since. He went after a garden hose, broke his tooth on the metal, and that was it. He's out of the ring."

"Forever?"

"Yeah. I guess dog shows are serious business."

"So, that's it?" Kat sounded upset, almost tearful. "He's not physically perfect anymore, and they just throw him out into the cold?"

"They re-homed him with loving new owners," Josh pointed out. "Us."

But Kat wasn't listening. "He didn't turn out exactly the way they expected, so they got rid of him. No blue ribbons, no love."

Cammie and Ginger abandoned all pretense of stealth and tromped down the stairs to meet Jacques.

"He's adorable." Cammie scratched the little dog behind the ears. Jacques licked her wrist.

Kat reached for the dog, then pulled her hand back. She took a deep breath and folded her arms. "I'm already taking care of my mother and a field full of grapes. This is not a good time to get a dog."

Ginger elbowed Cammie in the rib cage. "Did you hear that? She lumped me in with a *dog*." She scooped Jacques out of Josh's hands and gave him a thorough snuggling. "You did always used to say you wanted a French bulldog, Kat."

"So I hear." Kat slumped her shoulders, clearly not enjoying her role as the killjoy. "But I can't deal with one more thing to worry about right now."

"Ooh, that reminds me." Cammie looked out the window at the gentle green slopes. "I've got to figure out the irrigation system today."

"Katherine, you're being ridiculous," Ginger admonished. "Dogs and grapes are two entirely different things."

"Yeah, but shouldn't we pace ourselves here? Limit ourselves to one challenge at a time?" Kat glanced guiltily at Josh.

"He won't be much trouble," Josh said mildly. "He's already socialized and house-trained. He's a good boy."

"Every vineyard needs a dog," Ginger said. "I read that somewhere."

"I can't believe this." Kat was regressing into a sullen preteen right before their eyes. "How are you so breezy about this? You never let me have a dog. Not even when I begged."

"But now your wish is granted," Ginger put down Jacques, who started sniffing the wine barrels. "Thanks to your doting husband. Now, who wants breakfast?"

Josh looked at Kat. "I'm taking you to breakfast." This was not a request.

Ginger kissed her son-in-law on the cheek. "Good idea. You two lovebirds go have some alone time. I'll babysit my little grand-puppy while you're out. So glad you came, Josh."

"I'll get dressed." Kat practically dragged Cammie up the stairs with her. Jacques followed them, surprisingly nimble for such a short, stout creature.

Kat made it to the top of the stairs before she collapsed against the wall and dropped her face into her palms. "What is he doing?"

"What are *you* doing?" Cammie countered. "The man shows up to take you to breakfast, with the dog you always wanted, and you're hiding up here, freaking out?"

Kat's head sank even lower.

"Tell me," Cammie urged. "What happened? What'd he do?"

"Nothing." Kat's voice was muffled. "Nothing happened. He didn't do anything. That's the problem."

Cammie ushered Kat into the bedroom, closed the door, and waited.

"The problem isn't Josh." Kat sank down on the whitewashed wood floor. "The problem is me."

"Okay."

Kat addressed the ceiling beams. "When he first asked me out, I almost said no because, let's face it, he wasn't really my type."

"That's true," Cammie agreed. "I remember that. We had a three-hour text debate about it."

"But you told me to give him a chance, and I did. I made a conscious decision to be with a guy who was nice and smart and trustworthy."

"An excellent decision," Cammie said.

"It was." Kat looked more pallid by the second. "Even though the spark wasn't there in the beginning, I told myself that it would come. I told myself that eventually my heart would catch up with my head, and I would fall in love with him."

Cammie sat down next to her cousin.

"And I did," Kat finished. "By the time we got married, I was madly in love."

"Then what's the problem?"

"The problem is, I don't know if I still love him." Kat's whole body trembled. "I don't feel anything. I want to, but I don't."

Cammie didn't know where to start, what to ask. "How long?"

"The past six months? I'm not sure. And the problem is me—I know it is. I used to be this badass boarder with my own identity. I had tournaments and sponsors and a publicist. I did photo shoots and speaking gigs. I had a life, you know?"

"You still have a life."

"Yeah, but now I'm just another wife living in the suburbs, and I hate it." Kat lifted her head, her eyes both furious and glinting with tears. *"I hate it."*

"Okay."

"All day long, I do stuff like go to the grocery store and the dry cleaner. I go to events at the university, and I'm just Josh's wife. It's like the past fifteen years never happened."

Cammie nodded. "I'm sure that's hard for you, but it's not Josh's fault."

"I know. I know!" Kat threw up her hands. "He's so great and supportive, and I know he deserves a wife who's crazy about him."

Cammie planted her hands behind her and leaned back. "But . . . ?"

"But I'm not attracted to him. At all. I don't want to kiss him, let alone have sex with him."

Cammie blew out her breath. "That is a problem."

"I'm just going through the motions with the marriage." Kat paused. "With my whole life right now, really. I'm just . . . empty." Kat hung her head again. "And now he's here. With my dream dog. Like the perfect husband he is. And I don't want to deal with him."

They both pondered this in silence for a minute.

Finally, Cammie ventured, "Don't you think some of this should be expected after a big career transition?"

"Yeah, but knowing that doesn't help me. I want to be in love with him, Cammie. I want the butterflies so badly."

Cammie was surprised by the depth of her response—she felt angry and almost betrayed. "But you guys are great together! You're the couple I thought of as my role model."

Kat laughed drily.

"That's how I survived the dating scene in Los Angeles—every time I went out with a guy who left me at the bar with the bill or spent the whole time talking about his ex-girlfriend or said he'd call but didn't, I'd tell myself, *Don't give up hope. There's a guy like Josh out there for you, too.*"

"Why are you telling me this?" Kat asked. "I already admitted I was wrong. I know I'm a shitty wife, but I can't change my feelings."

"Try," Cammie urged her.

"We don't have kids." Kat heaved a heavy sigh. "He's young enough that he could go find someone else and start a family."

"Do you want kids?"

Kat nibbled her lower lip. "I thought I did. Someday. When I was done with the whole boarding thing. But now that I'm done and there's nothing to stop me from getting pregnant, I couldn't be less interested. Hell, I don't even want the dog right now." She turned to Cammie with dark, hopeless eyes. "Something's wrong with me. I'm broken."

"You're not broken," Cammie assured her with more confidence than she felt. "Let me ask you this: If you don't want the dog and you don't want Josh, what do you want?"

Kat closed her eyes. "I want everything to go back to the way it was." Another pause. "Do you think the strawberry wine's ready?"

"No. Ginger says she has to mash it again and then drain the berries and throw the yeast in there. I think the whole thing takes, like, two weeks."

"Two weeks? I need a drink now!"

"Mimosas with breakfast?" Cammie suggested.

"Kat!" Ginger called from downstairs.

"Coming!" Kat hollered back. She got to her feet and walked toward the stack of suitcases next to the dresser. "I'd better get dressed. Hey, do you want to come with us?"

"To a breakfast date with you and your husband? I'll pass."

"Please? I need someone to take the pressure off."

"No way. While you're off having breakfast and your mom is babysitting her grandpuppy—"

"That word is officially forbidden in this house." Kat grimaced.

"—someone has to get to work figuring out how to grow grapes. And that someone is me."

"How about this?" Kat winced as she stubbed her toe on the dresser. "I'll go ten rounds with the irrigation system, and you go have French toast with Josh. Sound good?"

"Sounds great. But it's not going to happen."

"Kat!" Ginger called again.

"Just a minute!" Kat yanked off her T-shirt and donned another clean shirt that was nearly identical.

"The man drove all the way from Maryland," Cammie said. "At least pretend you're excited to go out with him."

"Fake it till you make it?" Kat shrugged. "I'll try anything at this point."

"That's the spirit." Cammie headed for her room. "And have a mimosa or three for me while I'm out there in the fields."

Seven years before, when Ian had asked Cammie to stay, Cammie had worried she'd made a mistake. She'd wondered if maybe, perhaps, she had an undiscovered penchant for working the fields and relishing the feeling of dirt on her hands. Maybe she'd given up on farm life too soon.

Today, sweating and swatting at bugs under the merciless summer sun, Cammie knew she had made the right choice. She no longer wanted to find her inner farmer. All she wanted was to go watch Netflix in a dark room with the air-conditioning on full blast.

"Farming sucks," she said aloud, smashing yet another bloodthirsty mosquito against her forearm.

While Ginger washed the breakfast dishes and prepped the strawberry wine in the house, Cammie walked along the rows of vines, searching for clogged sprinkler lines and any sign of blight or disease. After only five minutes, she was covered in sweat and dust. She knelt in the dirt, attempting to dislodge a tiny rock from the irrigation line. Her fingernails looked like they were covered in crude oil.

As she swore softly and peered down at the rock, a black nose and a pair of bright eyes appeared next to her. Jacques the French bulldog sniffed the irrigation line thoroughly, then turned to her expectantly.

"Aw, that's so cute." She patted him on the head. "Someone thinks he's a working dog."

Though Cammie failed to locate her inner farmer, Jacques seemed to have found his inner farm dog with no problem. He stayed right by her side, wheezing slightly and looking concerned while she wrangled the irrigation lines.

But even after she vanquished the clog, she realized that she was too late. The young, delicate vines had been subsisting without water for too long, and at least three dozen plants at the far end of the field had died. The leaves had fallen off, leaving a snarl of dried brown twigs under the brutal summer sun.

She had to keep the remaining vines healthy. Everything depended on the grapes, and the grapes depended on her.

She pulled out her cell phone and searched for an app that would tell her humidity levels and hourly forecasts. And then she froze, her finger poised over the screen.

This is the first step down a slippery slope. Next thing you know, I'll be buying the Farmers' Almanac.

She hit "install." Jacques snorted with approval.

Gazing around at the vines, with only a cell phone app to assist her, Cammie decided that a little nervous breakdown was in order. She had no idea what to do or how to do it. She wanted to cry. She wanted to scream. Instead, she located a shovel and tried to dig out the dead vines. Even as she did so, she knew that this was futile. All her hard work and effort weren't going to make a difference. Not in California, not in Delaware.

After an hour of hacking away at the dirt, she conceded defeat. A shovel was totally inadequate for this job. So she returned her attention to the live vines. They looked like miniature trees at this stage of growth, with bare, twisted trunks on the bottom and a profusion of green leaves at the top. If she watered them too much, the grapes would bloat and the wine would be too thin. If she didn't water them enough, the grapes would shrivel and the wine would be too sweet. Too much heat, cold, bugs, birds, or even excess fruit could also ruin the grapes. Ian had been right all those years ago when he sliced away the first fruit from the strawberry plants: Judicious pruning and water deprivation in the early stages could result in better-quality fruit. But she didn't know how much to prune, or how much water to provide.

How could Ian love this? How could anyone?

When she finally trudged back to the house, sunburned and exhausted, Ginger greeted her on the porch with a cold glass of lemonade.

"Thanks." Cammie downed most of it in one gulp.

"Well?" Ginger prompted. "How's it looking out there?"

"I fixed the sprinklers." Cammie headed inside. "But a bunch of vines are dead."

"Dead? Oh no."

"Yeah, they got dehydrated. I think. I hope."

"What do you mean, you hope?"

"Well, if they didn't get dehydrated, that means they have some kind of disease that can spread to the other plants." Cammie hated to say this out loud.

Ginger looked aghast. "We need to take them out."

"I'm working on it." Cammie walked back to the kitchen and stuck her head into the freezer, savoring the arctic blast. "One thing at a time."

"You're doing great, honey! Just look at you." Ginger gestured to Cammie's filth-covered body and the mud-caked little dog beside her. "And look at Jacques. I almost mistook him for a border collie! Remember what I always used to tell you girls: The beginning is the hardest part."

Cammie had to smile. She did remember her aunt saying that. She turned to her canine sidekick and asked, "When do we get to the easy part?"

chapter 9

Kat and Josh were gone all day. After another few hours of watering the fields, Cammie and Ginger drank some awful iced wine, cleaned the house, made fruitless attempts to teach Jacques to sit, had dinner, and went to bed while the sun was still high in the sky. Cammie's last coherent thought as she passed out was, *I hope I find my inner farmer soon. And I hope she's a morning person.*

Five hours later, she awoke as Kat climbed into the queen-size bed.

"Hey," Kat said directly into her ear. "Are you awake?"

"It's the middle of night!" Cammie mumbled.

"No, it's not. It's barely ten o'clock. Why are you guys asleep?"

"Go away."

"Move over." Kat shoved Cammie out of the center of the mattress.

Cammie kicked in Kat's general direction. "When did you get home? Why aren't you in your room?"

"Move over and I'll tell you." Kat stole one of Cammie's pillows and helped herself to most of the covers. "It's the dog."

"The cute little French bulldog that you always wanted?"

"The cute little French bulldog that won't shut up," Kat corrected. "He snores like a bulldozer."

"You're exaggerating," Cammie said.

"Am I?" Kat huffed. "Listen."

They both froze for a moment. Sure enough, Cammie could hear the faint but unmistakable sounds of snores drifting down that hall.

"That's Jacques?"

"Yeah."

"Damn." Cammie paused. "Where's Josh?"

"In the bedroom. He could sleep through a typhoon." Kat yawned. "Now go back to sleep. Pretend we're sharing a room like when we were kids."

"What are you going to tell Josh when he wakes up tomorrow and you're in here?"

"I'll tell him that he shouldn't have bought a dog without consulting me."

Cammie struggled to wake up enough to carry on this conversation. "How was the breakfast date?"

"Um, pretty good."

"You guys were gone all day."

"Yeah, we had to go buy stuff for the dog." Kat slowly, slowly, started stealing the fluffiest pillow.

Cammie tightened her grip on the pillow. "Yeah, well, you should know that he thinks he's a farm dog. He walked the fields with me all afternoon."

There was a long silence, during which a land war ensued over the pillowcase.

"I wish . . . I just wish he didn't love me anymore." Kat sounded absolutely despondent. "Because then I could stop feeling so awful about not loving him."

"Good lord, what was that racket last night?" Ginger had already whipped up a stack of pancakes by the time Cammie and Kat came downstairs. "It sounded like a rock tumbler in your room."

"That was Jacques." Kat yawned and grabbed the carafe of coffee.

"It was? Good heavens." Ginger looked appalled. "Is he ill?"

"No, that's just what French bulldogs do," Kat said.

"Yes, it is." Josh's voice startled all of them as he walked into the kitchen. Jacques trotted along behind him, sniffing the air before sitting next to Ginger's feet.

"Well, we need to do something about that." Ginger picked up her spatula. "I'll die of sleep deprivation."

"Don't worry." Josh cast a pointed look at Kat. "Jacques and I are going back home today."

"You are?" Kat's expression and tone were oddly flat.

"That's what you want, clearly." He crossed his arms and leaned back against the cabinet.

"Who wants to help me weed today?" Cammie asked, feigning fascination in the steady drip of the coffeemaker.

"Oh, that sounds lovely," Ginger said loudly. "Count me in."

"Great. Want to join me out on the porch?"

"Why, yes, I'd love to."

The two of them hightailed it out of the kitchen. Cammie blinked in the bright morning light as they stepped onto the porch. She followed Ginger across the driveway to stand in the shade of a huge tree.

Her aunt sighed and shook her head. "I'm afraid Kat's making a very big mistake."

Cammie remained silent, determined not to get involved. Two seconds later, she caved. "She can't help how she feels."

"No, but she's a fool to be dictated by emotion. Love ebbs and flows in a marriage. You can't expect to feel head over heels every day. I thought she understood that." Ginger clicked her tongue. "This isn't about Josh at all; this is about Katherine having some kind of early midlife crisis because she can't skate anymore."

Cammie couldn't argue with that.

"If she lets him go, she's going to regret it later," Ginger predicted.

"Yeah, but you telling her that won't change anything. She has to see that for herself. And speaking of regrets . . ."

"Go on." Ginger kept a close eye on Jacques, who stumbled down the porch steps and sniffed a patch of flowers by the fence post.

"How are you feeling about the whole vineyard purchase now that we're actually here?"

"Why do you ask?" Ginger's eyebrows shot up. "Are you suggesting that I'm having some sort of *late* midlife crisis?"

Yes. "No. But sometimes the reality doesn't live up to the daydreams."

Ginger surprised her by giving her a big, warm hug and kiss. "Oh, honey. I know you had your own life going on in California. You girls are so good to come out here and indulge an old lady's folly."

Cammie frowned. "What? That's not—"

"That's exactly what this is, and we both know it. The sensible thing to do would be to sell this place to someone who knows what they're doing. Someone who has the time and money to make a real go of it. And I'll do that. I will." She lifted her chin. "Eventually. But I need the summer here. Just a little bit more fantasy before we all go back to reality."

Cammie understood exactly how her aunt felt. "I get it. But if we're planning to resell, we need to keep everything in good condition. We need to maintain. We need to *produce*."

Ginger nodded. "I'll help. Weeding, watering—whatever you need."

"Thank you, I appreciate that." *But it won't be nearly enough.* "I was thinking we could rent out the space for events. We could do weddings, bridal showers, maybe wine tastings for the tourists."

"You're so clever!"

"The first thing is, we should probably update the website."

Ginger frowned. "What website?"

"The vineyard's website."

"We have a website?"

"Well, I'm assuming . . ." Cammie trailed off when Josh and Kat strode out of the house, both of them visibly upset. Jacques raced over to them as fast as his stumpy legs would carry him, snorting with joy.

"Josh! You don't have to go." Kat pulled back her hair in frustration.

"Why would I stay here when you're acting like this?" Josh opened the car door.

"I'm sorry." Kat reached out her hand. "I'm trying. I'm working on it."

Josh reacted as if she'd slapped him. "Don't try, Kat. I don't want you to try." He slammed into the car and peeled out, sending a spray of gravel toward the grapevines.

Kat turned to Cammie and Ginger and tried to pretend the whole thing hadn't happened. "What're you guys doing out here?"

"Just talking about our website," Ginger trilled with forced cheer.

Kat perked up. "We have a website?"

"We don't have a website," Cammie confirmed a few minutes later as she scoured the Internet on her tablet.

"That would explain why I couldn't find out anything about this place online." Kat popped a handful of chocolate chips into her mouth. "Mmm. The only good thing about being forced into retirement is that I can eat candy with wild abandon."

"Since when do skateboarders not eat candy?" Cammie asked. "I thought you guys were all badass and devil-may-care."

"The devil does care . . . about empty calories. And so do athletes." Kat rummaged through the cupboards for more treats. "I know a little bit about Web design. I can slap something together after I help you with the vines today."

Cammie was overcome with relief. "How do you know how to make a website?"

"Well, I have one—I mean, I had one for skate stuff, and I figured out how to update it. It's not that hard to put a basic site together."

"Great, then we'll delegate that to you. Nothing fancy—just a few photos, a phone number, a map, and a reservations portal."

"Reservations portal?" Kat asked. "Reservations for what?"

"Events," Cammie replied. "Wine tastings, tours, parties."

"Who's going to coordinate all that?"

"You, me, and your mother."

Kat groaned and let her head drop back. "I'll do the website, but I ain't dealing with a bunch of hysterical brides. That's on you."

"Fine. I'll deal with the hysterical brides; you deal with the dead vines."

"The what now?"

Cammie summed up the situation at the far end of the field. Kat listened attentively, then gave a single nod. "I'm on it."

Cammie gaped. "Really?"

"Yep. Don't you worry your pretty little head. I've got this."

Cammie furrowed her brow "But . . . how? It's really complicated."

"It's not that complicated. All we have to do is get a tractor and rip them out."

"Oh, okay." Cammie had to laugh. "We'll just get a tractor? Just like that?"

"Yep." Kat hummed as she started scrolling through her phone. "Look, there's a big farm equipment auction in Lewes this weekend. Problem solved."

"We don't have the budget to buy a tractor."

"It's my treat. Now stop micromanaging. I said I'm on it and I'm on it."

Cammie stopped micromanaging.

"And what am I going to do?" Ginger demanded, hands on her hips. "While you two are whipping up a website and hosting weddings and buying tractors?"

Cammie shrugged. Kat blinked. "Um . . ."

"I'm not purely decorative, you know. I'm smart, I'm a hard worker, and, may I remind you, I own this place."

"Good point." Cammie considered the options for a moment. "You're on strawberry-wine duty."

"Strawberry wine?" Ginger threw her hands up. "What about the grape wine?"

"We can't make that until fall. In the meantime, we're going to need a lot of booze and we can't serve the swill the old owners left. We need to you make strawberry wine. Like, vats of it. Start making new batches every day. That way we'll have a steady supply."

"But you don't even know if you like it yet," Ginger protested.

"Based on the taste of the strawberries and the smell of what you were pouring in those bottles, I think it's safe to say we're going to like it."

"We have a feeling," Kat agreed.

Ginger glared at them. "You're patronizing me."

"No, ma'am," Cammie vowed.

"Well, if I'm going to make strawberry wine every day, I'm going to need a lot more strawberries," Ginger said.

"We better go back to the roadside stand." Kat winked at Cammie.

"You go," Cammie said. "I'm sitting this one out. Whatever was going on between Ian and me is deader than the gnarly brown vines out there."

"Are you sure?" Ginger wheedled.

"Positive."

chapter 10

"It smells like a square dance out here." Cammie wrinkled her nose as she and Kat arrived at the farm equipment auction.

"No, it doesn't. It smells like horse stables. In hell." Kat paused to sneeze three times in succession. "And seasonal allergies."

Cammie breathed through her mouth and slathered on an extra coat of sunscreen. She'd assumed that the auction would be held indoors, with a podium and some semblance of order, but this was nothing more than an open dirt field lined with tractors, backhoes, and combines. A group of men, all of whom seemed to know one another, eyed Cammie and Kat with a mixture of curiosity and derision.

When she and Kat had arrived a few minutes before, the smell of dust and manure had felt overpowering. But now that her nose had acclimated, she could detect ripe undernotes of hay, fertilizer, tobacco, and body odor.

"Maybe we should go home and change." Cammie glanced

down at her high-heeled sandals, which were sinking into the soil. "We need better footwear." She glanced at the men, all of whom were clad in mud-spattered jeans, ancient T-shirts, and sweat. So much sweat. She could discern an actual rivulet of perspiration snaking down the neck of the guy in front of her. "And we don't really blend."

Kat, who was herself wearing jeans, agreed. "I knew I shouldn't have ironed this shirt." She shook her head at Cammie's yellow cotton sundress and woven straw sunhat. "You are way overdressed." She indicated a man a few yards away. "Look how tight that dude's jeans are. Is that the John Deere version of jeggings? They're like a tourniquet."

Cammie surveyed the sea of silver belt buckles and sun-bleached cowboy hats. "Maybe we should try digging out the vines one more time."

"Too late. Let's make the rounds and figure out what we're going to buy." Kat led the way and together, they strolled the perimeter of the field. None of the rough-hewn men spoke to them or even made eye contact. Cammie hadn't felt so awkward and self-conscious since middle school.

"Is it just me, or do these all look the same?" Cammie whispered as she and Kat regarded a trio of tractors.

"What are you talking about? This one's way rustier than that one." Kat said. "Let's go over the plan again. We don't need anything fancy. It just has to be able to furrow the fields and yank out a bunch of grapevines. Ooh, let's get that one." She pointed out a tractor that had probably once been red. It was hard to determine the original color under all the rust.

Cammie tilted her head to assess the tractor. With a big, rectangular grille, two huge tires in back and two small ones in front, it would have fit right into an animated movie or an Old MacDonald storybook. "That one? Really?"

"It's red."

"So?"

Kat shrugged. "So it's cute."

"It's not a sports car, Kat."

"Yeah, but if we pretend it is, it'll be more fun to drive." Kat succumbed to another sneezing fit as she pulled her phone out of her pocket. "It's Josh. Should I—"

"Take it." Cammie waved her cousin away from the throng. "Talk to your husband. I can handle the bidding."

Kat blew her nose. "You're sure?"

"Of course I'm sure."

Cammie absolutely could not handle the bidding. The auction commenced without fanfare—all the men just clustered around a backhoe and started yelling. After about fifteen seconds, a barrel-chested, bearded guy in overalls announced, "Sold!" and everyone moved on to the next vehicle.

"Oh." Cammie hurried to keep up. "We're starting? Okay."

Three minutes later, the bearded auctioneer had sold two backhoes and two tractors, and Cammie felt rivulets of sweat trickling down her own neck. He spoke so quickly, she couldn't understand what the current bid was, although that was irrelevant since she couldn't seem to figure out how to bid, anyway.

She raised her hand. The men ignored her.

She waved her sunhat. The men ignored her.

She tried to push her way through to the front. The men ignored her, selectively blind and deaf.

Sales whizzed by in a blur of rapid-fire yelling and cursing. The crowd shuffled from one piece of equipment to the next. All of a sudden, there were only three tractors left. Cammie's desperation segued into full-fledged panic. What if she couldn't get a tractor? How would they get rid of the dead vines? What would happen to the rest of the harvest? How on earth was she going to—

"Hey!" A deep voice boomed out from the back of the crowd. *"Guys."*

All conversation ceased. Heads swiveled toward the back of the crowd. The only sound was a couple of tobacco chewers chomping away.

Cammie didn't have to look. She knew who had spoken.

"Give the lady a chance."

There ensued another moment of silence as everyone directed their attention to Cammie.

"Oh." She straightened her shoulders and smiled. No one smiled back. They coughed and muttered and waited with palpable impatience. But they gave her a chance.

She pointed to the rusty red tractor Kat had remarked upon earlier. "That one's great. I'll take that one." She named the price she and Kat had agreed upon, too flustered to try to bargain.

The auctioneer glanced toward the back of the crowd, then nodded. "Sold."

Cammie literally jumped for joy, then turned to locate Ian. He stood away from the group, watching her with the faintest trace of a smile.

She wended her way back to him, skittering sideways as a wad of freshly spit tobacco landed near her foot. "What are you doing here?"

He shifted his weight and lifted the brim of his cap, gazing down at her. "What are *you* doing here?"

She adjusted the strap of her sundress and tried to explain. "We have some dead vines. Well, they're either dead or diseased, and I'm worried that whatever they have is going to spread. We need to pull them out—so says the Internet—and also, we'll need to, um"—she strained to think of the correct terminology—"furrow the field."

"Furrow the field."

"That's right. I think." She twisted her hands together.

He watched her intently. "You're pretty hot when you talk like a farmer."

Cammie didn't know where to look. She could feel her thin cotton dress clinging to her back. "Thanks for your help."

"My pleasure."

"But I was holding my own, just so you know. I would have figured it out."

His smile deepened. "I have no doubt."

Kat bounded back into the field and looked around in dismay. "It's over already? What'd I miss?"

"I got the red one." Cammie gestured to the Old MacDonald tractor. "This lovely, um . . ."

"International Harvester," Ian supplied.

"This lovely International Harvester."

Kat high-fived her. "It'll be like the autobahn on the back forty."

Cammie rested her hand on the steering wheel, then pulled away when she felt the gritty combination of dirt and oil. "Here's hoping they'll wash it before they deliver it."

Ian laughed.

"What?"

"Wash it. Deliver it. You kill me."

"They're not going to deliver it?" Kat demanded.

Ian kept laughing and pointed out a little black puddle beneath the tractor. "You're going to have to change the oil, too."

"Details, details." Kat charged after the auctioneer, yelling, "Hey! Take my money and give me the keys! Will you take a check?"

Cammie turned back to Ian. "Can you believe it? I officially own a tractor. What next? Black is white? Up is down?"

"Next, you have to learn to drive it." His voice held a hint of a challenge.

She folded her arms and regarded the International Harvester.

"I drove the Los Angeles freeways every day. I think I can handle a tractor in an open field."

He sidled closer, just inside her personal space. "If you ask nicely, I'll come over and show you."

She sidled a bit closer, too. "Oh yeah? That sounds kind of like a date."

"More like a tutorial."

"Ooh." She framed her face with the brim of her hat. "I'm excited."

"You should be," he drawled. "How about Friday?"

She considered her options. "Let's say Thursday."

"Big plans for Friday?"

"Friday night's for dates. You said this was a farming tutorial." She smiled sweetly.

He didn't hesitate. "Fair enough. See you Thursday. Five o'clock?"

"Six," she countered.

"Five thirty." He leaned over and kissed her on the cheek. She closed her eyes and inhaled, picking up the scent of fresh soil and cut grass.

"Sold."

chapter 11

"Is the tractor all ready to go?" Cammie asked when she returned to the house after yet another day of weeding and watering the vines. She was covered in dust and sweat, but felt surprisingly energized after a full day's work. "Ian's going to be here in half an hour."

"No. They just dropped it off about an hour ago." Kat sat down on the hall floor, kicked off her flip-flops, and put on her sneakers. "It was supposed to be here yesterday, but they wouldn't take a personal check, so I had them call Josh and he worked everything out."

"You got them to deliver it? Good for you."

"Yeah, I had to pay extra. But now it's leaking all over the barn floor. We better go give it some more oil before Ian gets here for your, ahem, tutorial."

"You should worry less about my, ahem, tutorial and more about your own relationship. When are you and Josh going to see each other again?"

Kat took her time tying her shoelaces. "Unknown."

"Do you want to see him?"

"Kind of. I do but I don't."

"Fake it till you make it, remember? Call him."

"Why do you care?"

"I care because I love you, I love Josh, and I want you two to work this out and be happy." Cammie took off her sunhat and shook out her hair. "I believe in you."

"I'm glad somebody does."

"Call and invite him for this weekend."

"*You* call him and invite him for the weekend."

"Fine, I will." Cammie whipped out her phone.

"Stop. Stop!" Kat got to her feet. "Okay, I'll call him."

Cammie waited.

"As soon as we're done with the tractor." When Kat opened the screen door, Jacques materialized at her side.

"Is it dinnertime?" Kat asked as she took in the panting and beseeching canine eyes.

"No, he wants to help with the tractor. He's a farm dog," Cammie explained. "Just roll with it."

They headed out to the barn, which was dark and suffocatingly humid, to inspect the tractor. Jacques opted to wait outside in the grass.

Cammie folded her arms as she regarded the dilapidated red machine. "It just looks more jacked up every time I see it."

"It's about to look slightly less jacked up." Kat pointed out six bottles of motor oil resting on the dusty concrete floor. "At some point, I'll have to change the oil, but we can just top it off for now."

"And how do we do that?"

"I'm so glad you asked. I did some reading while you were out whipping the grapes into shape." Kat extracted a folded piece of paper from her pocket. "Behold, instructions on how to add oil to an International Harvester."

"All right, let's get down to it. I've got a tutorial in thirty minutes and I have to shower."

"Here we go." Kat gave directions with great authority. "First thing we do is check the oil level."

She lay down on the concrete and scooted underneath the tractor. "Come on. What're you waiting for?"

"If that thing falls on you, it'll kill you," Cammie said.

"Fall on me? How would that even happen?" Kat scoffed. "Get down here. Oh, but first, grab the wrench. I left it next to the oil."

Cammie obligingly grabbed the wrench and got down there. The underside of the tractor was impossibly claustrophobic, reeking of motor oil and diesel.

"I'll give you five minutes and then I'm showering," she told Kat.

"Then I better work fast." Kat applied the wrench to a rusty bolt and twisted. "Oof. This thing is stuck."

"Maybe it's a sign," Cammie suggested. "A sign that we should deal with this later."

"There is no 'later.' There is only now." Kat grimaced as she twisted the wrench with all her might. "I think it moved. Where's the oil pan?"

"What oil p—" Cammie broke off as a spray of black oil streamed onto her forehead. She flailed around on the filthy floor, shielding her face with her hands.

"Whoops." Kat sounded cheery and chipper as she tightened the bolt again. "Got a little carried away there."

Cammie gagged and sputtered, wiping her eyes.

"The good news is it wasn't rusted shut."

"Kat." Cammie wriggled out from under the tractor, dripping oil.

"Sorry. My bad."

"Kat."

Kat peered up at her. "I'll make it up to you. What can I do?"

Cammie mulled this over for a moment. "Call Josh."

"But—"

"I'm covered in used tractor oil and dust, Kat. I smell like a truck stop. Do not test me."

"Okay, okay. I'll call him."

But Cammie wasn't finished. "Ask him to have dinner on Saturday."

"All right, but you have to come with us." Kat emerged from beneath the tractor and stood up. "I can't make it through another meal like we had last time. It was deathly awkward."

"Look at me." Cammie held out her arms. "Do I look like I'm in any mood to chaperone you people?"

Kat nibbled her lower lip. "Please?"

"Ugh." Cammie wiped her face on the hem of her T-shirt, realizing too late that she'd left oil stains all over the fabric. "Fine."

"Thank you. You're a rock star." Kat pulled out her phone. "I'll text him right now. Wow, look at the time. You better go shower. No offense, but you look like a farmer."

While she shampooed her hair and shaved her legs, Cammie reflected that dating in Los Angeles had conditioned her to keep her expectations low and her bullshit detector finely tuned. Every time she sat down to have coffee with a new prospect, she had the feeling that he was looking over her shoulder just in case something better came along.

That was the thing about Los Angeles: Something better *always* came along. A younger girlfriend with bigger boobs. A newer, faster European sports car. A hot lead on a major studio deal that was mere minutes from being signed. How could anyone be expected to commit when the carousel of shiny new temptations was always turning?

Cammie had become as guilty of this as anyone else. She'd spent the past few years telling herself that she'd be happy as soon as she got a bigger apartment, made a profit at her dream job, found the love of her life.

She hadn't accomplished any of that, of course. She'd tried her best, given it her all, and ended up completely bankrupt, in more ways than one. But as she turned off the shower and wrapped her wet hair in a fluffy towel turban, she knew that she had something worthwhile to show for all her trials and tribulations in California.

Her magic jeans.

Blue, soft, and produced by an obscure Moroccan designer whose name Cammie couldn't even pronounce, these jeans were the real-life equivalent of airbrushing her lower half. She'd tried them on at the urging of a salesperson on commission at a boutique on Robertson Boulevard, and once she'd put them on, she never wanted to take them off. Her only regret was that she hadn't bought multiple pairs.

She was still drying her hair and debating her lipstick shade when she heard the crunch of tires on the driveway.

"Cam!" Kat hollered up the stairs.

"Coming!" Cammie stopped fussing, took a calming breath, and walked her magic-jeans-clad ass downstairs to talk farming with the one man she'd sworn she'd never farm with.

"I'll give you this—at least you got the soil right." Ian greeted her in the entryway, his expression both impressed and incredulous.

Cammie paused on the second step and struck a pose. "Hello to you, too."

"This is the best ground for growing grapes in all of Sussex County." He was too busy looking at the house and the fields to be awestruck by her beauty. "I didn't realize the owners were selling."

"Neither did I—this is all my aunt's doing." Cammie gave up waiting for him to ogle her and descended the final steps.

He continued to look at everything but her. "Why'd your aunt buy it?"

"I believe a bucket list was involved."

He nodded and finally gave her his full attention. "And here we are."

"Here we are." She looked into his warm brown eyes and her anxiety ebbed away.

"You ready to get acquainted with your tractor?" He started rolling up his sleeves.

"We can't." She gave him a quick rundown of the oil fiasco. "Kat says it's not safe to drive right now."

"It's not!" called Kat from the parlor, where she'd positioned herself for maximum eavesdropping potential. "Plus, I think the battery's dead. I can't get the engine started."

"So we can't have our tutorial. Not tonight, anyway." She had no idea how he'd respond to this.

Ian kept looking at her, assessing. "All right, then let's take a walk."

"A walk?" Cammie frowned.

"Yeah. I want to see the grapevines."

She squinted up at him. "So now is this a date?"

"It's a walk." He paused and checked his phone as an alarm sounded. His expression tensed as he read the message on the screen.

"Everything okay?" Cammie asked.

"Yeah." He glanced back up. "Just a weather alert. There's a heat advisory for tomorrow."

"Oh?" Cammie tried to sound casual. "Which app are you using?"

He told her, and Cammie made a mental note to download it later.

"Let me get you something to drink." She led him to the kitchen, where a strawberry pie was cooling on the counter, filling the room with a mouthwatering aroma. Then she glanced at the top of the refrigerator, where the strawberry wine was still fermenting. It wasn't ready yet.

"Iced tea?" she offered.

One corner of his mouth tugged up. "We need something stronger than iced tea."

"We only have really bad wine. Really, really bad wine. Like, someone should be in jail for this wine."

"I'll drink it if you will."

They headed out to the fields with plastic cups of really, really bad wine in their hands. The fading sunlight cast a golden glow across the vineyard. Cammie inhaled deeply, smelling sky and soil and grapes, and relaxed to the point that she could stop focusing on herself and start focusing on him. As he walked along a row of vines, she noticed that he, too, appeared to have a pair of magic jeans.

She was smiling when he turned around to face her, and her expression seemed to take him off guard.

"What?" He sounded wary.

She started talking and couldn't stop. "I have no clue what I'm doing. I'm reading as much as I can and watching a billion videos on wine making on YouTube, but none of it's going to matter if all the grapes die before the harvest."

"The grapes aren't going to die." He stated this as a fact. "You're going to keep them alive."

"You don't know that." She pointed to a shriveled brown leaf on the nearest vine. "Look! Dead already."

He plucked the leaf off and tossed it to the ground. "So you prune. No problem. You'll focus on quality, not quantity."

"But what if they all die?" She couldn't keep the fear out of her voice. "A bunch of vines already died back there." She pointed to the other side of the hill. "Hence the tractor."

Ian pointed out the rosebushes at the end of every row of vines. "Watch the roses. They're your early-warning system. If there are bugs or mildew or rot, the roses will show it first."

"Oh." She felt the tiniest twinge of relief. "I was wondering why those were there."

"They're there to help you. Check them every day."

Amid the rows of full, lush rosebushes, she'd noticed one that didn't fit in. It was scrawny and sparse, with thin green tendrils that clung to the grapevine stake. She pointed it out to Ian. "What's up with that one?"

He strode over to examine it. After inspecting the stalk and the leaves, he crouched down to look at the base and roots. "It's new. And it's a mistake."

"A mistake?"

"Yeah, it's a climbing rose." He showed her a tiny yellow metal tag at the base of the plant. "It shouldn't be here. It's the wrong kind and it's really young—it's not going to bloom for at least two more years."

"Who planted it, do you think?"

"Someone who didn't know what they were doing. We can pull it out right now." He looked enthused by the prospect.

"No." Cammie felt sorry for the poor little plant. "It's not doing any harm."

"It's not doing any good, either."

"I have bigger problems than a climbing rose," Cammie assured him. "Like keeping the grapes alive."

Ian stood up, still scowling at the errant, bloomless rose vine. "You'll do fine. Remember the strawberries?"

She didn't have to ask for clarification. "Of course."

"You kept those alive."

"So did you," she said. "For seven years now. What happened?"

"After you left?" he said pointedly.

She didn't respond directly to that. "I thought your family had been growing corn for generations."

"The corn crops took a big hit about five years ago. My dad was in danger of losing the farm. We needed to diversify our income stream, and one of the strawberry plants threw a sport."

Once again, Cammie felt like farming was a foreign language. "A sport?"

"A genetic mutation," he clarified. "Happens all the time with plants. A rosebush that should have red roses suddenly blooms with yellow flowers."

"What kind of sport did our strawberry plant grow?" she asked.

"A bigger berry. It was redder, juicier." He shook his head at the memory. "I almost didn't notice it at first; it was from the plant that you refused to let me prune."

Cammie was pleased that after all these years, her instincts had been proven correct. "See? I told you so."

"You did." He didn't look at all chagrined. "So, I took the seeds from that strawberry, hybridized them, and started growing more of them."

"And our magic strawberries saved your farm. It's like a fairy tale."

"The patent I got on those seeds saved the farm," Ian corrected.

"You can patent seeds?"

"Sure. There are patents for citrus fruit, berries, roses, shade trees . . ." He shrugged. "Those berries won agricultural awards and a company made me an offer to produce and distribute the seeds. The patent will be good for twenty years."

"So I could buy these berries out of a seed catalog?"

He nodded.

"What are they called?" she persisted. "I want to look them up."

"It's a passive stream of income to supplement what we make from the crops," Ian finished. "It was a fluke. A fluke that saved the farm."

"What did your dad have to say about all that?" Cammie asked.

"He and my mom retired to Florida. Spent some of the strawberry money on a condo by the ocean and turned the farm over to me and my brother."

They had fallen into step together and were slowly walking the perimeter of the field.

"Your brother's the father of the girls who sold us the strawberries the day we got into town?" Cammie asked. "A family of entrepreneurs."

"Yeah, Mike keeps the books, and I take care of the fields." Ian turned his face up to the setting sun.

"He doesn't want to be out in the fields? He's an indoor type, like me?" Cammie teased.

"He just moved back to town last year," Ian said. "He thinks he's ready to run the day-to-day operations because he grew up on the farm."

"But he's not?"

"Not yet." Ian's expression was obstinate, his eyes intense. "I'll know when he's ready."

"How will you know?"

"I'll know." His expression softened. "So, yeah, we're doing well. All because you don't like sweet corn."

"There you go." Cammie couldn't quite meet his gaze. "That summer wasn't a total waste."

"Changed my life," he said, his voice deepening.

She took a sip of tart, acidic wine and tried not to gag.

"Back to the grapes. You're off to a good start—the soil here is sandy loam."

She stared at him. "What does that mean?"

"It means you have good drainage. Drainage is good for grapes."

"If you say so."

"And the land here is pretty flat." He stretched out his arm to indicate the gently sloping hills. "You know where else it's flat?"

"Iowa?" Cammie guessed.

"Bordeaux, France. Where they grow the best wine in the world."

"I think Napa would beg to differ with you on that point." She took another sip of wine and started to enjoy the fact that she and Ian were out here, walking and talking and getting along. Even though their summer romance had been short-lived, their strawberries would live on forever.

It was almost as if that final, bitter conversation had never happened.

The planes of Ian's face were cast in shadows by the setting sun. "The angle of the land determines how much sun the grapes get."

She rocked back on her heels, marveling. "How do you know all this?"

"It's my life's work." He hesitated for a second, then reached up to push a stray piece of hair from her forehead. "What kind of wine are you going to make?"

She thought about the labels on the bottles the previous owner had left behind. "Cabernet and seyval blanc."

"What's seyval blanc like?" he asked.

"It's a white wine."

He waited for more details.

"I'll let you know more as soon as I find out." She grinned. "Whatever it is, we can make it work if we market it right. That much I learned from a few years in the restaurant business: There's a ton of peer pressure. Everyone's afraid to admit they like uncool wine."

"What makes a wine uncool?"

"It's affordable and other people can get it."

He groaned. "Are you sure you want to get into this business?"

"I'm sure I *don't*, but my aunt does, so here I am." She spread out her arms. "Keeping the grapes alive." Even as she said this, she noticed a little geyser of water spurting from a nearby vine. "Crap. The irrigation system's broken again."

He knelt down and tugged the thin tube of water from the soil. "Give me a minute to look at this, and then we'll fix it together." He examined the system in silence for a few moments, heedless of the water soaking his shirt.

"We're making wine with your strawberries," she mentioned as the wine from her plastic cup started to kick in.

He glanced over his shoulder at her. "Yeah?"

"Yeah. It was my mom's recipe, but my aunt's made it tons of times. It's going to be really good."

"I see how it is." He shook his head, his tone both teasing and not teasing. "You don't want me. You just want my strawberries and my tractor expertise."

"Not true." She sank down into the soil next to him. "I mean, I do want your strawberries. And also your tractor expertise. But . . ."

"But?" he finally prompted.

She scooped out a little hole in the dirt for her wine. "We should probably finish this conversation when I'm not tipsy."

He looked incredulous. "You've had half a glass of wine. How are you going to be a winemaker if you're tipsy after that much?"

"I'll work on it," she vowed, watching his hands as they sifted through the dirt.

"You do that. And this conversation is not over." He got back to work. "To be continued."

She couldn't tell what he was thinking, but she had a feeling it was juicy and salacious. And after several seasons of drought and despair, she was ready for juicy and salacious. "When are we going to continue it?"

"Saturday night?" he suggested. "Dinner?"

She could only blame the really bad wine for what came out of her mouth next. "Is *that* a date?"

"You tell me." He tried and failed to hide a smile. "Is Saturday night a date night?"

"Yep."

"Well, then . . ."

Cammie's eyes widened as she remembered her promise to Kat. "My cousin's husband might be in town Saturday. Double date?"

He glanced at her, his brown eyes darkening, and she felt a little frisson of anticipation. "Okay, but I'm driving you home."

He leaned in toward her. She leaned in toward him. Then she closed her eyes, parted her lips, and . . .

Woof!

The short, indignant bark startled both of them. Cammie whirled around to find Jacques standing behind her, his eyes bright and his ears pricked forward. His expression could be described only as one of betrayal.

"This is Jacques," Cammie told Ian. "Our farm dog."

Jacques started panting, which exposed his missing tooth.

"I like the snaggletooth." Ian reached down to pet him.

"Yeah, he likes to come with me and . . ." Cammie trailed off. She didn't want to talk about counting the rows right now. She didn't want to say anything that would remind Ian of everything that had come before.

Ian watched her, waiting.

"He likes to keep an eye on the grapes," she finished.

After Jacques escorted them around the remainder of the field, Cammie walked Ian to his truck. She strolled back to the house with a huge smile on her face.

When she stepped into the parlor, Kat glanced up from her website work on the laptop. "Tell me everything."

"It went well?" Ginger hurried down the stairs. "Oh, I'd better give him some pie before he leaves." She hurried outside, waving at the pickup truck with a dish towel.

"Spill your guts," Kat commanded. "Hurry up and tell me the good stuff before she comes back."

"It was all good." Cammie sank down on the worn green brocade sofa. "I feel like I'm twenty-two again."

"Wow." Kat sounded a bit envious. "That is good."

"Yeah." Cammie stretched out, all warm and tingly. "Oh, and we're going to dinner on Saturday. You, me, Josh, and Ian."

"What?" Kat's jaw dropped. "You were supposed to get in, get a tractor consult, and get out! What happened?"

"Bad wine and magic jeans." Cammie kicked her feet up as the wine went to her head. "How could I resist?"

chapter 12

"Our double date is at a place called the Jilted Café." Cammie sat in the passenger seat of Kat's car, looking up at the brick building with mounting trepidation. "Promising."

"This was your doing," Kat said. "Too late for cold feet now."

"It seemed like such a good idea at the time." Cammie smoothed her skirt. When she'd agreed to this, she'd been drunk on sunset and sky and the prospect of keeping the grapes alive. And wine. But over the past two days, she'd realized that the whole situation was fraught with pitfalls.

"Come on, let's get this over with." Kat reached for the door handle. "I'm having dinner with my husband, you're having dinner with the swarthy strawberry guy, and we're all going to have fun, dammit." She got out of the car and waited for Cammie to follow.

"Why did I agree to dinner? Dinner's a lot of pressure." Cammie shut the passenger-side door with a bit more force than was necessary. "We'll have to sit there, staring at one another, small-talking for an hour and a half, and we'll have to deal with menus and servers—"

"Oh, I know what this is about." Kat smote herself on the forehead. "This isn't really about the restaurant, is it? This is about the restaurant *guy*."

"NO." Cammie spoke so loudly, several nearby pedestrians turned to look at her.

"It's okay." Kat nodded. "Of course you're all triggery about restaurants after what Zach put you through."

"This has nothing to do with Zach," Cammie insisted. "This has to do with me. I'm just not ready for this—with Ian or anyone else. My life is complicated enough right now."

Kat stopped with the pep talk and started commiserating. "Listen, I'm not ready to face my lawfully wedded husband, either. But we made a commitment—well, *you* made a commitment—and now we have to honor it."

They stood on the sidewalk, Kat in jeans and a blouse, Cammie in a flowery dress, both of them primped and powdered and petrified. Kat grabbed Cammie's elbow and hustled her into the cozy café. "And remember: If you can get him talking about farming, everybody wins."

They entered the café and spotted Ian at a table by the back wall. Cammie smiled, though just the sound of clattering silverware from the kitchen made her heart rate pick up. He stood to greet them. She sat down next to him and picked up her menu with trembling hands.

He noticed the shaky hands. She noticed him noticing and put down the menu.

He directed his attention to Kat. "We're meeting your husband, right?"

"Yeah. Josh." Now Kat looked edgy. She kept glancing at the doorway.

Cammie tried to reassure her. "I'm sure he'll be here any minute. You know how bad beach traffic is on Friday evenings."

"Where's he driving in from?" Ian asked.

"Maryland," Kat said.

"But you live here?"

Kat's smile was as huge as it was fake. "Just for the summer. We're figuring out a few things."

Ian turned to Cammie and wisely changed the subject. "You look nice."

"Thanks." She knew it was her turn to make small talk or ask a question, but she had no idea what to say.

Kat jumped in on her behalf. "So, Ian! Did you always know you wanted to be a farmer?"

Ian shrugged. Cammie could see the faintest trace of sunburn near the collar of his shirt. "My parents made me get up every morning at four thirty to check the fields and feed the horses, so yeah."

"But you like it?" Kat persisted.

He seemed confused by the question. "That's what my family does. We've had the land for generations and it's not going to farm itself."

"It's your calling?" Kat rested her chin in her hand, a captivated listener.

"I guess."

Josh arrived, his shirt and khakis rumpled from a long drive in a hot car.

"Sorry I'm late." He settled into the chair next to Kat. "Traffic was brutal."

Kat gave him a quick peck on the lips. "Thanks for coming all the way out here."

"Well"—Josh doffed his baseball cap—"it's not like you were ever going to come to me."

Kat ignored this. "I'm so glad you're here. We're going to have a lovely dinner. No distractions." She shot Cammie a look of desperation. "Isn't it great to be able to just focus on each other?"

"It certainly is," Cammie said brightly. "Ian, this is Josh. Josh, this is Ian."

Everyone shook hands and complained about traffic and scanned the menus. Cammie started to relax. This wasn't so bad. They were normal people having a normal double date.

As the server arrived with their drinks, Kat's phone chimed. She reached for it, and Josh said, "No distractions."

After they ordered their entrées, Summer Benson walked through the front door. Kat waved and prepared to get up to say hi. Josh intoned, "No distractions."

A few seconds after their meals arrived, a teenager with spiked hair and tattoos galore approached the table. He stared at Kat as though she were an exotic zoo animal.

"May we help you?" Josh asked.

"Are you Kat Milner?"

Kat nodded and smiled, though her eyes were bleak. "That's me."

"You guys!" the boy shouted to his table mates in triumph. "I told you it was her! Can I please have your autograph?"

"Sure." Kat scribbled her name on a napkin and hissed at Josh out of the corner of her mouth, "I'm not going to be rude."

Josh set his jaw.

Her fan pulled out a phone and prepped for a series of selfies. "Can me and my friends take a quick picture with you?"

"Um, sure." Kat turned to her dining companions. "I am so sorry. This will just take a second."

And Josh was out the door.

Two minutes later, still smiling and waving as her fans snapped photos, Kat dashed out after him.

Ian and Cammie regarded each other over the bread basket.

"And that's my family," she announced. "We're a little . . . intense."

"What does your cousin do that she gets autograph requests at dinner?" Ian asked.

"She's a professional skateboarder. Well, she was. She just retired. Spine injury."

"I didn't realize there were professional female skateboarders." He offered her a wedge of bread, and she passed him the butter.

"There aren't very many. She was one of, like, three. But she was big-time—she had posters and corporate sponsors and a line of boards she designed and everything." Cammie took out her phone and showed him some photos of Kat modeling her gear.

"That was her calling?"

"Oh, yeah. She really, really loved it."

"What's yours?" he asked. "I thought you were going to be a restaurateur in California."

"Yes, well . . ." Her whole body felt aflame with humiliation. "That didn't work out."

He hooked one arm over the back of his chair and waited for her to elaborate.

"I opened a restaurant. It went bankrupt." She glanced up at him, expecting a long-overdue "I told you so," but she could see in his eyes he wasn't thinking that.

"What happened?"

"My original plan was to open a bar, like a fancy cocktail lounge–type deal. But my boyfriend wanted to be a chef. We decided to open a restaurant together. He'd run the back of the house, and I'd run the front." Somehow, they'd also decided that since Zach would be providing all the culinary know-how, Cammie should provide all the start-up capital.

Ian remained carefully neutral.

"A wise man once told me that ninety percent of restaurants

fail in their first year," Cammie informed her napkin. "I couldn't beat the odds."

"What happened to the boyfriend?" Ian wanted to know.

"He was part of why the restaurant failed." Cammie had to close her eyes to endure the burn of shame. "Two months after we opened, he left."

"For someone else?"

She shook her head. "For another restaurant. One of the big-name New York chefs was opening a place down the street and needed an executive chef. He jumped ship." And now he was lapping up accolades at a Hollywood hotspot where everyone wanted reservations, while she was broke. In Delaware. Farming against her will.

Ian was still listening, so she wrapped up her story with, "So now I'm in the wine business, which also has a pretty high failure rate."

"But you're keeping the grapes alive."

"They were alive when I left them tonight." Cammie allowed herself a little smile. "So far, so good."

"And you're going to have help from an expert."

She looked at him quizzically.

"I'll be your consultant," he offered. "You can pay me in strawberry baked goods."

"But why?" She had to ask. "We didn't exactly end on the best note."

He didn't break eye contact. "That was a long time ago."

She nodded, trying to remember what she had felt like before life got so convoluted and expensive. Before she'd put up all the defenses she couldn't take down.

"Farming's a community." His voice was matter-of-fact. "Everyone helps each other out, because everyone needs help eventually."

"Well, that's very enlightened."

"Yeah." He reached across the table and squeezed her hand. "Plus, I have a thing for you."

"Oh." She rearranged herself in her chair and tucked her hair behind her ear. She knew she should say something. Anything.

"You liked it?" Ian's gaze intensified as he let go of her hand.

"I . . . What?" She blinked.

"The restaurant you opened."

"It had its moments." Her knee rested against his under the table. She could feel the coarse denim of his jeans against her bare skin. "I liked the pace. Something different every day, new people every night. In a weird way, I liked running around, putting out fires. It was a challenge. And you know I'm a night owl." She shifted her leg against his. "Which is why this whole getting-up-with-the-sun thing is killing me."

He acknowledged this with an incline of his head. "Yeah, it's work, work, work, work, work all morning, and then nothing to do all evening."

"Except check the weather," she said.

"Yeah, except that. Hey, did you see that it might rain tomorrow morning?"

"It might?" Cammie frowned. "My app didn't say anything about that."

"Oh, you can't just look at the app." He pulled out his phone to show her. "You always have to check Weather.com. It's the best."

They huddled over his phone, comparing sites. And, just like that, they were completely at ease. She asked about his family and his house and his crops, and then, finally, when the waitress came to ask if they wanted dessert, she asked the question she'd been wondering about since she first saw him on her way into town:

"How are you not married? I figured you'd have settled down by now."

"'Settled down' is a state of mind." He signaled to their server and pulled out his wallet. "Come on. I'll drive you home."

. . .

Cammie looked around for Kat and Josh as she followed Ian out of the café, but they had vanished. Maybe they were having a mature, productive talk that would lead to a clear resolution. It wasn't likely, but it could happen.

Anything could happen, apparently.

"I'm serious," Cammie said as they walked toward his truck. "A guy with your agricultural expertise? You must be knee-deep in women."

"Don't forget the strawberry-seed patents," he said drily.

"How could I possibly?"

"We do get a lot of women in this town," he allowed, "especially in the summer."

"I heard! All the heartbreak tourists."

"We even had a designated rebound guy for a while."

"Get out." Cammie loved everything about this. "That was his job?"

"It wasn't an official position or anything. He just hung out at that wine bar down the street, buying drinks for women who had bad breakups."

"Is he still there?" Cammie turned toward the Whinery. "I need to get a look at this guy."

"Too late. He retired." Ian steered her back toward the parking lot. "I think he met someone."

"What about you?" Cammie tried to sound casual. "Did you meet someone?"

"While you were off opening a restaurant with your California boyfriend?" He pulled out the keys to his truck. "I met several someones."

She expected this, had set herself up for it, but was still surprised by the twinge of jealousy. "And . . . ?"

He looked at her for a moment. "And they were all great."

She crossed her arms, feeling more defensive by the moment. "But . . . ?"

"But it was never the right woman at the right time."

She squinted through the evening shadows, trying to discern his expression. "You're telling me that all your exes were great but it was never the right timing?"

He nodded. "Timing's important."

"If you turn this into a farming metaphor, I won't be responsible for my actions."

"No farming metaphors." He opened the truck door for her. "Get in."

"Are we going to the wine bar?" she asked hopefully.

"Nope."

She didn't want the night to end. "You're taking me back to the house?"

He settled into the driver's seat and started the ignition. "Eventually."

chapter 13

The ocean looked amber under the light of the huge golden moon as they drove by the beach. "We could take a little stroll on the sand." Cammie inched toward Ian on the truck's wide bench seat. "I haven't been to the boardwalk yet."

"We're not going to the boardwalk." Ian gave her a knowing look. "We're going back to the fields. Putting it off is just making it worse."

"I have no idea what you mean."

"You're scared," he said.

She pulled back a bit. "Of what?"

"The grapes. The dirt. All of it."

"I'm not scared of the grapes," Cammie insisted.

"Have you tasted one yet?" he challenged.

"No," she blustered. "They're for growing, not for eating."

He turned off the coastal highway and headed inland. "You and those grapes are going to be spending a lot of time together. You need to get comfortable with them."

She shot him a sidelong glance. "Because grapes can smell fear?"

"Damn straight." He draped his arm along the back of the seat. "We just had a lovely dinner and drove by a gorgeous full moon over the ocean. This night has potential. Let's not ruin it with grape talk."

"I'm not ruining anything." He let his arm settle across her shoulders. "I'm about to make your whole life better."

"In the vineyard? At night?" She considered what she just said. "That sounds so romantic. Too bad the reality is so . . ."

"So what?" he prompted.

"Nothing." She sighed. "There's just so much to know. There's nothing arty or creative about growing grapes. Everything's technical and exact." Her voice got thinner, higher. "Water, but not too much water. Heat, but not too much heat. Fertilizer, but not too much fertilizer. If you make one mistake, everything's ruined for the season. You fail."

All she could hear was the rush of the wind through the open windows. Then Ian said, "Don't ruin this for yourself."

"I'm not."

"They're just grapes. It's just sun and earth and water. Think of it like this," he suggested. "A few years ago, this vineyard didn't even exist. It's an experiment."

She held one hand just outside the window, feeling the push of cool air against her palm. "How can you be so relaxed about it?"

"I have to be. That's how it goes with farming. You can't control the weather or the soil or the bugs. All you can do is work with what you have. If it doesn't pan out, wait for a season and try again."

"Timing is everything?"

"Exactly." He brushed her hair aside and rested his palm on the nape of her neck.

Cammie knew she should be enjoying the here and now, but her anxiety mounted with every mile they drove. Facing down a field of grapes in the dead of night was the stuff of nightmares. She would have to admit all her ignorance and inadequacies to him. Again.

She lapsed into silence until Ian turned down the winding gravel road and parked by the grapevines. "Let's go." He walked around, opened her door, and offered his hand. "Come on."

"We could just sit in here and make out," she offered.

He took her hand in his and led her toward the field. She could smell the faint trace of roses in the humid night air. Ian kept going until they reached the center of the vineyard, where all she could see was tender young vines and the man next to her. When she looked up, the vast, starry sky stretched out forever.

He looked down at her. She looked up at him.

"Now what?" she murmured.

He rested his index finger on her lips. "Listen."

She tilted her head and strained her ears. After a few moments, she heard the soft, persistent whisper of the breeze against branches. The rustle of growth and greenery. Undetectable, unless you knew to listen for it. The sound of life.

She gazed up at him, a smile spreading across her face. "I hear it."

He leaned down and kissed her softly, and she felt something spark within her. Everything shifted, even as the earth remained solid beneath her and the stars remained fixed overhead.

Cammie made it back to the house just after eleven. All her warm, fuzzy feelings faded when she saw Kat crying on the sofa in the parlor.

When she sat down next to her cousin, Kat hugged a throw pillow to her chest and turned her face away. "I can't talk about it."

"Okay." Cammie made herself comfortable, anyway. "But you can watch TV, right?"

"No one is watching TV at this hour." Ginger's voice floated down from upstairs. "Both of you are going to bed this instant."

"Do we have a curfew?" Cammie asked Kat.

"You shouldn't need a curfew," Ginger called. She had always had superhuman hearing. "You should have enough common sense at your age to know that you need to be in bed at this hour. But since you don't have common sense, I'll be the voice of reason. As usual. Upstairs, both of you. *Now.*"

Cammie and Kat were getting to their feet when the doorbell rang. The chimes echoed through the dark, quiet house. Jacques let out a single bark from his dog bed on the second floor.

Cammie looked at Kat. Kat looked at Cammie. Jacques started trundling down the stairs, snorting with every step.

"Who on earth is that?" Ginger demanded.

Kat's expression was both hopeful and horrified. "Maybe it's Josh again?"

They were all still standing around, staring and wondering, when the doorbell rang a second time.

Ginger marched down the stairs and bestowed a withering look on the younger women as she reached for the doorknob. "*Somebody* has to take action."

She yanked open the door, which blocked Cammie's view of the porch.

"Oh." Ginger sounded both annoyed and confused. "*Oh*. May I help you?"

Kat jumped off the couch and hurried to her mother's side. Cammie was right behind her. They jostled for position as they regarded the quartet of middle-age tourists bedecked in Bethany Beach sweatshirts and tennis visors.

"Is this the winery?" a tall brunette with blindingly white teeth asked.

"Yes." Kat frowned. "Are you guys lost?"

"Not anymore. We've been driving around looking for this place for almost an hour."

The man behind the dazzling-toothed woman nodded. "Not to tell you gals how to run your business, but you should really consider getting some better signage."

Kat's eyebrows went all the way up to her hairline. Cammie hastened to intervene. "Signage. Got it. We'll take that under advisement."

The tourists started to look peeved. "So . . ."

Cammie, Ginger, and Kat waited for them to finish the sentence.

"Can we come in? Your website says you do wine tastings."

"It's past eleven," Ginger pointed out.

The visitors looked sheepish—for about five seconds. "I know, but we have to fly back home tomorrow, and we were so looking forward to this."

"No offense," said the guy who had made the helpful suggestion about signage. "But you ladies don't look like you're in a position to turn away business."

Ginger and Kat opened their mouths in unison, but before they could utter a syllable, Cammie slipped into restaurateur mode. She was used to dealing with last-minute requests and overinflated egos. Her guests wanted a certain experience, and she was going to provide it. "Come on in." She stepped back and held the door open. "Make yourselves comfortable. I'll be right back with the wine."

When her aunt rounded on her, Cammie held up her palm and whispered, "In the kitchen."

While she located wineglasses and checked them for water spots, she said, "You guys go to bed if you want. I can handle this."

"It's the middle of the night!" Ginger was outraged. "The nerve of them, traipsing into our house at this hour. Who do they think they are?"

"They can take their signage," Kat growled, "and shove it up their—"

"You know who they are? They're paying customers," Cammie

replied. "Who will leave big tips after they get some cabernet into them."

"The website says we offer wine tastings by appointment," Kat said. "Not by demand, whenever your punk ass happens to show up. That's not how we operate."

Cammie grabbed a corkscrew, poured a bottle of water into a carafe, and rummaged through the pantry for a box of crackers. "It is now. Grab some ice and see if we have any soda in the fridge."

"What are we doing with soda and ice?"

Cammie washed her hands and flexed her fingers, preparing to do culinary magic. "Making bad wine slightly less bad."

"This is . . . interesting."

Cammie smiled as everyone sipped the strawberry sangria she'd made with the cabernet. "It's *delicious*."

"Yes! Delicious!" By midnight, the well-heeled tourists were thoroughly soused and easily persuaded. "Delaware is the next Napa."

"I'm flattered you think so." When the sangria was gone, Cammie poured seyval blanc into the wineglasses and encouraged everyone to cleanse their palates by nibbling the oyster crackers. "Here, try this and see what you think."

"Sweet," proclaimed the brunette.

"Dry," her husband asserted.

They both looked to Cammie to determine who had the more discerning palate.

"You're both right," she assured them. "That's the beauty of wine—taste is subjective."

Behind the tourists, Ginger gave her a silent golf clap.

"You're drinking the same thing, but having entirely different experiences. There's no such thing as a great wine—there's only what you like and don't like." Cammie was one hundred percent making this up as she went along, but her guests were nodding in agreement.

"That's why there's no point in being snobby about wine." She handed out fresh napkins and offered everyone more crackers. "You're supposed to enjoy it, not judge it."

"So it's okay if I like Riesling, even though all my fashionable friends say it's awful?" The second female tourist seemed so earnest and hopeful.

"It's not awful if you love it," Cammie decreed. "Remember: It's just wine."

"It's just wine," they all murmured.

"Just sun and soil and grapes." Cammie glanced at her watch, then made a point of yawning loudly. This set off the desired chain reaction, and everyone started exclaiming about how late it was and how early they had to leave for the airport in the morning.

"This is such a beautiful area," the brunette said as she regarded the night sky with boozy appreciation. "And so romantic."

"You gals are so lucky. Living the dream."

"While we have to go back to the real world. Meetings and dentist appointments and morning commutes. What's it like? Not having to deal with any of that crap?"

Just tractor auctions and broken sprinklers and snowballing debt. "What can I say?" Cammie shoved a handful of oyster crackers into her mouth. "Living the dream."

chapter 14

Two days later, Cammie was on the phone with Ian when the male stripper showed up.

"Grapes still alive?" Ian asked.

"So far, so good," Cammie confirmed. She tucked her feet underneath her on the sofa. At almost five o'clock in the afternoon, her muscles ached and her limbs felt leaden with exhaustion. Ginger, Kat, and Jacques had joined her shortly after dawn to pull weeds and check the moisture levels in the soil. She let her eyes flutter closed for a moment, tipped her head against the back of the sofa . . .

"Hey." Ian's voice brought her back to reality. "Still with me?"

"What? Yes." She could hear a faint mechanical rumbling on his end of the connection and pictured him out in the fields, surrounded by soil and strawberries. "Sorry—I'm a little drowsy. We've had people show up at all hours." She recounted the story of the midnight tourists.

He sounded both amused and incredulous. "And you invited them in and poured them wine?"

The doorbell rang. Cammie froze. "Oh no."

"What?"

"That might be another wine-tasting group right now."

"Are you kidding me?"

"I'll get it." Ginger hurried out of the kitchen, through the living room and into the front hall.

Thirty seconds later, she returned, her face scarlet.

"Hang up the phone," she ordered Cammie.

Cammie covered the mouthpiece with one hand. "What's up? More wine tasting?"

Her aunt plucked the phone from Cammie's hand and hung up.

"Hey!" Cammie protested.

Ginger shut her down with a withering glare and yelled up the stairs for Kat.

"You paged me?" Kat ambled down, in no particular hurry.

Ginger folded her hands primly and drew a shuddering breath. "Why is there a scantily clad man dressed like a sailor on my front porch?"

Cammie and Kat practically knocked each other over as they headed for the foyer. Sure enough, an almost cartoonishly buff and tanned guy was standing on the welcome mat. He had on tight white pants, a jaunty white sailor's cap, and a navy neckerchief, and no shirt. Despite the gratuitous display of pecs and abs, he had the demeanor of a sheltered high schooler dressed up for a musical. A topless musical.

"This place just gets weirder every time the doorbell rings," Kat said to Cammie. Then she turned her attention to their guest. "Hi there. How may we help you?"

Cammie elbowed her cousin out of the way. "I like your hat."

He reached up to touch the brim and gave her a heartbreaking smile. "Thanks."

"Why is he here?" Ginger yelled from the kitchen. She banged some pots around for emphasis.

"Don't be shy. Come in, come in." Kat ushered their guest into the house.

The poor guy wandered around the parlor, looking completely confused. "I'm here for the party."

Cammie's brows snapped together. "The what, now?"

"The bachelorette party?" He adjusted the navy neckerchief.

"I don't think we have anything like that scheduled," Kat said.

"I'm sure there's a party tonight. They said five p.m." The strapping young lad pulled up an e-mail on his phone as proof. "Here it is: five p.m."

"We'll get this figured out," Kat assured him. "And while we do that, why don't you sit down and have some wine?"

"Oh, I can't drink."

"I guess it makes sense that there are laws against imbibing while, um, entertaining," Cammie mused.

"Yeah, plus I'm only twenty."

"How about cookies and milk?" Kat offered.

"Gosh, that sounds great." He ducked his head, abashed. "But I don't want you ladies to go to any trouble."

"Oh, it's no trouble." Kat led the way down the hall. "We should find you a shirt, though."

"Okay," the guy agreed. "If it's not too much trouble."

"No trouble at all. I've got a hundred promo T-shirts from boarding expos. What's your name?"

"Theo," he replied.

Cammie's heart warmed as she imagined the cozy tableau: stripper and skateboarder about to sit down to cookies and milk.

She startled when she heard Ginger's voice hissing in her ear: "Since when are there strippers in Black Dog Bay?"

Cammie gasped and whirled around. "Don't sneak up on me like that."

"And since when are we inviting them in for a snack?" Ginger brandished a strawberry juice–stained potato masher as if it were a weapon.

"His name is Theo," Cammie informed her aunt. "And he seems like a very nice young man."

Ginger gave a little squeak of disbelief. "Nice young men wear shirts."

"Kat is getting him a shirt right now."

"I don't like this." Ginger crimped her lips as they heard the clatter of glassware in the kitchen.

"Come on, just say hi. He's very polite. And he's only twenty." Cammie strolled into the kitchen to find Theo regarding Kat with wide-eyed sincerity.

"Did you know she's a professional skateboarder?" he asked.

Cammie toasted Kat with her water glass. "I did know that."

"That's pretty badass." With his earnest blue eyes and a milk mustache, Theo looked more like an Amish farm boy every minute.

"Here." Kat opened a fresh package of cookies and informed Cammie, "We figured out what happened: He went to the wrong winery."

"You did?" Cammie frowned. "I thought we were the only winery in Black Dog Bay."

"You are. I'm supposed to go to one in Lewes." Theo checked the time on his smartphone. "I have to leave in three minutes."

"There's a winery in Lewes?" Cammie filed away this tidbit for future reference. "I'll have to hunt down the owner and find out, well, everything she knows, basically."

Theo, still starstruck, handed his phone to Kat. "Are there any videos of you on YouTube?"

"Probably." Kat looked self-conscious.

"What? You haven't watched them?"

"I don't need to be some pathetic has-been, watching clips of my glory days. That's gross. And sad. And . . ."

"Ignore her." Cammie nodded at Theo. "Type in 'Kat Milner.'"

He did, and watched a few clips of skating competitions. "Cool. You *are* badass."

"I *was* badass," Kat corrected him. "I'm retired now."

"Yeah?" He looked at her, considering. "But you're not completely old yet."

Kat laughed. "Not completely; only moderately. I'm trying to figure out how to be a housewife in the suburbs."

Theo looked horrified. "Dude, why?"

"Well, what else am I going to do?"

"I don't know. Can't you, like, coach or something?"

"Not too many guys want to hire a woman as their coach."

"That's sexist," Theo said.

"Yeah, it is. But it's a fact. It's hard enough trying to make it as a female skater, never mind as a coach."

"Is your husband an athlete, too?" he asked.

"No." Kat looked away. "He's a professor." Then she deliberately, almost aggressively, changed the subject. "What about you? Are there any videos of *you* on YouTube?"

Theo looked appalled at the very idea. "Gosh, I hope not."

"There must be," Kat said. "All those boozy bachelorette parties full of cell phones?"

"Oh, well, uh, this is actually my first bachelorette party." Theo stared at the table and confided, "I've only been doing this for a month and a half."

Ginger materialized behind Cammie and hissed in her ear. "I need a word."

Cammie groaned and followed her back into the hallway. "Aunt Ginger, look at the poor kid. He's sweet. We're just giving him a snack and sending him on his way."

"That's the problem! I may not know much about strippers, but I know about men. Once you start feeding them, they never leave!" Ginger threw her hands up. "We do not need any more projects or complications."

Cammie was about to ask Ginger when she'd become so snippy and coldhearted, and then she looked at the duo at the kitchen table. Kat and Theo were leaning in toward each other, watching a video clip on Theo's phone.

The two of them seemed very cozy, and, suddenly, Cammie didn't like what she was seeing, either. No wonder Ginger wasn't thrilled. Josh wouldn't be thrilled, either.

Cammie strode back into the kitchen, brisk and businesslike. "Tick-tock, tick-tock. Theo, you'd better run along if you want to get to Lewes by five."

"Yeah, okay." Theo got to his feet and pulled off the T-shirt Kat had given him. "See you tomorrow, Kat?"

Cammie side-eyed her cousin. "What's happening tomorrow?"

"Theo and I are going down to the boardwalk," Kat said.

"The boardwalk?" Cammie's glance bounced between the thirtysomething redhead and the barely-legal boy toy. "Why would you do that?"

"Kat's going to teach me some tricks." Theo's face lit up. "I've always wanted to learn to do a bubble flip."

Cammie turned to Kat. "Isn't that what you used to call the hospital flip?"

"'Hospital flip' is sort of a basket term," Kat hedged.

Cammie looked back at Theo. "But his face is his fortune. His face and his um, physique. He can't be going to bachelorette parties all bloody and bruised."

"That reminds me." Kat flexed her fingers in anticipation. "If you're serious about growing your business, Theo, you'll need a website. Let's throw something together. We'll brainstorm tomorrow."

Theo gazed at Kat with worshipful, puppy-dog eyes.

Cammie tried to catch Kat's attention. Kat studiously ignored her.

Then Kat walked Theo out to his car, the pair of them laughing like old friends. When she returned to the house, Cammie and Ginger were waiting with grim expressions.

Kat's smile wilted. "What?"

"You tell me," Ginger said.

"What are you doing?" Cammie said. "He's twenty."

"And shirtless," Ginger added.

"And twenty."

Kat set her jaw and mimicked their defensive posture. "So what? We're discriminating against genetically blessed twenty-year-olds now?"

"You're married," Cammie reminded her.

"I'm aware of that," Kat snapped. "I'm going skateboarding and building a website with this kid. Not having a sordid affair."

"Yet," Ginger muttered.

Kat's nostrils flared. "What did you say?"

Cammie stepped in between them. "She just means that it's a slippery slope. You start out having fun, being friends, but then you're talking and sharing emotional stuff, and next thing you know . . ."

"No. I don't know." Kat's eyes were cold and furious.

Cammie kind of shrugged. "It's just that, given what's going on with you and Josh . . ."

"I might cheat on him? Is that what you're saying?"

Cammie held out both palms. "No one's saying you'll cheat on him."

"Yeah, actually, you are. You're saying I'm going to go behind Josh's back and sleep with a twenty-year-old."

"Well, when you put it like that . . ."

"There's no other way to put it." Kat had gone from chilly to subzero. "That's what you think of me."

Cammie took a moment to collect herself. "Let's start over."

"Too late."

Ginger rested her hand on Kat's shoulder. Kat jerked away.

"You're in transition right now," Ginger said. "With your career and your marriage. You're still recovering from surgery. You've vulnerable and you need to be careful."

Kat's temper detonated. After rattling off a string of obscenities, she said, "I can't believe this is how you see me: weak and superficial and ready to sleep with any guy who throws me a scrap of attention."

"We don't—"

"Let me finish." Kat looked ready to tear a wine barrel apart with her bare hands. "Why are you two allowed to make mistakes and act on impulse, but I have to stay the course at all times?"

Cammie had never thought about it that way. Kat's career had meant that taking risks and making split-second decisions *was* staying the course.

"I'm not going to cancel on Theo just because you're not comfortable with it," Kat said. "You can think whatever you want, but keep it to yourself."

"Okay, but—"

"Don't talk to me." Kat strode toward the staircase, whipping out her cell phone as she went. "I'll be talking to my husband. And not being vulnerable."

"That's probably why the two of you are having problems!" Ginger called after her.

"Don't you have some grapes to worry about?" Kat slammed the door behind her.

Cammie sighed. "Yes. Yes, we do."

chapter 15

"Well? How was skateboarding?" Cammie emerged from the grapevines, brushing dirt from her palms and knees, as Kat returned from her boardwalk rendezvous with Theo the next day.

Kat slammed out of the car and threw her wrist guards to the ground in disgust. "I suck. That's how it was."

Cammie wiped the sweat off of her forehead, realizing too late that she'd left a smear of dirt across her face. "Oh, Kat, I'm sorry."

"No, you're not." Kat was clearly frustrated and looking for any target to unload upon. "You're checking up on me to make sure I didn't get handsy with the twenty-year-old."

"Kat . . ."

"I told Josh all about him, okay? I told him everything." Kat's face flushed pink under the blazing midday sun. "And he's fine with it."

"Great." Cammie paused. "So, you want to come count the rows with me?"

Kat reached down and retrieved her wrist guards. "Yeah, okay."

As soon as the phrase "count the rows" left Cammie's lips, Jacques appeared at the farmhouse's porch door. He squashed his already-squashed face against the screen and whined pathetically until Kat climbed the porch steps and let him out. He trotted over to Cammie and waited at her feet, staring up at her impatiently.

Kat trailed behind the French bulldog. "What does he want?"

"He wants to count the rows." Cammie scratched Jacques behind the ears.

"He knows what 'count the rows' means?" Kat started petting Jacques, too, and he luxuriated in the attention, wriggling his stocky little body and snuffling.

Cammie led the way to the farthest corner of the vineyard and started to walk, silently counting the rows of vines as she went. Kat fell into step on her right side, Jacques on her left.

"So, why did skateboarding suck?" Cammie asked.

"Because I can't skateboard." Kat balled up her fists. "I tried to show Theo a basic inward heel flip, and I couldn't do it."

"It's been months since you've been on a board. And you've had a serious injury. Cut yourself some slack."

Kat raked her hands through her helmet-matted hair. "My ankles and knees don't work the way they're supposed to anymore." She pressed a palm to her lower back and grimaced. "And my back hurts. I have lower back pain. Like I'm *old*. I'll need like five ibuprofen and a fifth of vodka just to get through tonight."

"Hang on." Cammie stopped to assist Jacques, who was knee-deep in a pile of loose soil.

Kat stopped, too. Her hands fell to her sides, her fierce facade fell away, and she looked helpless under the bright blue sky. "I can't do any of the things I spent my whole life doing. My body has betrayed me." She sank down to sit in the dirt. Jacques took the opportunity to drape himself over her lap. "What am I going to do?"

Jacques lunged up, bonked his forehead against Kat's, and licked her right on the mouth.

"Ugh." Kat made a face. "You taste like dirt and desperation." But she calmed down, snuggling Jacques against her chest. "See, he gets it. Forced to retire at the height of his career because of a little dental snafu."

Jacques started panting, his tragic broken tooth on full display.

"But you don't see him drowning his sorrows in a fifth of vodka," Cammie pointed out. "He has a good attitude. He's reinventing himself."

"Our scrappy little farm dog." Kat seemed lighter as she got to her feet.

Cammie leaned down to examine the rosebush at the end of a row of vines. "Hmm." She peered at a cluster of leaves that appeared to be shriveling. "This doesn't look good."

"What's wrong with it?"

Cammie took out her cell phone and snapped a few pictures. "Hopefully, someone at the garden-supply store will be able to tell me."

Kat surveyed the rosebushes lining the fields. "Why are we growing roses again?"

"They're our early-warning system for drought, blight, and pests." Cammie summarized what Ian had told her. "Except for that one over there." She pointed out the climbing rose. "That one was a mistake, and it won't bloom for two more years."

"You sound so knowledgeable."

"Don't I?" Cammie patted her leg, and Jacques scampered back to her side.

When they'd walked the perimeter of the field, they found Ginger waiting for them on the porch. "The first bottle of strawberry wine is officially ready to drink. Come on in!"

The cool, shaded parlor was a welcome refuge after hours in

the scorching heat. Ginger had draped a green-and-white tablecloth atop the tasting bar, and Cammie could smell the oak of the upended wine barrels in the humidity.

"Here's to us." Ginger distributed three glasses of pink liquid.

"Are we supposed to drink this cold or at room temperature?" Kat peered into her goblet.

Ginger turned to Cammie. "I'm not sure. What's the proper temperature for fruit wine, dear? Do you know?"

"I don't need to know," Cammie said. "It's our wine, so we can drink it however we want."

"Then I'm getting ice." Kat started for the kitchen. "Some for my wine and some for my back."

"What happened to your back?" Ginger asked.

"Cast your mind back," Kat said. "Remember a few months ago when I had major surgery and that giant scar?"

"But I thought that was healing well!" Ginger fluttered around Kat, brimming with maternal concern. "The doctors said you were on the mend."

"It's never going to be the way it was." Kat opened the freezer and pulled out an old-fashioned tray of ice cubes. "I'll be lucky if I can do fifty percent of what I used to."

"Knees and backs don't last forever," Ginger conceded. "But you're still so young and healthy. You have years and years ahead of you."

"That's the problem. I have all these years and nothing to do with them. I don't even want to think about the future." Kat distributed ice into everyone's glasses. "He'll never admit it, but I think Josh was kind of excited when I got hurt. He keeps saying that now we can do all the things we were putting off. Travel for fun, watch all the movies I never had time for." She swallowed hard. "Have kids."

Ginger squeaked with joy at this prospect, then forced herself to temper her enthusiasm. "Well. Not that it's any of my business—"

"Agreed."

"—but this *would* be a good time to have children. The clock is ticking, you know."

Cammie expected her cousin to bristle, but Kat looked contemplative. "I know you're right. But I don't want to do anything. When I think about having kids, I just feel . . . flat."

"But you'll do it, anyway." Ginger said firmly. "Right?"

Cammie curtailed the conversation by raising her glass. "Let's drink. To my mother."

They all clinked glasses and sipped. "Hmmm," Cammie said.

"Hmmm," Kat said.

"And by 'hmmm,' you mean 'delectable.'" This was a statement, not a question. Ginger took a second sip.

"Tastes like summer," Kat said.

"I don't think I've ever had fruit wine before," Cammie said between sips. Clean and bright and subtly sweet, the wine did indeed taste like summer. "Where has this been all my life?"

"It's classy," Ginger informed them. "Ladylike."

"I don't know about 'ladylike.'" Kat threw back the rest of her wine in one gulp. "I like it, and I'm no lady."

"And you never get tired of proving that to me." Ginger put her glass down on the counter. "Well, there's more where this came from. I've got bottles and bottles in the basement. I'm refining my technique."

"How much do you think we're going to drink, Mom? We do have to work sometimes."

"It's not for you, you goose." Ginger waved this away. "It's for the tastings. I'll make strawberry wine all summer while we wait for the grapes to grow." She appealed to Cammie. "Do you think people will buy it?"

Cammie appealed to Kat. "You're the marketing guru, right? Can you whip up a pretty little label?"

Kat snickered. "Have you ever seen me draw?"

"No, now that you mention it."

"There's a reason I went into extreme sports instead of the visual arts."

"But what about your gear?" Cammie asked. "The boards you designed? All those T-shirts?"

"I told a design team what I liked and they took care of the details." Kat reached for the bottle and poured a second helping. "Oh, and we had focus groups tell us what they thought of the products before we finalized production. That, I remember. We should round up a focus group."

"I hate to be a killjoy, but we're in Black Dog Bay," Ginger said. "Where are we going to find a focus group?"

Cammie put down her still-full glass of wine and snagged Ginger's car keys from the little brass hook on the cabinet. "I think I know just the place."

"Refreshing," Jenna, the Whinery's owner, decreed.

"Sweet." Hollis, who owned Black Dog Books, took another sip. "But not *offensively* sweet."

"Makes me want to get a tattoo," Summer Benson said.

Cammie turned to Summer, her pen poised above her yellow legal pad. "Is that a good thing?"

"I only get tattoos when I'm in a really good mood," Summer assured her.

Cammie wrote down the feedback. "So, you would buy a bottle of this if you got a sample at a tasting?"

"I would," Jenna said.

"That's very encouraging." Ginger saw her opening and took it. "Any chance you'd be willing to stock it here? I have a bunch more bottles brewing in the basement."

"That's a lot of *b*'s," Hollis marveled.

Cammie addressed Jenna, wine slinger to wine slinger. "Please excuse her. She doesn't understand how this works."

"Don't patronize me," Ginger said.

"I'm not, but it's not that easy to add a new menu item." Cammie tried to explain. "You've got to reprint the wine list, rearrange existing inventory, figure out your price point. . . . It's a lot."

"Well, you can come in here one morning and take care of all that for her, since you know so much." Ginger put her arm around Cammie's shoulder and told Jenna, "I volunteer her."

Jenna tilted her head, considering.

"It's local, it's seasonal, it's pink," Kat the marketing guru threw in.

"It'd fit right in with our house specialties." Jenna pointed to the chalkboard overhead, which described a cocktail called the Cure for the Common Breakup.

Cammie glanced around, taking in the bar, the tables, the candy dishes with a pang of longing and envy. "This place is amazing. You've really built something special."

Jenna's smile tightened. "Eh."

"No, really. You've got ambience and a distinct customer base. This place stands apart from all the driftwood-and-life-preserver beach bars up and down the coast."

"Plus, you give us M&M's," Summer pointed out. "You win. Everything. Forever."

"This is exactly what so many people want to create when they go into the restaurant business," Cammie said. "I wish I could've done what you've done."

Jenna stood up straighter. "You want it?"

Cammie blinked. "What?"

"Make me an offer. I'm serious."

This sparked a small riot among the clientele:

"Don't even joke about that!"

"You can't sell this place. We need you, Jenna."

"You don't need me." Jenna rubbed her palm against her forehead. "You need the bar. The community. The candy. You guys could get along just fine without me." She turned to grab a pink dishtowel.

"We could not," Hollis insisted. "We would wither away and die."

"Why would you walk away from all this?" Cammie asked.

"You mean the late nights? The working weekends? The constant stream of people on their worst behavior after a breakup?"

"But . . . but the *ambience*," Cammie countered. "The location. You have my dream job."

Jenna kept smiling, and Cammie thought about how the impromptu wine tasters had said those very same words to her and Ginger and Kat, while they dealt with leaky irrigation systems, crack-of-dawn fungicide application, and dwindling cash reserves.

"You want my job?" Jenna asked. "Dream no more. Write up a halfway decent offer, and your wish is granted."

Cammie allowed herself to imagine it for a moment, then faced reality. "I can't."

"That's right." Ginger patted her hand. "She's already working on *my* dream job."

"Plus, I have no money," Cammie admitted.

"Well, if you know anyone else who'd like to buy a bar full of M&M's and pink toile . . ."

"No one's buying this bar," Summer declared. "Because you're not selling it. All you need is a little vacation."

Jenna gave up arguing and sampled the strawberry wine again. "Before I can even consider adding this to the menu, let's talk volume. How much of this can you supply, and how often?"

Ginger winked at Cammie. "You can get us a good deal on the strawberries, right?"

"Here we go again." Kat dropped her forehead into her hands.

"Ian already gave you a great deal," Cammie said.

"Oh, I'd bet you can get us an even better deal," Ginger said airily. "With your powers of persuasion? Maybe when he picks you up for that date he asked about?"

Cammie narrowed her eyes. "How did you know he asked me out?"

"I have my ways."

"Do your ways involve going through my phone?" Cammie turned to Kat. "Help me; I'm being pimped out for produce over here."

But Kat's attention had gotten snagged earlier in the conversation. "You're going out with Ian again?"

"I . . ." Cammie trailed off as she glanced around and realized that the music had died and everyone in the bar was listening to her. "Maybe."

"You guys should come here for your date," Jenna said. "The Whinery has an impressive track record with romances."

"What? I thought this was the epicenter of drama and heartbreak."

"Oh, it is. But it's so much more than that." Jenna twirled her pink dishtowel. "I don't mean to brag, but this is basically the hot-husband emporium."

Summer chimed in. "She has a point. Just think about all the people who have hooked up with their soulmates here: me and Dutch, Malcolm and Lila, Brighton and Jake . . ."

"And yet I'm still single." Jenna tossed the dishtowel on the bar top in frustration. "Unfair and unexplainable."

Ginger placed her hand on Kat's forearm. "You should take Josh here."

"Who's Josh?" Jenna asked.

"Her husband," Cammie said aloud. Then she silently mouthed, "It's complicated."

"By all means." Jenna uncorked a bottle of chardonnay. "Bring him over."

"Mom, stay out of it." Kat's expression darkened. "He's not going to come here with me." Her voice barely audible, she added, "And I'm not sure how much longer he'll be my husband."

Jenna turned the music back on, and everyone gave Kat some space. Everyone except Cammie and Ginger.

"There." Kat's tone was tinged with relief. "I said it. My marriage is failing, and it's my fault."

Cammie couldn't remember her cousin ever conceding defeat before. "Failure" was not a word Kat used. Ever.

"It's not like you to quit," Ginger said.

"Maybe it is." Kat shrugged. "First I quit skating; now I'm quitting marriage."

"You didn't quit skating," Cammie said. "You got injured. You had to retire."

"And if you're having a hard time with that, you should let him know. Talk to him," Ginger urged. "He'll understand."

"I know he will." Kat sounded increasingly glum. "But I don't want help or encouragement. I just want to . . ." She trailed off. Cammie and Ginger leaned in, waiting for the rest of the sentence.

"I just want to sit on the couch for the rest of my life. Although, obviously, I can't do that with my lower back all messed up."

"I'm no expert," Cammie said, "but that sounds like depression."

"I'm irritable and avoidant. When the going got tough, I ran off to a vineyard with my crazy mother."

"I beg your pardon," Ginger huffed.

Kat rested her chin in her hand. "I wouldn't want to be married to me, either."

"I am not crazy," Ginger insisted.

Cammie and Kat made vague conciliatory noises in her direction.

"Don't brush me off." Ginger pounded the bar top. "I am a visionary. While you girls are busy talking about your boy trouble, I'm doing all the hard work."

Cammie choked on her ice water. "Um."

"Excuse me?" Kat said.

"Strawberry wine." Ginger pointed to the proof. "A bar that's going to stock it."

"Maybe," Kat emphasized.

"Well, what have *you* done?" Ginger countered.

"I made a website," Kat shot back. "And bought a tractor."

"I'm pimping myself out for produce," Cammie said. "And weeding. And walking the fields. And keeping the grapes alive. You're welcome."

"Well, there you go." Ginger said, satisfied. "We're a stellar team."

"So, how are the grapes?" Jenna asked when she refilled the candy dish near Kat. "Other than alive?"

"You know. Great. Growing," Kat said.

The bar owner nodded. "I assume you have your plan in place for harvest and wine making?"

Kat looked at Ginger, who looked at Cammie, who looked at Kat. "Um . . ."

"You have a vintner lined up this late in the season, I'm sure." Jenna started to look a bit worried. "Right?"

"We're working on it," Cammie said. "Any day now."

Jenna stopped doling out candy and regarded them with huge, horrified eyes. "Oh."

"Don't worry about us." Ginger patted her hair and took a sip of strawberry wine. "We have a plan."

"We do?" Kat whispered.

Jenna looked dubious as she replenished the other candy dishes. "There's a wine festival in Maryland this weekend. Lots of wine growers, winemakers, and wine tastings. It'd be a good place to network and meet potential vintners."

"Where and when?" Cammie demanded. "We're going."

"Yeah, we are," Kat agreed.

"It's so nice to be together as a family again." Ginger beamed.

When they got home, Ginger urged Cammie and Kat to come down to the cellar to admire her stores of strawberry wine.

"I can't. I have to go to the garden-supply store for— Wait." Cammie held up her hand, her ears straining. "Did you hear that?"

"Hear what?" Kat cocked her head.

"I think I heard a knock at the door."

The three of them fell silent, staring at one another.

Cammie heard it again: a soft but unmistakable knocking.

"We're ignoring it," Kat declared.

"Seconded." Ginger nodded.

"You guys." Cammie put her hands on her hips. "We're running a place of business here."

"But it's also our home," Ginger said.

"And every time that door opens, it turns out to be a bunch of demanding visitors," Kat said.

"Or a male stripper."

Kat grinned. "We don't mind the strippers that much."

"The point is, we need a little break from these surprises." Ginger opened the basement door. "Whoever it is can come back later."

Cammie glanced toward the parlor. "But—"

"I feel like we're bootleggers," Kat enthused as they disappeared down the shadowed steps. "Next stop, making moonshine in our bathtub."

"Hush your mouth," Ginger admonished. "I'm no bootlegger; I'm an artisan."

Cammie was not an artisan. She was a businesswoman—bottom

line. And a good businesswoman did not let potential customers languish on the porch in the hot sun just because she was feeling a little piqued. She marched through the parlor and yanked open the door, preparing herself for tourists, strippers, a traveling circus. Or Ian. *Please be Ian.*

But it was Josh. Again.

"Oh! I mean, hi. I mean, come on in." Cammie stepped aside to let Josh into the foyer. "Sorry about the wait, we were just . . . Um, is Kat expecting you?"

"Not until tomorrow." He held a bouquet of yellow flowers in one hand. "But she said you guys bought a tractor that needed some work?"

"We sure did." Cammie glanced toward the barn. "It's a beaut."

"So I thought I'd come a day early and see if I can help. I called her, but she didn't pick up." He looked around. "Is she here?"

"Downstairs in the basement with Ginger. They're bootlegging with strawberries."

Josh didn't seem the least bit fazed by this announcement. "So, she's back from her date with the muscle-bound teenager?"

"It wasn't a date." Cammie knew the expression on her face belied her calm tone. "She was showing him how to do an inward heel flip. Or something."

"Wait. They went skateboarding?" Josh's placid eyes darkened and his voice went cold.

"Yeah. I thought you knew." Cammie realized too late that she had made a huge mistake.

"Kat told me she was making a website for him. She didn't say one word about skateboarding."

"She is making a website," Cammie assured him.

"I cannot *believe* she went skateboarding with another man. After all we've been through together." He seemed furious, and Cammie remembered how she'd felt when Zach had left for another restaurant. When the person she loved shared their passion with someone else.

Josh pivoted and strode back out to the porch.

"Let me go get her." Cammie started for the cellar door.

"Don't bother." He strode down the porch steps. "I'm not going to keep begging her. If she wants to throw away our marriage for some stupid midlife crisis, that's on her."

Cammie started to argue that thirty-two was too young for a midlife crisis, but stopped when she saw his expression. "I promise you, nothing's going on." As soon as she voiced the promise, she wished she hadn't. How could she make such a guarantee? "She's just trying to figure things out."

"That's the problem." Josh was practically yelling at her from the driveway. "She does whatever she wants while I keep everything going at home. And I'm done. I'm done apologizing for living in the suburbs. I'm done apologizing for being a professor." He smiled wryly at Cammie's expression. "You don't think I know how she feels about that?"

Jacques ambled out from the parlor, his wrinkly brown-and-white face even more wrinkled than usual. He looked dismayed by the proceedings.

"I know she loves you," Cammie said softly.

"She loves me in spite of who I am and what I do?" The smile turned into a smirk. "How generous of her. She's willing to overlook the fact that I read Camus and go to faculty meetings and have a good, stable job with health insurance that covers all her trips to the ER." He stalked over to his car. "I'm supposed to be impressed because she was some sort of celebrity in the skating world? I'm supposed to put up with an endless amount of bullshit because she needs to keep breaking her bones to feel alive? As Camus would say, fuck that."

Cammie blinked. She'd never heard Josh curse.

"I'm done." And with that, he threw down the bouquet, slammed into his car, and drove away, running over the cheerful yellow flowers in the process.

Cammie watched him go, then headed back into the house. "Hey, Kat? I think you better come up here."

chapter 16

Cammie stood outside the garden-supply store, fighting back a sudden, strong urge to weep. The bags of potting soil and fertilizer stacked by the door triggered a total recall of sweat, frustration, and manual labor.

She closed her eyes and took deep, measured breaths. *It's just fungicide. No need to panic.*

Forcing herself to take one step and then another, she walked to the store entrance and opened the door.

The first thing she saw was Ian.

Okay, now *you can panic.*

He smiled when he noticed her. "Didn't expect to run into you here."

"I know, right? Of all the garden-supply stores, in all the world . . ." She turned up her palms.

"Yeah." He rocked back on his heels and held her gaze. "You never texted me back."

"I know. I'm sorry. I wanted to, but . . ."

He rested one hand on a bag of potting soil, as if he had all the time in the world.

She fiddled with the silver bangle on her wrist. "I think the roses need fungicide."

He held out his palm. "Let me see."

"You don't have to . . ."

"Let me see."

She took out her phone and pulled up the photo she'd taken of the rosebush leaves.

"Yep, they need fungicide. And if the roses need fungicide, the vines probably do, too." He started toward a stack of yellow bags. "Try this."

She followed one step behind him. "Thank you."

"I'll come over tomorrow and take a look at the plants," he said.

She wanted to touch him, to connect with him again on every level. It was all she could do not to rest her hand on his arm. But she held herself back because she wasn't a willful and selfish twenty-two-year-old anymore. She needed to consider his feelings, not just her own. "I couldn't ask you to do that."

"You didn't ask me." He picked up a pair of the yellow bags and walked her toward the register. "Three o'clock tomorrow?"

It would be so easy to give in and let him help. To rely on him. To say yes, to go out again, to kiss him, and much more.

"I appreciate the offer, but I can't accept it." Her tone was cheerful but firm. She turned to the cashier and handed over her credit card. "And I hate to brag, but the grapes are still alive."

"Grapes? Oh, you must be one of the ladies who bought the vineyard?" the cashier asked. "You settling in okay?"

"Absolutely. It's a steep learning curve, but we're figuring it out."

"It's nice to have some new full-time residents." The cashier seemed oblivious to the tension.

"I'm not really a resident," Cammie replied. "I'm just here for a few months."

"Mm-hmm." The cashier plucked a flimsy painted wooden sign from the revolving display atop the counter. "On the house."

Cammie glanced at the sign's message: BLOOM WHERE YOU'RE PLANTED. She returned the sign to its place on the rack. "You're too kind."

The cashier shoved the sign at her. "I insist."

"I couldn't possibly."

But she was no match for the sunny, smiley blonde. The cashier waited until Cammie had her hands full, then tucked the sign into her purse. "Enjoy."

"It's like shoplifting in reverse," Cammie muttered, heaving the bags of fungicide onto a rolling metal hand truck. Ian followed her out to the parking lot, where she opened the trunk of Kat's car and attempted to wedge the bags into the tiny space.

"There's no room in there," he remarked.

"I know. We're working on Kat to trade it in for a minivan."

"Yeah? How's that going?"

"It's a process." She managed to close the trunk, then studied the cracked, uneven asphalt.

He waited for her to glance up at him. "If you don't want me in your fields, come on over to mine."

She hesitated. "For what? Another farming tutorial?"

"For old time's sake." He put his hand on her back and walked her over to his truck. "And for fun."

She couldn't suppress a smile. "We do have fun together."

"Yeah, we do." His voice deepened and she forgot all about the roses and the grapes and the encroaching fungus. "Come on."

Cammie made small talk during the twenty-minute drive to Ian's farmland, but she had no idea what she'd said. Internally, she was grappling with a whirlwind of conflicting emotions—excitement and misgiving and desire.

She wondered what had become of the little patch of land where she and Ian had first planted strawberries. The strawberries that were supposed to entice her to stay with him, but had ended up helping him flourish long after she'd left. What would her life be like if she had stayed here with him all those years ago? Would she still be restless, longing for the dreams she'd given up, or would she have found new dreams to chase here in this tiny town by the sea?

Ian drove down a narrow dirt lane that led into the flat, dusty fields. When she glimpsed the rows of strawberry plants, Cammie felt as though she'd left civilization. They were surrounded by the simple, essential elements of soil and greenery. The sun seemed to shine brighter, and the air seemed fresher.

She could see the beauty in farming—when it was someone else's farm.

Ian stopped the truck and they both climbed out.

"So this is where you grow the magic strawberries," Cammie marveled as she stepped into the rich, loamy soil.

"Your legacy lives on." He reached down, plucked a ripe red strawberry, and handed it to her.

She bit into the berry and closed her eyes as sweetness flooded her mouth. "This is not natural. Nothing grown with plain dirt and water could taste this good. You're adding opium or crack or something. Admit it."

They regarded each other for a long moment, both of them remembering, neither of them speaking.

Then Ian broke eye contact. "Come on, you know you want to count the rows."

He took her hand and led her farther into the field. They walked in companionable silence and, for a brief moment, everything was perfect between them. No conflict, no regrets, no expectations. By the time they started back toward the truck, a layer of heavy gray clouds had rolled in, obscuring the sun.

Cammie glowered up at the sky. "My weather app didn't say anything about rain today."

"I keep telling you, you have to check the website I told you about," Ian said. "It's much better than your app."

They got back into the truck and sat on opposite ends of the bench seat. Neither one made a move to close the distance between them, but they both knew what was coming.

This isn't going to end well, but we might as well enjoy the beginning.

Ian looked at her, his gaze speculative. He seemed to debate with himself for a moment, then he turned the key in the ignition and put the truck in gear.

Cammie sat back in her seat, surprised at how disappointed she felt. The truck rolled along the bumpy dirt pathway bisecting the field. The gray clouds thickened, and a sprinkling of raindrops dotted the windshield as Ian attempted to make a tight turn over a concrete slab bridging a drainage ditch.

"Oh, I almost forgot to tell you," Cammie said. "My aunt wants to buy bushels and bushels of strawberries because— Whoa."

She braced her hand against the dashboard as the truck lurched, the back end dropping suddenly.

Two seconds later, she was looking up through the passenger-side window at the drizzly dark sky. She turned to Ian. "What was that?"

He looked mortified. "That was me turning into the ditch."

"Oh." She relaxed, repositioning herself against the bench seat.

"Sorry about that."

"No problem. I'm sure this kind of thing happens all the time."

He scrubbed his palm over his face. "Not really."

She shifted her weight to compensate for the change in elevation. "So, now what?"

"Now I try to get the truck out of the ditch."

Three minutes of futile tire spinning later, it became clear that the ditch had no intention of giving up the truck.

"Is this a farm-boy thing?" She couldn't resist teasing Ian as he assessed the situation, dirty and damp and frustrated. "Take a girl out in the fields, then 'accidentally' get stuck in a ditch?"

"If I were going to 'accidentally' get stuck in a ditch with you, I would have done it back there." He jerked his thumb over his shoulder to indicate the vast stretch of strawberry plants. "Not by a main road, where a car will be along any minute."

Cammie gazed out at the rock-studded dirt path. "I don't know that I'd call this a main road."

"It's all relative." He took one more rueful look at the truck's back end, kicked a tire, and helped Cammie out. "This isn't going anywhere without a tow truck. We'll have to walk into town."

Before they even set foot on the so-called main road, the drizzle intensified to a shower.

Ian glanced up at the clouds, then at Cammie.

"No worries," she said. "I don't mind a little rain."

"You sure?"

"I'm sure."

Thirty yards later, the shower progressed to a downpour and the wind picked up, blowing sheets of water almost sideways. Thunder boomed overhead, and a white bolt of lightning streaked across the sky. They looked at each other, joined hands, and raced back to the truck.

Cammie sprinted next to Ian, freezing and soaking, heedless of the mud splashing on her shins. For a moment, she lost herself in the elements—sky and rain and the warm pressure of his hand holding hers.

They reached the truck, gasping and laughing as torrents of rain poured down on them. Ian opened the passenger-side door and they scrambled inside. Because the truck was angled diagonally into the ditch, the long bench seat was slanted. Ian had to brace both feet against the floorboards to keep from sliding into Cammie.

Cammie took a moment to wring out her hair while she considered their circumstances. She was shivering, soaked, utterly bedraggled. . . . But she was in the driver's seat. Both literally and figuratively.

She held out her palm for the keys and he gave them to her. Metal clicked against metal as she started the ignition and turned on the heat. Warm air gusted out of the dashboard vents and raindrops drummed against the metal cab.

Ian glanced up. "Sounds like it's hailing."

The rain came down so hard that Cammie couldn't even see through the windows. As she started to warm up, Cammie realized that her thin cotton T-shirt was plastered against her torso. Ian wasn't ogling, but she was very aware of how she must look: drenched and disheveled but finally able to relax.

"We're trapped." She grinned, clasping her hands dramatically. "Helpless against the elements."

"A car will be along any minute," Ian predicted.

"In this weather? I don't think so." She glanced down as a square of paper on the floorboard caught her eye. A torn seed packet with a picture of ripe red strawberries. She reached down and picked it up. "What's this?"

Ian ducked his head and she caught a glimpse of the boy he'd been when she first met him. He looked almost . . . nervous? "Oh, that's just . . ."

She watched him stammer, bemused by his sudden change of attitude.

"Those are the strawberries we grow."

"Here in this field? These are your world-famous, patented strawberry seeds?" she clarified.

"Yeah, they have different kinds of packaging. This is for home gardeners." He reached out to take the packet from her. But she hung on.

She examined the back of the packet, which specified when and where to plant the seeds. And then she turned it over and saw the name of the strawberries.

COB strawberries. All caps.

She furrowed her brow. "COB?"

Ian looked like he was internally dying a thousand protracted, agonizing deaths.

She shook her head, trying to make sense of everything. "Is this COB, like . . . ?"

"Yeah," he told the windshield.

And Camille October Breyer was officially out of things to say.

He'd named the strawberries for her. Even after she'd left and broken both their hearts. He'd let her go and never contacted her.

But he'd named the berries after her. The berries they'd grown together right here in this field. The berries that could now be bought and planted all over the world.

"Oh." A bittersweet mix of loss and longing rushed through her.

"I know." He sounded chagrined. He still wouldn't look her in the eye.

She rested both hands on the steering wheel and watched the rain sluicing over the windshield. "That's the sweetest thing anyone's ever done for me."

He finally looked at her. She held out her hand, beckoning him closer.

A deafening thunderclap shook the truck. They both started laughing, and then they were kissing while the raindrops pelted against metal.

Twenty minutes later, they were both even more disheveled. The rain showed no signs of relenting.

"Do you have any bottled water in here?" Cammie asked. "Granola bars? It looks like we might be here for a while."

"No granola bars, but I do have a phone."

"Oh." Somehow calling for help, although the logical next step, didn't feel very adventurous.

He produced the phone and started dialing. "I can call for a tow truck."

She put her hand over his. "Five more minutes."

Twenty more minutes and several shirt buttons later, the rain ceased as suddenly as it had started. The sky was still dark and heavy with humidity, but the drops stopped falling.

The truck windows—including the windshield—were completely foggy.

Cammie used her index finger to write their initials in the condensation. "I feel like a girl of fifteen again."

Ian smiled.

"Confess: I'm not the first girl you've gone parking with in this field," she said.

He furrowed his brow, considering. "I'm not sure what we're doing here really qualifies as parking."

"I didn't realize there was a set definition."

"Oh yeah. We're very strict about that. It's a farm thing."

She narrowed her eyes. "Really."

He tried to look earnest. "Really."

"Then what—and I'm just talking hypotheticals here—what would we have to do in order for this to meet the technical definition of 'parking'?"

"I can't tell you." He grinned. "But I can show you. Come here."

"I can't believe I lived my whole life till now without a proper parking experience." Cammie was all aflutter and her clothes were askew as she and Ian started the long walk back to civilization.

"I'm glad you had fun." He glanced back at the foggy windshield with a smile. "You're a natural."

"I have many hidden talents." She flipped her hair, splattering droplets of water across his face. "Sorry. So, what else do you Delaware farmers do that I'm missing out on?"

He guided her around a huge mud puddle. Cammie eyed his long, confident stride and tanned forearms. "You're totally in your element out here."

"Pretty much. Were you in your element in the restaurant world?"

"At first I was. And then overhead costs and an absentee chef did me in. All those years of business education, you'd think I could have made it work, but no."

"All the education in the world can't prepare you for the realities of running a business." He squeezed her fingers. "Someday I'll tell you some of the crazy shit I did the first year I took over the farm from my dad."

She looked at him with one eyebrow quirked.

"Someday," he repeated. "You learned a lot from the first restaurant. The next one will work out."

She shook her head. "There will be no next restaurant."

"You're giving up after only one try?"

She wasn't going to argue this point with a man who had such superlative parking skills. "Well, before I can even think about another restaurant, I have to deal with the vineyard. Which brings me to what I was going to ask you before we drove into the ditch: Would you consider selling us your strawberries in bulk?"

He smiled. "They're really your strawberries, too."

"So says the seed packet." She pulled him in for a kiss.

He rested his forehead against hers. "How many strawberries are we talking here?"

"A *lot*." She described Ginger's foray into fruit wine. "And since that's the only thing that might actually make any money right now, she's completely obsessed with it."

"You're going to let me try this wine, right?" he asked.

"Absolutely. Bottles and bottles will be coming your way."

"I'll think about it." His tone was low and teasing.

She gasped in mock outrage. "You'll *think* about it?"

"Yeah. We'll have to negotiate."

She smoothed back her damp hair. "What kind of negotiating do you have in mind?"

His eyes gleamed. "We'll see. Everything's on the table."

She went up on tiptoe and murmured into his ear. "This table of yours . . . Is it sturdy?"

"Very sturdy."

"I'm looking forward to our discussions."

By the time Cammie finally got back to town and collected Kat's car from the garden-supply store, her shirt had dried but her hair was tangled, her lips were tender, and her perception of thunderstorms had changed forever.

She drove to the vineyard and picked up Kat, who wanted to go to the Whinery. So the two cousins returned to Main Street, Cammie hoping for a cup of warm tea and a bit of camaraderie at the wine bar. Instead, she found herself the center of attention.

"The old 'truck broke down in the middle of nowhere' routine, hmmm?" Jenna winked. "I've had a few guys try that on me."

"The truck didn't break down." Cammie plucked a blade of grass off her shirt. "It got stuck in a ditch."

Kat seemed fascinated. "How'd it get stuck in a ditch?"

"Ian drove it in there by mistake. What can I say?" Cammie fluffed her messy, snarled hair. "I'm just *that* distracting."

"Yes, we heard *all* about it," Jenna said.

Cammie frowned, confused. "You heard about what?"

Jenna ticked off the juicy details on her fingers. "The foggy windows, the lipstick smears on his cheek, the drama in the ditch."

"But even if they hadn't heard about any of that, your hair tells the story all by itself." Kat nodded at the coiffure chaos.

Cammie stared at Jenna, thoroughly bemused. "How'd you hear? It just happened."

Jenna was happy to explain. "Did you ever take physics?"

"Yeah, in high school, but I don't remember any of it."

"That's okay. Let me break it down for you: The speed of sound is fast."

Cammie nodded.

"The speed of light is faster."

Cammie nodded again.

"But the speed of gossip in Black Dog Bay is faster than both of those. By a lot."

Kat sipped her drink. "So, what does this mean?"

Cammie popped a miniature Milky Way into her mouth to stall for time. "What does what mean?"

"Is this just a one-time ditch date, or is it serious?"

"I . . ."—Cammie had no idea what to say—"need a drink."

Jenna produced a pitcher of sangria. "Your wish is my command."

"Did you have fun, at least?" Kat asked. "You must have, if your hair and your face are any indication."

"So much fun." Cammie thought about the strawberry seeds but didn't tell. "But it's tricky. Because really, nothing's changed." Even as she said the words, Cammie knew this was a lie. Everything had changed. She wanted to be back in the truck cab with Ian while the wind and rain and lightning raged outside. The prospect of a dinner-and-a-movie date seemed so boring in comparison.

"Did he ask to see you again?" Jenna wanted to know.

"Yeah." Cammie felt her face flood with heat. "We're going to get together and negotiate. For strawberries."

Kat rubbed her palms together. "Ooh, like strip poker?"

Cammie rolled her eyes. "It's a business deal. Which is separate from any pickup-truck parking sessions that may be happening. Which is why I resisted making out with him in the first place." Her girlish smile and blush vanished. "The last time I mixed boyfriends and business, look what happened."

"That was a onetime thing!" Kat passed the candy dish. "That won't happen again."

Jenna looked confused. "What happened?"

Cammie summarized the restaurant fiasco. "And now Zach is getting rave reviews and prepping playful little amuse-bouche plates for Jennifer Lawrence, while I'm living in disgrace with my aunt."

"You're living in disgrace with your aunt *and* your cousin," Kat amended.

"You're not living in disgrace; you're living in Delaware," Jenna said

Cammie glanced at the bartender's wristwatch. "I better get back to the vineyard. I have an appointment in an hour."

"A hot-and-heavy 'negotiating' session?" Jenna asked with a wink.

Cammie shook her head. "Meeting with a bride-to-be. I'm so glad the weather cleared up."

"You're going to have a wedding at the vineyard?" Jenna gushed. "How romantic."

"The mother of the bride contacted us through the website you built," Cammie told Kat.

"Glad I'm good for something," Kat said. "I know I'm useless in the fields with my back problems."

"What are you talking about?" Cammie offered her glass of sangria to her cousin. "We couldn't get along without you."

"Josh can get along without me just fine." Kat picked up her cell phone, which was resting on the bar top next to her napkin. "He's not even taking my calls now. He says he's said all he has to say."

Cammie hung her head as guilt washed over her. "Again, I am so sorry for what happened the other day. If there's anything I can do to fix it—"

"Cam, it wasn't you. You didn't do anything wrong." Kat blew out a breath. "This is all me. And I don't think it's fixable. I've called him, I've texted him, and I haven't gotten so much as an angry emoji in response."

Cammie hesitated to offer any solutions, given her own abysmal track record in this department. "Maybe you both need to stop saying things and start doing things. I mean, he took action, right? Showed up on your doorstep with your dream dog."

"But if I drive out there and show up on his doorstep, I better be damn sure what I want. I better be ready to commit to the future." Kat tapped her fingertips on the glossy black bar top.

"Think it over and we'll talk tonight." Cammie threw down some cash to cover her tab. "I've got to go meet the wedding people."

"Good luck with that," Kat called after her as she started for the door. "Tell the happy couple it's all fun and games until somebody fractures their spine."

chapter 17

An hour later, Cammie hosted a grand tour of the vineyard for the bride-to-be . . . plus her fiancé, her mother, her future mother-in-law, her maid of honor, her future sisters-in-law, and assorted aunts and grandmothers.

"Welcome!" Cammie had to project her voice in order to be heard by everyone in attendance.

She needn't have bothered—the members of the group were deep in conversation with one another. They didn't even glance her way when she greeted them.

"So, we'll do the yellow centerpieces," the woman to her right said. "And yellow boutonnieres for the groomsmen."

"Aren't you worried that they'll wilt in the heat?" someone else asked. "Last August was brutal."

"It'll be fine," the first woman replied. "I'll talk to the florist about keeping everything refrigerated until the last minute."

"You have such artistic vision," the second woman said admiringly.

"Well, someone has to take charge with this crowd, or they'd run roughshod over me." The woman put her hand on Cammie's forearm. "I'm Vanessa, the mother of the bride." She gestured to her companion. "And this is Jeanie. Mother of the groom."

"Pleased to meet you." Cammie introduced herself, then asked, "So, where's the bride?"

The two mothers looked at each other. "That's a good question. Where is Bronwyn?"

Vanessa scanned the crowd of people. "Oh, she's back there with James."

"She's terribly indecisive," Jeanie said. "Vanessa and I can answer all your questions." She pulled a little pad out of her purse and flipped through a dozen pages scribbled with notes. "We have some questions for you, too."

"I'm going to need to talk to the bride," Cammie insisted sweetly.

The moms muttered and rolled their eyes. "Oh all right. But don't say you weren't warned."

"Bronwyn!" Vanessa called into the throng of guests. "We need you up front, sweetie."

A tiny, wavy-haired waif hurried to her mother's side. "Hi, I'm Bronwyn."

Cammie shook the bride's hand and tried to conceal her surprise. Bronwyn must have been of legal marrying age, but she looked as though she were still in high school. She seemed as shy and soft-spoken as her mother was strident and determined.

Cammie introduced herself as the vineyard's official events manager—neglecting to mention that she herself had created and filled the position mere minutes ago—and asked Bronwyn to supply some information about the big day.

"What are you thinking?" Cammie asked. "Most importantly, *when* were you thinking?"

Bronwyn shot a quick, furtive glance at her mother. "Well, James and I originally thought—"

"They wanted to get married at their university chapel," her mother finished for her. "But there's no air-conditioning, and no reception area close by."

The mother of the groom piped up. "Then we thought we could use the same church where James's father and I got married—"

"*So* meaningful," Vanessa gushed.

"—but it's not big enough to accommodate all the guests."

Cammie looked at Bronwyn. "How many people are you expecting?"

Bronwyn cleared her throat. "We're hoping to keep it small."

"Two hundred," Vanessa declared.

"At least," Jeanie agreed. "The guest list's bursting at the seams, but the more, the merrier."

"Hmm." Cammie maintained eye contact with Bronwyn. "And when is this slated to take place?"

"The Saturday before Labor Day," Vanessa declared. "We know it's short notice, but our other venue fell through."

"Which I can't understand." Jeanie tapped her lip with her index finger. "I e-mailed them every day with updates, and they knew our schedule in detail. I called them twice a week for follow-up, too. It's so frustrating. I can't understand why they returned our deposit money."

"And we really need something definite so we can send out corrected invitations," Vanessa finished.

Cammie lowered her voice so only the bride could hear. "You're okay with this?"

Bronwyn shrugged. "Wedding planning isn't really my thing. I never had the whole pretty-princess fantasy."

Cammie nodded. "Then let's get the groom over here and figure this out."

Vanessa and Jeanie laughed uproariously. Even Bronwyn cracked a smile.

"What?" Cammie asked.

"The only person less interested than Bronwyn in wedding details is James," Jeanie said.

"It's true," Bronwyn confirmed. "He says to buy him a suit and tell him what day and time and he'll be there."

As the mothers debated the merits of a buffet versus a plated dinner, Cammie tried to figure out the dynamics at play. Everyone seemed to get along. Everyone seemed content with the way things were going, including the bride.

And yet . . .

She watched Bronwyn's expression closely as they continued the conversation. "There's no way we can accommodate two hundred people in the house," Cammie said. "Even the barn is going to be too small."

Vanessa waved this away. "As if I'd hold my only daughter's wedding in a barn."

Jeanie giggled at the very idea. "We're going to put up tents on the lawn. Over there, by the field."

Cammie studied the space, considering. "That could work. Unless it rains."

"It won't rain," Vanessa and Jeanie said in unison.

"Yes, hopefully it won't rain," Cammie said. "But we need a contingency plan, just in case."

Vanessa seemed to be taking this personally. Her eyes narrowed and her lips thinned.

Cammie pressed on. "Thunderstorms aren't uncommon in the summer here. Just yesterday—"

"I live here," Vanessa said tightly. "I'm aware of the weather."

"Then you understand why we need—"

Vanessa sighed, as if trying to explain a simple concept to a child. "It won't rain."

Cammie remained upbeat. "But what if it does?"

"It won't."

"But—"

"It. Won't."

Cammie turned to Bronwyn. "May I have a word, please?"

Bronwyn followed Cammie across the lawn until they were out of earshot of the bridal party.

"How old are you, if you don't mind my asking?"

"Twenty-two." Bronwyn grinned. "I only *look* sixteen."

"Ah."

The bride's smile faltered. "I know you think I'm too young to get married—"

"I don't think that at all," Cammie assured her.

"Twenty-two is pretty young by most people's standards. I mean, it's young by *my* standards. None of my friends are ready to get married. But James and I have been together forever. We met before preschool. Our moms made friends when they were in labor and delivery together."

"When you were born?"

"Yep. They both showed up fully dilated, there was only one room left, and they had to fight it out."

Cammie's amazement must have shown on her face, because Bronwyn added, "It was a full moon. I guess hospitals get really busy during full moons."

"So who got the room?"

"My mom, of course." Bronwyn looked ruefully at Vanessa. "There's no point fighting with her; she always gets her way. Jeanie had to deliver James on a gurney in the hallway. But they bonded during recovery and now they're BFFs." Bronwyn laughed. "My mom is impossible to fight with, but she's also impossible to stay mad at."

"So, you and your husband have the same birthday? That's quite a story."

"Oh, it gets better. Our moms talked about this wedding before they even took me and James home from the hospital. They thought it would be so cute if the two of us grew up and fell in love. And now here we are."

"Here you are," Cammie echoed.

"Of course, we wouldn't be getting married if we didn't really love each other. Our mothers just lucked out. We always got along—we even shared well as toddlers—and we started dating, if you can call it that, in seventh grade. Our wedding day will be the tenth anniversary of our first official date."

"That explains why you'd rather change reception venues than the ceremony date."

Bronwyn glanced down, interlacing her fingers. "It's sentimental and kind of cheesy, but that's who we are."

"It's not cheesy at all," Cammie assured her. "I think it's beautiful, and I'll do everything I can to make it happen." She took a breath. "But. Here's the thing."

Bronwyn laughed. "I know. Don't worry, we'll try to rein my mom in."

"It's not that I don't respect the mother of the bride, it's just that you're the *actual* bride. It's really your day."

Bronwyn swept her long, light hair back. "I don't mind if she takes over. The menu and flowers don't really matter to me."

"Did you get to pick out your own wedding gown, at least?"

"Yes. It's kind of simple for her taste, but she'll live. She picked an extrafancy mother-of-the-bride dress to make up for it. Sequins for days." Bronwyn glanced back at her mother, smiling fondly.

"You're very mature for twenty-two."

"That's what they tell me." Bronwyn nibbled her lower lip. "Sometimes I think . . ."

Cammie waited.

"I wonder if I should have taken a few risks before settling down."

"What kinds of risks?" Cammie expected the bride to talk about dating other people, but Bronwyn surprised her.

"Well, I love James—I know he's the right one for me—but he's starting a job in September and so am I, and I know our mothers are both dying for us to give them grandchildren, and it's all happening so fast."

Cammie thought about Kat and how trapped she felt in the suburbs. "It's a bit overwhelming?"

"I never told my mom this—I didn't even tell James—but right after we got engaged, I applied for a research assistantship in the Galápagos. I majored in biology, and I always wanted to go." She lowered her voice as this little tidbit slipped out. "Don't tell anyone."

"I won't," Cammie promised.

"It didn't work out, anyway. I knew it was a pipe dream when I applied—it's really competitive." Bronwyn now looked determined to accept her fate. "When I got the rejection letter, I figured it just wasn't meant to be."

"It was only one rejection letter," Cammie said. "Most people who achieve their pipe dream deal with way more rejection than that."

"Yeah?" Bronwyn looked intrigued. "Like who?"

"Bronwyn, meet my cousin Kat. Kat, this is the bride who's planning the reception here."

"Great to meet you." Kat offered a handshake, and Bronwyn stared at the scars and tattoos. While the rest of the wedding party strolled inside to enjoy a wine tasting with Ginger, Cammie arranged a tête-à-tête in the slice of shade afforded by the red barn.

"You're a professional skateboarder?" Bronwyn asked.

"I was." Kat's cheerful facade never wavered. "I broke too many bones too many times, so now I'm a retired skateboarder."

"And you run a vineyard? That sounds so cool."

"Yes," Kat said with an almost undetectable trace of irony. "Doesn't it?"

Before Kat could delve into the sordid truth about running a vineyard, Cammie jumped in. "I was telling Bronwyn here that rejection is part of success."

Kat rubbed her lower back. "Well, you know, it wasn't my favorite part of my job, but I got over it. Like, a million times."

Bronwyn was still eying the scars. "I've never set foot on a skateboard."

"Most women haven't. Which is too bad, because it's such an incredible experience. It's spiritual, in a way—mind and body and soul all working together."

"Can we go sometime?" Bronwyn asked. "I could really use a spiritual experience right now."

Kat's blue eyes brightened at the prospect. "Tell you what—if you want to try skateboarding, I'll take you out for a lesson. But you're going to have to split my time and attention with another student."

"Okay."

"A male stripper," Kat added.

Bronwyn shrugged. "Okay."

"And your fiancé's going to be fine with that?"

Bronwyn rolled her eyes. "He's my fiancé, not my father."

"See?" Kat looked pointedly at Cammie. "*Some* men aren't threatened by skateboarding with a stripper."

"They've known each other since birth," Cammie said, and Bronwyn told the story of their courtship to Kat.

Kat's expression vacillated between awed and appalled. "You've been together since seventh grade?"

Bronwyn nodded. "I can't imagine being with anyone else."

"And you're sure you're ready for this kind of commitment?"

Cammie snapped her brows together. "Kat."

"What? I'm just asking a question. Marriage is a big deal."

Bronwyn's eyes were wide and solemn. "I know."

"A *big deal*," Kat emphasized. "You think you know what it'll be like, but you don't. No matter how well you know your partner, how long you've been together, how much you love each other, you just. Don't. Know."

"What *is* it like?" the young woman asked.

"It's great," Cammie said quickly.

Bronwyn turned to her. "You're married?"

"Well, no."

Bronwyn turned back to Kat, noticed the simple platinum band on her ring finger. "You're married?"

"For now," Kat muttered.

"What does that mean?" Bronwyn asked.

"I have no idea." Kat ran one of her fingers along the thin white scar on her forearm. "When we got married, I was sure. This was it, this was the one. And now we're living in different states. Full disclosure: It's all my fault."

"Do you love him?" Bronwyn pressed.

"I think so."

"You *think* so?" Now it was Bronwyn's turn to look appalled. "What kind of answer is that? You make the decision to love someone every day."

Kat stared down at her sneakers, ashamed.

Bronwyn regarded both of them with indulgent amusement. "You guys. I've known my fiancé since before we could talk. We've been dating for ten years. Don't you think the butterflies have worn off by now? James is my best friend, but he's also my soul mate."

"That's what we all say in the beginning," Kat intoned.

"He cleans the bathroom every Saturday morning," Bronwyn added.

"For real?" Kat conceded defeat. "I give you my blessing. Marry him and never look back."

"What happened?" Bronwyn asked her. "To make you stop loving him?"

Kat thought for a bit before answering. "Nothing. He's the exactly the same as he's always been. I'm the one who changed. I keep telling him it's not about him—it's all about me."

"It's all about you," Bronwyn repeated back to Kat. "Hear how that sounds?"

Kat looked chagrined. "I do now."

"When does he get a turn to have it be all about him?"

Kat started to reply, stopped, then finally said, "*How* old are you again?"

"Twenty-two. I'm an old soul, or so people tell me."

"No kidding."

"Tell her about the Galápagos," Cammie urged.

Bronwyn hemmed and hawed for a few minutes, but ended up confessing the details about her failed attempt to research marine ecosystems in South America.

"How long have you wanted to do that?" Kat asked.

"Since high school." Bronwyn nibbled her lower lip. "But I always knew it wasn't realistic." She sounded apologetic. "Grant money is really hard to get these days, and I didn't have a lot of research experience."

"Twenty-two is too young to give up on your dreams," Kat said.

"Yeah? How old are you?"

"Thirty-two."

"Thirty-two is too young to give up on your dreams," Bronwyn said.

"Great." Cammie clapped her hands to signal an end to this increasingly existential conversation. "We all agree we should chase our dreams. In the meantime, let's talk about reception sites and weather contingencies, shall we?"

"It's not going to rain." Bronwyn shot her a pointed look. "You heard my mother."

Cammie studied the clouds on the horizon, fighting the urge to check the weather website Ian had recommended. She hoped it wouldn't rain again tonight—too much rain could cause rot in the rosebushes and bloat in the grapes. "I'm aware that your mother is very strong willed, but even she can't control the weather."

"Ha. That's what you think."

Kat looked intrigued. "She can ward off thunderstorms with her mind? Is she part of the X-Men?"

"She's a different kind of superhero: the Indomitable MOB."

"Listen." Cammie sat down next to Kat on the green velvet sofa in the parlor after the bridal party departed. "I don't want to tell you how to run our little family business here—"

"But you're going to, anyway?"

"In the future, maybe don't discuss all your marriage problems with the bride. She wants the happily ever after. The fairy tale. Let the girl enjoy her engagement."

"But she should know—"

"Maybe she should," Cammie conceded. "But we're not the ones who should tell her. That's what therapists and passive-aggressive relatives are for. We're just here to make sure the reception goes well."

"You're right. It won't happen again." Kat tipped her head back and stared up at the wooden ceiling beams.

Cammie helped herself to one of the orange slices on the plate next to Kat. "You seem a little distracted."

Kat let out her breath in a rush of air. Cammie expected another conversation about Josh, but Kat surprised her. "My old sponsor is hosting a major competition in California in three weeks. Since I can't compete, they've asked me to come judge."

"Oh, good for you!" Cammie stopped enthusing when she noticed Kat's dour expression. "Not good for you?"

"I can't decide if I should say yes. It'd be great to get back into the boarding world, but it'll be a bitch to just sit on the sidelines." Kat paused. "And flying off to California's not going to help things with me and Josh."

Cammie inclined her head in agreement.

"But, honestly, I'm not sure what *would* help me and Josh, so I might as well go. A check is a check, right?"

"That's pretty much my motto." Cammie grinned. "And look how great my life is turning out. Planning weddings for child brides, and making out with farmers in ditches."

Kat offered a high five. "Living the dream."

"Every day."

chapter 18

Ginger, Kat, and Cammie entered the wine festival linked arm in arm in arm. After much controversy over what to wear, they'd decided to stick to basic black, in an effort to look like serious wine growers while simultaneously blending into the background.

Ginger had opted for a demure black wrap, a huge gold bag, and flashy gold earrings, while Kat had gone with a no-fuss black wool crepe dress with a cowl neckline and minimal jewelry. Cammie had landed somewhere in the middle, in a V-neck cocktail dress with vampy pink stilettos and a pink garnet pendant she'd borrowed from her aunt.

The trio paused at the entryway for a moment, taking in the twinkle lights overhead, the throngs of well-heeled wine enthusiasts, and the bow-tie-bedecked waiters carrying trays of wine and champagne.

"Oooh," Ginger breathed.

"Wow," Kat said.

"I left something in the car," Cammie mumbled. "Go in without me. I'll be back in a minute." She retreated to the parking lot, sternly admonishing herself. *Pull it together.*

This was a family outing. Also a business trip. With wine and schmoozing and twinkle lights. So why did she feel as though she were on the verge of a panic attack?

She leaned against a concrete slab for a moment, forcing herself to breathe deeply in an effort to steady her shaking hands and feet. Her shoe heels were high and spindly; her trembling would result in a snapped ankle if she didn't calm down.

After a few minutes, she calmed down.

And then, the moment she stepped back into the swanky soiree, she started trembling again.

Everywhere she looked, there were people who had succeeded in life: winemakers, sommeliers, judges, and journalists. All of these people had somehow managed to thrive in an industry littered with bankrupted businesses and misguided marketing campaigns.

And Cammie had lost everything, including her mother's legacy. She bowed her head, suffused with shame.

"Cammie!" Ginger glided up beside her. "There you are! I've found some people you simply must meet." Her aunt dragged her toward a cluster of merrymakers who were passing around a goblet of dark red wine.

"Cammie, dear, this is Tasha and Reyna and Geoffrey and Max. Everyone, this is my niece, Cammie."

Everyone stopped laughing and chatting just long enough to politely acknowledge her, then went right back to partying.

"She's the entrepreneur," Ginger confided to the man next to her, who was wearing a purple velvet jacket and a black bowler hat. "Very business savvy. She went to graduate school. Moved to Los Angeles all by herself and opened up her own restaurant. Fearless, I tell you!"

Geoffrey put down his wineglass and looked at Cammie with renewed interest. "Very impressive."

"It's not, really." Cammie decided it was definitely time to start drinking. "She's exaggerating."

"What part am I exaggerating?" Ginger turned to her male companion with a sassy little wink. "I'm very honest."

"I have no doubt." He winked back.

Cammie didn't know what was up with all the winking, but she didn't like it.

"My restaurant didn't work out the way I planned," she found herself confessing to the stranger in the purple jacket. "We didn't even last a year."

He waved this away. "Neither did my first restaurant. And my second, third, and fourth restaurants were all disasters, too. You won't really hit your stride until number six or so."

"You had six restaurants?" Ginger asked.

"I had three successful restaurants and five dismal failures." He seemed almost proud of this.

Cammie stared at him. "How did you keep going? After five failures?"

He laughed. "I had no other options. I'm not qualified to do anything else."

"Where are your restaurants?" Ginger asked. "Are they nearby?"

"Two in D.C.; one in Virginia. Sold them all last year," Geoffrey replied. "I'm supposed to be retiring, but really I'm just shifting gears. That's why I'm here tonight—I'm getting into wine."

After spending a few years in LA, Cammie recognized a line of BS when she heard it. "Uh-huh."

"I've made wine as a hobby for years. Studied with masters in France, Italy, and Spain."

Ginger batted her eyelashes. "Really?"

Cammie leveled her gaze at him. "Really?"

"I didn't settle down and get serious about it until after my divorce." He looked meaningfully at Ginger.

"So, you're single?" Ginger pressed.

"At the moment." More meaningful glances.

"And you know a lot about wine?"

"I'm not a professional, but I know a few things."

"Here." Ginger heaved her massive gold lamé bag onto the table. "Try this."

"Aunt Ginger!" Cammie swatted at the bag, but Ginger would not be deterred. "What are you doing?"

"I want him to taste our wine." Ginger pulled a bottle of strawberry wine out of the bag. "Made with my late sister's recipe. Everyone says it's delicious."

"I'd love to try it." Geoffrey gallantly dumped the rest of his wine into a metal spit bucket, then produced a Swiss Army–style corkscrew from his jacket pocket. "May I?"

While Geoffrey poured the wine and charmed her aunt, Cammie went in search of Kat, who was drowning her sorrows in the corner.

"We have a problem," Cammie announced without preamble. "It's your mom. She's met a guy."

"Oh good! I've been telling her do to that for the last twenty years."

"No, not good." Cammie lowered her voice. "He's shady."

Kat glanced over toward her mother. "Go on."

"He claims he owned a bunch of restaurants, but he just sold them. He's conveniently divorced. He claims he studied wine making all over Europe. It's a little too good to be true."

Kat narrowed her eyes. "You think he's a lying liar?"

"I kind of do."

Kat craned her neck to get a better look at her mother's companion. "What's up with the outfit? He's like a cane and two green socks away from being the Riddler."

"Exactly. Just look at him!"

"I don't want to look at him." Kat straightened her shoulders and started toward her mother. "I want to talk to him."

"Okay, but no fistfights. This is a black-tie event."

"Fistfights?" Kat looked aghast. "What kind of hooligan do you take me for?"

"The kind I've seen brawl in a bar fight on two separate occasions."

"Then you should know I never throw the first punch." She grinned again. "I always throw the last."

As the two cousins started across the room, Ginger motioned for them to hurry up.

"Kat!" Ginger looked absolutely delighted (and totally buzzed). "I'd like to you meet Geoffrey."

"What?" Geoffrey turned to Ginger with a big display of shock and awe. "Surely this isn't your daughter? Why, the two of you must be sisters!"

"Yep," Kat muttered under her breath. "Total grifter."

"I told you," Cammie muttered back.

"What are you girls whispering about?" Ginger demanded.

"Nothing," Cammie said. "We were just—"

"Hoping for a glass of that incredible strawberry wine, I'm sure." Geoffrey poured out two more servings of the wine and handed the glasses to Kat and Cammie. "Playful, subtle, not too sweet. Meant to be savored."

Kat clicked her tongue. "Hey, Mom, can I talk to you for a second?"

"Drink your wine first," Ginger commanded.

Kat obligingly chugged half the pink liquid in her glass.

"Not like that! For heaven's sake, Katherine. Don't waste it; this is meant to be *savored*. Didn't you hear the man?"

"Oh, I heard him."

"He's an expert, I'll have you know. Studied with the finest vintners in France and Italy. You should listen to him." Ginger glanced at him with admiration.

Cammie took another swig of the strawberry wine, which, she had to admit, tasted even better this time around. "Ooh. This is really good." She held up her glass, examining the blush-colored liquid.

"You don't have to sound so shocked." Ginger appealed to Geoffrey. "You see what I have to put up with?"

Kat took another sip. "What'd you do to it?"

"Nothing you couldn't do, if you'd bother to follow directions."

"I don't bother, so why don't you just tell me?"

Cammie glanced at Geoffrey, expecting the suave older man to retreat in the face of mother-daughter squabbling. But he didn't seem uncomfortable in the least. In fact, he seemed intrigued by the family conflict.

"You two are close," he said.

Kat and Ginger stopped bickering for a moment.

"Absolutely," Ginger assured him. "We hardly ever fight."

"What are you talking about? We fight all the time." Kat turned to Cammie. "Can I get a witness?"

Cammie raised her wineglass to her lips, which rendered her unable to reply.

"All families fight," Geoffrey said. "You're lucky you have a great family to fight with."

"Exactly." Ginger was practically radiating happiness. "That's just what I always tell her."

Kat finished off her strawberry wine and pulled out her cell phone.

"I'm calling Josh." She sounded almost threatening.

"What about?" Cammie asked.

"I don't know." Kat started to dial. "But I feel like I should call him. I think it's that strawberry wine."

"Ooh, it's like a love potion." Cammie regarded the pink liquid with renewed interest.

"More like a potion that makes me pathetic. Whatever. I'm dialing. He can't ignore me forever. And you know, that twenty-two-year-old bride had some good points." Kat's eyes looked dazed and detached, almost as though she were hypnotized. "He's a great guy. We have a great life together. I would be stupid to let that slip away."

Cammie cleared her throat. "You know what I *don't* hear? An impassioned declaration of how much you love him."

"Love is a decision you make every day," Kat replied.

"Spoken like a twenty-two-year-old bride."

Kat hummed a little tune as she dialed her phone and held it to her ear.

As her cousin stepped outside, Cammie had the urge to dial her phone, too. She decided to also blame the strawberry wine. *Why not?*

She pulled up Ian's name in her contacts list. As soon as she heard him say hello, she felt tingly all over. "Hey, it's me. No, I'm not calling about grapes. We're done talking about grapes and we're done talking about strawberries. Want to come pick me up?"

chapter 19

"I never know what's coming next with you." Ian looked wryly amused when he got out of the truck and opened the passenger-side door for her.

"Keeps life exciting." Cammie practically bounced into the truck cab. "What's up with you?"

"I was hanging out at home, watching the ballgame."

Cammie scooched toward him as he settled into the driver's seat. "And?"

"And halfway through the third inning, my phone rings."

"And you picked up." She moved all the way to the middle of the bench seat.

"Well, yeah."

Cammie could smell the traces of shampoo in his freshly washed hair. "And you're wondering what kind of farming help I need from you?"

"The thought did cross my mind."

Cammie nestled closer, her body heat commingling with his. She lowered her voice to a throaty whisper. "I don't want to do anything related to farming with you. I want to do everything else." She reached up and brushed her fingertips against his cheek.

He rested his hands on the steering wheel, the truck still in Park. His jaw twitched under her touch. "Why now? What's changed?"

She considered this for a moment, trying to piece together an explanation that would make sense to him—or to herself. But all she knew was that she didn't want to spend the next decade regretting letting him go. Wondering what might have been.

She smiled up at him. "Everything."

He bowed his head, brushed his lips against hers once, twice.

"You taste like strawberries," he told her.

"I taste like the wine we made with your strawberries. And we're not talking about either of those things, remember?" She slid her hand to the back of his neck, urged him to kiss her again. When they finally pulled apart, he put the truck in gear.

"Where are we going?"

"First, to the grocery store."

"What's at the grocery store?"

"The opposite of wine and strawberries."

Cammie rested her head on his shoulder, feeling safe yet buzzed with anticipation. She was able to appreciate this in a way she hadn't when she was younger. Right now, in this moment, she felt like her chances were infinite, like her luck would never run out.

They ended up at the beach after stopping to buy tequila, lemons, and fixings for s'mores. Ian parked by the north end of the boardwalk, where the public-beach crowds ended and the deserted private beaches began.

He unbuckled his seat belt and grabbed the grocery bags. "Let's go."

Cammie stared at him. "Go where?"

"Looking for ghost crabs."

"What's a ghost crab?" It sounded decidedly unromantic.

He strode around the front of the truck, opened her door, and pulled a flashlight out of the glove compartment. "They're little white crabs that only come out at midnight." He held out his palm, offering to help her alight.

She blinked at him. "But I . . ."

"You said you wanted the opposite of walking the fields in the hot sun. Baby, this is it."

She took his hand and climbed down to the crumbling asphalt in her spindly high heels.

"Take your shoes off," he said, and she complied, leaving the peep-toe pumps on the truck's floor mat. He took his shoes off, as well, then helped her over the low metal guardrail and onto the sand.

The afternoon had been unrelentingly hot and humid, but the air had cooled as night fell. The sand felt refreshing against her bare feet.

Strands of hair whipped across her face as the breeze picked up. She pulled out the jeweled combs, letting her hair tumble loose around her shoulders. Ian watched her. When she was through, she folded her arms over the bodice of her cocktail dress and said, "Really? Ghost crabs? Really?"

He nodded, his eyes glinting in the moonlight. "Really."

"This sounds like a hoax. Is this like a snipe-shooting expedition?"

"No. If I wanted to take you on a wild goose chase, I'd ask you to come look for the ghost dog."

She frowned. "Wait. There's a ghost dog?"

"Not really. That's why it's a wild goose chase."

"Wait, *what*?"

He laughed and turned on his flashlight. "Come on. Stop stalling."

"What are we looking for?" Cammie asked as they started across the dunes toward the water's edge.

"Little white crabs. They usually hang out right at the edge of the waves."

Cammie could see the flicker of a bonfire farther down the shoreline. Teenagers, no doubt, flouting the strict policy against open flames on the beach. She turned to Ian to ask if they'd be roasting s'mores out here later, when she registered a blur of movement at the edge of the flashlight beam.

"Is that one?" She pointed. "Right there."

He swept the flashlight beam across the sand. "Yep. Good eye."

She hopped back as she got a good look at the creature scuttling along the wet sand. "That's not little, that's huge! Look at those claws!"

"They don't pinch."

She grabbed his shoulders, putting him between her and the crab. "Are you sure?"

He wrapped one arm around her and spun her back toward the shoreline. "I'm positive. They're more afraid of you than you are of them."

Right on cue, the white crab scurried back into the water.

"Come on." The flashlight beam bounced off the water as Ian started walking again.

She relaxed, curled her toes into the cool, wet sand . . . and shrieked as a tiny pincer speared her heel.

"Aigh!"

Ian was at her side immediately. "What?"

"It pinched me!" In an attempt to shake off the little hitchhiker, Cammie raced into the waves, shivering and sputtering as the crab dropped into the frigid, foamy water. For a moment, she lost her breath, overwhelmed by the adrenaline surging through her veins and the tang of saltwater in her mouth. Her eyes burned, her lungs burned, the freshly pierced skin on her heel burned.

And she felt completely, gloriously alive.

She emerged from the sea, laughing and shaking her fist at Ian, whose expression went back and forth between amusement and chagrin.

"I've never seen anyone get attacked by a ghost crab. Ever."

She held out her dripping, shivering arms. "Well, take a good look."

He did, letting his gaze slowly sweep from her head to her toes. Her hair was tangled and dripping, her expensive dress was ruined and clinging to her skin.

She stared back at him, and she knew she would think of him every time she saw the moon shine down on the ocean, every time she felt a sea breeze on her cheek. This was the opposite of fear. The opposite of failure.

"Come here." He opened his arms to her. "You're freezing."

She flung herself into his warm embrace, savoring the feel of her body against his. She knew she couldn't stay with him forever, but she could stay with him tonight.

He tightened his arms around her as she shivered in the cool evening air. "You okay?"

She nodded, her teeth chattering almost too much to talk. "Mm-hmm."

As they started back toward the truck, he kept her close to him, warming her with his body heat and fending off any crabs. He settled her into the passenger's seat, pulled a small first-aid kit from under the driver's seat, and dabbed disinfectant on her heel.

She sucked in her breath at the sting. "Ouch. I think I'm ready for a shot of tequila."

He applied a Band-Aid, lifted her foot, and bestowed a light kiss on the arch.

And just like that, she wasn't cold anymore. All of her senses thrilled at the feel of his lips on her bare skin. His hands, deliciously rough and callused, slid up past her ankle to cradle her calf. His lips progressed, too, trailing light kisses up her shin.

He paused, glanced up at her face, and kissed her knee. Then he stopped.

Cammie held her breath.

He trailed his fingers back down to her ankle. She shivered with anticipation.

"Cold?" he asked.

She shook her head. All she could hear was the steady crash of the surf and the pounding of her own heart in her ears. The rush that swept through her was faster and stronger than any wine-induced buzz.

Finally, she whispered, "What are you waiting for?"

His fingers slid back up toward her knee. "We're taking our time."

She wrapped her hands around his shirt collar, urging him closer. "I'm in a hurry."

His face was so close to hers, she could feel him smiling against her cheek. She turned her head and kissed him. He kissed her back and settled his hands on the curve of her hips.

They stayed there, making out by the light of the huge golden moon, for what felt like hours.

Finally, Ian pulled back, his eyes hooded.

"What's wrong?" she murmured.

"Nothing." He rested his palm on the back of her head. "It's late. I should take you home."

"What?" She had to force herself to unhand his shirt. "No, you shouldn't!"

"You have to get up early tomorrow."

"Not as early as you." She ran her hands through his hair, then wrapped her arms around him and held him close. "And we haven't even cracked open the tequila or the lemons or the marshmallows."

"We have time," he promised. "Not just tonight." He gave her one last kiss. "We'll both have something to look forward to."

She knew this was the sensible choice. She knew they had all summer. The anticipation would be delicious.

But there was a lot to be said for instant gratification.

chapter 20

Cammie lay awake for hours that night, tossing and turning, her body primed and her heart racing. The house had been empty when she went to bed, but she could hardly spare a thought for her aunt and her cousin. She was consumed with longing, and it felt good to want something so much. She hadn't let herself really want anything—or anyone—for a long time.

She finally drifted off but awoke at dawn, feeling refreshed despite the lack of sleep. She glanced over at her phone to check the time—still fifteen minutes before her alarm would ring. Ian had promised her that her brain and body would adjust to the vineyard lifestyle, and he'd been right. She was officially shifting over to Farmer Central Time.

She stretched, padded out of bed, and sent a text to the man who'd been on her mind all night:

Up with the sun. No rooster required.

Moments later, he replied: Coffee required?

She smiled and replied: More like a caffeine IV.

He responded: Meet at Jilted Café at nine?

She wrote back: Nine a.m. is the new nine p.m. It's a date.

"Hey." Kat was sitting at the kitchen table when Cammie came downstairs. Jacques was curled up under her chair. "What are you doing up?"

"I could ask you the same question."

Kat was still wearing her dress and makeup from last night. Her face looked pale and drawn. "I'm just thinking."

"Yeah?" Cammie pulled out a chair. "What are you— Hang on." She squinted at a little magnet on the refrigerator door. "What's that?"

Kat leaned back in her chair and grabbed the flowery magnet made of felt. Jacques snorted in protest as the chair legs scraped against the hardwood floor. "That's my mom's idea of folksy charm."

"'Bloom where you're planted?'" Cammie read the message embroidered around the flower petals. "There's a lot of that going around."

"What do you mean?"

Cammie told her cousin about the wooden sign she'd been forced to take at the garden-supply store. "That's two 'Bloom where you're planted's' this week."

"Maybe it's a sign from the universe," Kat suggested. She glanced down at Cammie's bandaged heel. "What happened to your foot?"

"Crab attack. I went to the beach last night with Ian."

"Ooh, the plot thickens. What's going on with you two?"

"Not much." Cammie cleared her throat. "Just, you know, setting up our second date in twelve hours."

"Rawr."

"Here's hoping." She leaned in and confided, "We made out."

"And?"

"And then he took me home."

Kat made a face. "Well, that's boring."

"*Au contraire.* The sexual tension is blowing my mind."

"Know what else might blow your mind?" Kat sipped her coffee. "Actual sex."

"I know. But right now, I'm in that can't-sleep, can't-eat, can't-concentrate infatuation stage."

"I think I have vague memories of that from high school."

Cammie fanned her face. "I'm feeling *all* the feelings."

Kat smiled wistfully. "Well, enjoy them while they last."

"Speaking of which, how'd it go with Josh last night? Did he finally answer the phone?"

"Wait. I need a PopTart if we're going to have this conversation." Kat rummaged through the cabinet, ripped open a foil packet, and handed a strawberry pastry to Cammie. "Okay, where was I?"

"Josh."

"Okay, so yes, he did answer the phone. I told him I was sorry for pushing him away. I told him I was deeply remorseful and I'd prove it to him. I offered to do anything he wanted."

Cammie took a little nibble of frosting. "What'd he say?"

"He said no." Kat put down her pastry.

"Oh, honey."

"I can't blame him. I have this coming."

"He's angry, but he'll get over it," Cammie declared with a confidence she didn't feel. "Give him some space and some time."

Kat straightened up. "I've given him too much space already. We need to stop spending time apart and start spending time together."

"But if he said . . ."

"You know what else we need?" Kat crumpled up the foil wrapper. "Less talk and more action. I got us into this mess, and I'll get us out of it."

"Okay, but if I could just be the voice of reason for one second—"

Kat rolled her eyes. "If you must."

"You guys are partners. So you both have to take action. Together."

"That's what I'm saying—I'll start the train rolling, and he'll get on board."

Cammie gave up on reason and common sense. "What do you think you'll do?"

"Well." Kat toyed with her paper napkin. "There's a chess tournament in Rehoboth Beach next week. I could sign him up for that."

"Josh plays chess?"

"He loves chess."

Cammie wondered if this whole thing would make more sense after the caffeine kicked in. "And a chess tournament is going to save your marriage *how*?"

"It'll show him that I'm willing to do anything to spend time with him. Including watching chess for hours on end. Something that's all about him and not about me. It's a start, right?" Kat brightened for a moment, then went back to looking glum. "But what if it's too late? What if I threw away a great marriage because I had some stupid midlife crisis?"

"For the last time, Katherine, you're too young for a midlife crisis." Aunt Ginger strolled into the kitchen, still wearing her cocktail dress and chandelier earrings.

Cammie heard the faint rumbling of a car engine outside. She gaped at her aunt. "Are you just getting home from the wine festival?"

"As a matter of fact, I am. What are you girls doing in here?"

"We're up for the day."

Ginger glanced at the clock, her expression horrified. "Oh God. It's practically time to start weeding."

"That's life on a farm."

"I need a nap, at least, before I can work in the fields." Ginger stretched her hands above her head and yawned.

"Take today off." Cammie remembered all the mornings in high school and college when she'd slept in while her aunt made breakfast and cleaned the house. "Jacques and I can go count the rows."

Jacques jumped to his feet and wagged his stump of a tail.

Ginger didn't argue. "Fine. I'm going to turn in. So if there's nothing you need . . ."

Cammie pointed at Kat. "She's trying to save her marriage with a chess tournament."

Kat pointed at Cammie. "She went parking with her ex."

"We will sort out both of those issues after I get some shut-eye." Ginger started for the staircase.

"Not so fast," Kat called after her. "Where have *you* been all this time?"

"The very best thing about being the parent is that I don't have to answer those questions." Ginger hummed a little tune. "But I will tell you this much: While you two were creating all sorts of drama with all sorts of men, I was networking and lining up business contacts."

Cammie narrowed her eyes. "What business contacts?"

"That lovely gentleman I introduced you to, for one."

"The one you were flirting shamelessly with?"

"That's the one." Ginger nodded. "He's going to make our wine this fall."

Cammie and Kat exchanged a look. "Uh . . ."

Ginger tapped her fingernail on the doorjamb. "What?"

"We get that he's lovely and all . . ."

"But he's not actually qualified for that."

"He's more qualified than any of us," Ginger retorted.

"Jacques is more qualified than us," Kat said. Jacques's ears pricked up at the mention of his name.

"We don't have to make a decision right now," Cammie said.

"It's already made. It was made hours ago," her aunt declared. "It's my vineyard, and I've selected my winemaker. Deal with it."

Kat and Cammie exchanged another meaningful look.

"Don't." Ginger's tone sharpened. She walked back toward the kitchen table so she could tower over them. "I know you think you know better because you're young. But let me tell you something: I've had to be tough to make it this far. Do you really think I'd risk my financial future over a one-night flirtation?"

Cammie and Kat shook their heads and mumbled apologies to the tabletop.

"If I say he can do it, he can do it. And with that, I bid you both adieu. Hold my calls." Ginger strode up the stairs and shut her bedroom door firmly enough that the sound echoed down the stairwell.

"We're going to have to give her a curfew," Kat said.

"I don't know, maybe she's on to something," Cammie mused. "Maybe we should watch and learn. She's nothing if not a survivor." She glanced over at the freezer door. "She's blooming where she's planted."

"Whatever. I'm off to do damage control on my marriage." Kat shoved the rest of the PopTart into her mouth.

"Smile when you say that."

Kat twisted her face into a positively macabre grin. "Have fun counting the rows."

Jacques yipped and wriggled with joy.

Cammie got to her feet and started looking for sunblock. "Oh, I will."

Two hours later, Cammie knelt on a blue piece of foam, her fingers sifting through the cool soil, the warm sunlight filtering through the brim of her woven straw hat. Jacques scampered up and down the row, tripping over his own feet and trying to catch a fly in his mouth. When she looked up, all she could see was green and gold.

She should be wearing gloves. She should apply a fresh coat of sunscreen. But right now, she didn't want to interrupt the flow. She wanted to keep checking the budding vines, pulling weeds, and smelling the faint trace of roses on the morning breeze. This was hard work, but she welcomed the opportunity to do something productive. To be part of this cycle that had started before she arrived in Delaware and would continue long after she left.

Maybe, just maybe . . . she was starting to like farming.

Maybe, after all her frustration and trepidation and disparagement, she was starting to understand why Ian would never be able to walk away from this life. Because that's what it was—a *life*. Not a job with an eight-hour shift you could forget about once you clocked out. This was an ongoing relationship with the land and the seeds and the rain and the sun.

Maybe she, too, was blooming where she'd been planted.

Her spirit soaring, she doffed her hat and looked up to the sky.

A majestic bird flew overhead . . .

And pooped on her forehead.

Screaming and swearing as she wiped her skin with the hem of her shirt, Cammie accepted the unfortunate truth: She *wanted* to like farming, but she didn't. She *wanted* to have the kind of relationship with her grapes that Ian had with his strawberries, but she never would.

She wanted Ian, but not enough to give up everything else she wanted. There had to be a compromise here somewhere—some way they could be together without one of them having to sacrifice too much.

The phone in her back pocket chimed as a text message from Ian arrived:

Mite emergency. Have to cancel breakfast. Will make it up to you.

"Farming sucks, yo," she said aloud, so that the grapes and the roses and the birds could all hear her.

She had to figure out what she was doing with Ian. She had to figure out what she was doing with her life. And figure it out she would—right after she took a hot, steamy, soapy shower to get all this freakin' nature off her.

chapter 21

"What happened to you?" Kat asked when Cammie straggled back into the house.

"Farming." Cammie made a face. "Farming happened to me."

Kat got off the couch and put her laptop aside. "I'll come help you."

"I don't need help." Cammie wrinkled her nose at her stained shirt hem. "I need a shower, a spa day, and a ticket back to civilization. Oh, and a working tractor would be nice. Those dead vines aren't going to uproot themselves."

A knowing grin spread across Kat's face.

"What?" Cammie demanded.

"You know what you look like right now?"

"Hell?"

"You look like Ian McKinlay's dream girl. You guys are living the R-rated version of *Green Acres*."

"We're not living the R-rated version of anything. I don't think we're going to move beyond making out in a pickup truck." Cammie pointed to her besmirched forehead. "Now, if you'll excuse me, I have to go wash off bird poop."

"What?" Kat got to her feet and motioned for Cammie to follow her to the kitchen. "You're a grown woman. Why on earth wouldn't you go all the way with him?"

"Because, for one thing, grown women don't use the phrase 'go all the way.' And for another, he made it very clear that he's not ever going to ask me to settle down again."

"What? When did he say that?"

"The summer we were twenty-two."

Kat pulled a cold bottle of water out of the refrigerator and handed it to Cammie. "That doesn't count! He doesn't even remember that."

"Oh, I assure you, he does."

Kat looked unconcerned. "Well, then, you'll just have to make him change his mind."

"Gee, it's so easy. Why didn't I think of that?"

"It sounds like you did." Kat winked. "In the pickup truck in the ditch."

Cammie got serious. "The thing is, before I ask him to change his mind, I have to be really, *really* sure I've changed mine."

Kat's expression sobered. "I know exactly what you mean."

"It's one thing to spend a summer growing grapes and pretending to be a vintner—"

"There's nothing pretend about it. I've seen the bank statements."

"—but it's quite another to give up on the city and my career, such as it is, and decide to devote the rest of my life to growing strawberries. Farming isn't just his job; it's his *life*. He comes with a lot of baggage—the early mornings, the uncertainty of the weather, the constant responsibility . . ."

"Plants never sleep?" Kat said.

"Exactly. At least a restaurant has a closing time. In LA, I just had to commit to the late nights, the uncertainty of the reviews, the constant responsibility . . ."

"See? You've spent your whole life prepping for this!"

"To be a farmer's wife? Or even a farmer's girlfriend?" The phrase sounded just as jarring to Cammie now as it had when she was twenty-two. "That's not who I am. Anyway, I can't talk about this anymore. I have to clean myself up for another meeting with the bride and groom who have been together since seventh grade."

"Let's talk about strawberries for a moment," Vanessa, the mother of the bride, examined her manicure as she considered her options. "I've heard the local produce is delicious."

"COB strawberries." Cammie couldn't suppress a smile. "They're incredible."

"We'd like to do a shortcake for dessert instead of a traditional cake. Do you happen to know any good local bakers?"

"I'll get you some names." Cammie jotted down the request, then glanced up to confirm with Bronwyn that this was acceptable. But Bronwyn was no longer following the mothers around the vast green lawn. And Jeanie and Vanessa were only too happy to plan without the bride.

"Now." Vanessa strode over to a patch of grass near the barn. "I'm thinking we start the aisle runner here. The officiant will stand right over there."

Jeanie nodded approvingly. "I can see it. I like it."

"We'll put the reception tents right over there, with lots of twinkle lights. Dance floor there, tables there, band on that side."

"Perfect," Jeanie agreed.

"Yes. Well. We'll hope for beautiful weather, of course, but we still need to come up with a plan for rain." Cammie tried not to show fear. "Just in case."

Vanessa heaved a weary, put-upon sigh. "We've been over this already. It won't rain."

Cammie didn't blink. "But it might."

"It won't."

"But if it does . . ."

"Moving on." Vanessa dismissed these petty concerns with a wave of her hand. "What appetizers should we serve while Bronwyn and James are doing photos?"

Cammie managed to keep her screams of frustration contained as she scanned the vineyard grounds for the only member of this bridal party who could be counted on to be reasonable. But she didn't see Bronwyn anywhere.

While the mothers prattled on about canapes, Cammie excused herself and walked toward the barn. When she rounded the corner, she glimpsed the beautiful bride-to-be clutching her smartphone in both hands.

"Bronwyn?" Cammie approached slowly. "Everything okay?"

Bronwyn glanced up, her expression flickering between amazement and horror. "I . . . yeah. I just need a minute."

"Take as much time as you need. Your mom and Jeanie are filibustering about reception food."

As Bronwyn stared down at the little screen, a pink flush spread from her chest and crept up her neck and face. She seemed to be short of breath.

Cammie frowned. "Maybe you should go inside and sit down. Do you need some water?"

The young woman swallowed hard. "I don't need water."

Cammie backed off. "Okay. Well, if you change your mind—"

"I just got an e-mail," Bronwyn blurted. "From the research program I applied to last fall."

"The one in the Galápagos?"

"Yeah. They have a spot for me now. One of their graduate assistants dropped out."

"That's great!" Cammie's enthusiasm faded as she watched Bronwyn's expression. "It's not great?"

"They said no." Bronwyn twisted a lock of hair around her finger. "I put everything I had into that application, and they said no. And then James asked me to marry him and I said yes."

"Ah."

"And I want to marry James. I've wanted to marry him since we were in kindergarten." She tipped her head back and gazed up at the clear blue sky.

Cammie waited.

"But I want this, too." Bronwyn sucked in a ragged breath. "So, so badly."

"You don't have to choose," Cammie said. "You can get married and still go to the Galápagos."

"I can't, actually." Bronwyn looked back down at her phone. "The team is leaving for South America on my wedding day."

"Just change your wedding date."

Bronwyn laughed mirthlessly. "Hi. Have you met my mother?"

Cammie watched the bride's expression flicker between doubt and determination. "It's not her wedding or her life; it's yours. If you want to do this, you should. You're young, you're chasing your dreams—"

"I'm engaged." Bronwyn looked resigned. "I can't go."

Cammie knew this was her cue to stop talking and walk away. Anything else would be unprofessional. Kat would have a conniption.

And yet.

"Have you told James about this yet?" Cammie asked.

Bronwyn's flush deepened. "No. What am I going to say? 'Hey, I know I promised to love you forever and ever, but something better came along so I'm bailing'?"

"You're not bailing; you're postponing."

"It's never a good sign when someone postpones their wedding," Bronwyn declared. "Besides, I can't put it off. We're supposed to be moving three weeks after the wedding."

"Where are you moving?"

"Oklahoma."

"That's a big move. What's in Oklahoma?"

"James's new job." Bronwyn looked wistful.

"Well, there you go. You're so committed to the man you love that you're willing to uproot your life and move to Oklahoma for him."

"Of course. I'd do anything for him."

"Don't you think he feels the same about you?"

Instead of answering directly, Bronwyn said, "I'd never ask him to give up that job offer. The Galápagos thing is an unpaid internship. It's the chance of a lifetime, but it's not a career. We've graduated college. We're adults now." She clicked off her phone. "And in twenty or thirty or forty years, I won't even remember I got this e-mail."

Cammie didn't say anything.

Bronwyn squared her thin, pale shoulders. "You don't get to do everything you want. That's not how life works. Like my grandmother always says, you have to bloom where you're planted."

Cammie's jaw dropped. "What did you say?"

"I said you've got to—"

"Never mind. I heard what you said. Listen. You've been planted your whole life already. Maybe it's time for you to fly."

"I'd be gone for eight months." Bronwyn dabbed sweat from her brow with a tissue. "We've never been apart for more than a week and a half."

"Well, surely they have Skype or FaceTime or whatever down in the Galápagos."

"Yeah, but it's not the same as seeing him in person every day.

Kissing him and holding him and eating with him and sleeping with him . . ." Bronwyn trailed off. "I don't know what to do."

"At least tell him you got the offer," Cammie urged.

Bronwyn let her hair fall across her face, hiding her expression. "What if he tells me to go, and I do, and then everything falls apart? What if he goes to Oklahoma and finds someone new? Or I find someone new? Or one of us decides they're never coming home? Or we both come back, but things are different between us?" Her voice got higher and tighter as she listed all the possible scenarios.

"Bronwyn?" Vanessa's voice drifted across the fields. "Where are you?"

Bronwyn gave herself a little shake. "Oh, forget it. No one's going to the Galápagos. I have to get married." She set her jaw. "If I was meant to go, I would've been accepted months ago. It's not meant to be."

Cammie gave her a long look. "Then let's go talk about chair bows and appetizers. But, Bronwyn?"

"Yes?"

"You need to have a talk with your mother. About rain contingencies."

Bronwyn looked resigned. "I'll try."

"I know she's decided it's going to be a clear day, but I can't make any guarantees."

"I'll talk to her." Bronwyn raised one eyebrow warningly. "But that's *all* I'll talk to her about."

"And you should know that the *Farmers' Almanac* predicts thunderstorms for your big day."

Bronwyn blinked. "The *Farmers' Almanac*? I didn't think that actually predicted anything."

"It doesn't." Cammie lowered her voice. "But it *might*."

chapter 22

The next afternoon, after a long, hot day of weeding, watering, and taking calls from Bronwyn's mother about everything from silverware to string quartets, Cammie decided to treat herself to a drink at the Whinery.

Every time she walked into the bar, she felt a pang of longing. The cozy little lounge was completely different from what she'd tried to create in Los Angeles, but in this setting, with this clientele, it worked perfectly.

This early in the evening, the bar was sparsely populated with tourists and the music was turned down. Cammie took a seat at the very end of the bar and waved to Jenna.

"Hey." Jenna approached with a friendly smile. "What can I get you?"

Cammie scanned the offerings listed on the chalkboard above the bar. "Anything but wine."

"Vodka and cranberry?"

"Perfect."

While Jenna poured the cranberry juice, her nemesis returned. The health inspector's suit, tie, and clipboard looked completely out of place against all the pink and silver and toile. Jenna slammed down the cranberry-juice bottle, visibly panicked.

Cammie, too, scanned the barroom for any possible violations. She spied a metal scoop in the ice well, which she knew from personal experience would incur a penalty. She leaned over the bar as casually as possible and extracted the scoop.

"Thanks," Jenna mouthed over the guy's shoulder.

When the inspection was over, Jenna retrieved the scoop with a sheepish expression. "You're a lifesaver. I know better than to leave that in there."

"It's the least I could do; you're pouring me booze."

"Yes, I am, and your booze is on the house." Jenna was still visibly anxious. "He couldn't find anything to cite me for today, which means he'll be back soon to harass me again." She frowned. "Do I sound paranoid?"

"Slightly."

"How'd you know, anyway? About the scoop in the ice?"

"Back when I was in the restaurant business, I got dinged on the ice well so many times, my nickname was Scoop."

Jenna looked intrigued. "I always wanted to open a restaurant."

Cammie glanced around at the customers and the cocktails. "But you already did."

"No, no, I opened a *bar*—big difference. Restaurants have food and menus and kitchens."

"And fickle, temperamental chefs," Cammie finished for her.

Jenna waved as a new customer walked through the door. "Had a bad chef experience?"

"The chef was great, actually. Supertalented. The problem was, he was also my boyfriend." Cammie explained how she and Zach had decided to open the restaurant together. "He jumped ship and he still has a career. He moved on without a backward glance."

"He'll be sorry someday," Jenna predicted. "He'll end up poor and disgraced."

"I don't think so. I just read in *Us Weekly* that he's going to be a judge on a rip-off of *Top Chef*."

"Then I hope he gets singed on a flattop in front of a live audience." Jenna excused herself to pour a drink for someone at the other end of the bar. When she returned, she asked, "So, how did you get started in the restaurant business? Did you have to line up investors?"

"No." Cammie's smile faded. "I had my own capital. If I were going to do it again, I would definitely try to get a business loan or find a partner. But I had an inheritance from my mother. And now it's gone. I wasted it all."

"You didn't waste it," Jenna said firmly. "I bet you learned a ton about the business."

"I learned that the health inspector will ding you for having a scoop in the ice well."

"There you go." Jenna offered her a tiny bag of M&M's.

"I know that I'm supposed to look for the lessons and learn from failure and all that, but I just can't get there." Cammie sipped her drink. "I'm done with the restaurant chapter of my life."

"Are you sure?" Jenna pressed. "I was serious about selling before. Make me an offer. If I have to deal with one more health inspection, one more piece of relationship memorabilia flushed down the toilets . . ."

Cammie frowned. "Relationship memorabilia?"

"Jewelry, letters, stuffed animals. You wouldn't believe some of the stuff we've pulled out of the sewer line. I have a plumber on retainer." Jenna pointed out a huge cardboard box in the corner. "We encourage people to throw all their unwanted crap in there, but some people just love the drama of the flush. The plumber once fished out a strand of opera-length pearls."

Cammie's jaw dropped. "Real pearls?"

"Real and very, very expensive."

"Wow." Cammie shook her head. "That's . . ."

"Just another day at the Whinery," Jenna concluded. "You sure I can't interest you in a quick sale?"

Cammie closed her eyes and allowed herself to imagine this—starting fresh—for a moment. This place would be easier to run than a full-menu restaurant; there'd be no chefs or line cooks; there was an established clientele and a prime location. She'd have to go over the books, of course, but all other things being equal, this wine bar could be a great opportunity. That's what she should be doing with her life—*selling* wine. Not growing it.

She opened her eyes and returned to reality. "I'm broke."

"Damn."

"Just as well. The locals here would never get over it if you sold this place. Besides, what would you do if you didn't have the Whinery?"

"Move back to Boston," Jenna said without a moment's hesitation. "Become a plumber. They make great money, if my bills are any indication. No, seriously, I'd open a café with my sisters. We'd focus on breakfast and brunch. Those kinds of places can do really well in the right location, and there are no late nights."

"But there are early mornings. Those are much worse."

"That's a matter of opinion," Jenna said.

Cammie considered this for a moment. "Boston, huh? So you didn't grow up here in Delaware?"

"No. Boston, born and raised."

"Then how . . ."

"Same way all these heartbreak tourists ended up here. There was this guy."

Cammie grinned. "Isn't there always?"

"Well, this particular guy was ten years older and I thought he knew everything. He dragged me out here one summer and said he and his buddies were going to open a sports bar."

"This place was supposed to be a sports bar?" Cammie squinted, trying to envision it.

"Yeah, if you can believe that. I knew a sports bar would never work with this clientele, but I was still in the 'he knows everything' phase, so I went along with it." Jenna pointed to the far wall. "There used to be two giant TVs over there. Golf and football and baseball all day, every day."

"Stop. I can't."

"Neither could anyone else. Sports bar went under six months after he opened it." Jenna rinsed off the metal ice scoop. "And, by that time, I stopped thinking that he knew everything, and started thinking that *I* knew everything."

"Sometimes that's an asset in the business world."

"He'd lost so much money, he said I could have this place if I'd just take on his debt. So I did."

"And turned it into a decadent pink paradise."

"That part was actually an accident," Jenna confessed. "We had a summer resident who was an interior designer, and she was redoing one of those huge mansions by the beach. The owners were getting rid of all their old furniture, and the designer donated it to me in exchange for a month's worth of chardonnay."

Cammie looked around at all the lace and pastel. "That must have been some mansion."

"She showed me the before pictures." Jenna grinned. "It was like a My Little Pony bordello." She indicated the chandelier. "That used to hang over the bathtub."

Cammie glanced at the little silver candy dishes. "What about those?"

"Those were my idea," Jenna said. "I was so sick of pretzels and peanuts."

"Brilliant."

"These dishes are kind of special. Every now and then, one of them gets lost or 'borrowed,' but customers keep bringing in replacements. I don't know how they know; I never ask. But that one"—she pointed out the one next to Cammie—"is new. Lila Alders said she spotted it at Goodwill and thought of me."

"See? People think of you. This bar is special."

"Make me an offer," Jenna repeated.

"I would if I could."

"But you can't." Jenna grabbed a clean, folded pink dish towel. "It's okay. I've actually gotten a few calls from business brokers over the past few months."

"I'll keep my fingers crossed for you." Cammie felt an irrational pang of remorse and disappointment, like she'd lost something she'd never had in the first place.

"Thanks." Jenna refilled Cammie's water glass. "So, what's going on with you and the farmer?"

"That's classified."

"Oh, you're so cute." Jenna waved as Lila Alders strolled through the front door. "Hey, Lila—I just asked Cammie here what was going on with her boyfriend, and she said it's classified."

"Adorable." Lila all but pinched Cammie's cheeks before sitting down next to her. "Once upon a time, I, too, thought I could have a private life in Black Dog Bay. When Malcolm and I got together, it was all very *Mission: Impossible.*"

"The 'impossible' part being keeping it secret," Jenna said.

Lila nodded. "The walls here have ears. And ESP and X-ray vision. Anyway, just give me a call when you guys are ready to pick out an engagement ring."

Cammie choked on her water.

"What?" Lila asked, the picture of wide-eyed innocence. "Too soon?"

Cammie just kept hacking and coughing.

"Don't die," Jenna pleaded. "I'll definitely get cited for that."

"I'm not dying," Cammie assured them when she recovered the power of speech. "But I'm not getting married, either."

"Well, sure, not right now."

"No, no, no. Not ever. Not to Ian, anyway."

"I've made a decision," Bronwyn announced when she arrived—sans mothers—at the vineyard the next morning. She planted her tiny, flip-flop-clad feet on the uneven planks of the porch and announced, "James and I are getting married as scheduled."

Cammie nodded, keeping her expression neutral. After all, this wasn't her marriage, her life, or any of her business. "That's great."

Bronwyn grinned mischievously. "In a year. I told him about the Galápagos. And he obviously didn't want me to go, but he gets that I need to go. So . . ." She took a deep breath. "We're going to be apart for the first time. He'll go to Oklahoma, I'll go to South America, and a year from now, we'll have the wedding."

Cammie smiled. "You look so happy."

"I am. I'm also really nervous, but I'm going to have an adventure. And then I get to come home and marry the man I love."

"I'm thrilled for you." Cammie was afraid to ask the next question. "Did you two break the news to your mothers yet?"

"Yep. I'm surprised you couldn't hear the screaming from two counties away." Bronwyn grimaced at the memory.

"Well, think of it this way: The hard part's over." Cammie opened the screen door and invited Bronwyn inside. "Come with me and I'll give your deposit back."

"Keep it." Bronwyn waved one hand. "For next summer."

"You're sure?"

"Very." Bronwyn beamed. "I may be leaving James temporarily, but our story's not over."

"Oh, that's lovely." Aunt Ginger sighed that evening as she, Kat, and Cammie had dinner at the cramped but cozy kitchen table. "He'll wait for her; she'll wait for him. It's so romantic."

"Romantic, yes." Kat helped herself to a crab leg. "Good business, no." She pointed the empty crab shell at Cammie. "Do we have any other big events on the calendar?"

"No."

"Then why'd you talk the bride out of getting married? We need that money."

"I kept the deposit," Cammie said.

"Only because she insisted." Kat tsk-tsked. "And the deposit is, what? Half of the total?"

"More like thirty percent," Cammie admitted.

"What?" Kat looked outraged. "You should ask for at least half up front. No wonder—" She stopped herself, but Cammie knew exactly what her cousin had been about to say. *No wonder your restaurant went out of business.*

"You have a lot of opinions for someone who didn't want to be involved," Cammie retorted. "If you'd like to review the contracts and make changes, be my guest. And feel free to wrangle the mother of the bride, line up the caterers, and obsessively check the weather."

"I'm sorry," Kat muttered. "You're right."

"I am right," Cammie agreed. "And the bride is right, too. They can come back and get married here next summer."

"If we're still here next summer," Kat said.

Ginger froze, a homemade biscuit halfway to her mouth. "What do you mean?"

"How are we going to keep this place going?" Kat said. "We're hemorrhaging money."

Ginger turned to Cammie. "See how negative she is? I don't know where she gets it. I never raised her to be negative."

"Mmm." Cammie crammed a piece of biscuit in her mouth in an effort to avoid further discussion.

But Ginger would not be deterred. "You've known me all your life, Cammie. Am *I* a negative person?"

"Mmph," Cammie replied.

"You're not negative; you're delusional," Kat countered.

"I *beg* your pardon." Ginger put down her silverware and stared icily at her daughter. "I realize that you think you're terribly fancy and important because you've traveled and secured a few corporate sponsors, but you do not talk to your mother that way."

Kat started stammering an apology, but it was too late. Ginger was on a roll. "Katherine, I love you—I will always love you—but I cannot abide a daughter who criticizes her cousin for trying to make the best of a bad situation and tells her mother, who's feeding and housing her while she works through some ridiculous existential crisis, that she's delusional." Ginger got to her feet and threw her napkin onto her chair. "I will take chances and I will live with the consequences, but I will not be judged by the child I gave up everything to raise." She stalked out of the kitchen, her head held high, and slammed the screen door.

The sound startled Jacques from his nap under the table. Kat and Cammie regarded each other with wide eyes. A few seconds later, they heard a car engine in the driveway, and headlight beams bounced off the kitchen wall as Ginger drove away into the night.

"Wow." Cammie shook her head. "Do you want an ice pack for that burn?"

Kat sat back, obviously shaken. "She's right."

"She's upset," Cammie corrected. "No one ever accused this family of being subtle and restrained."

"But she is right," Kat said. "You both are."

"It's been a long day. Everyone's stressed and tired—"

Kat stood up and started to clear the table. "I don't like who I am anymore. I used to be so disciplined and productive, and now I'm lazy, critical, feeling sorry for myself. It's unacceptable." She raised her head, her eyes aglow with determination. "And it stops now."

"Okay, but before you recommit to all that discipline and productivity, I'd like to point out that there's ice cream in the freezer. At least have some of that before you go all hard-core."

Kat looked appalled at the very suggestion. "I'm serious, Cam. I have been unbearable these last few weeks, and I apologize."

"Apology accepted," Cammie said. "Now, about that ice cream . . ."

Kat responded by grabbing a bowl and spoon. She retrieved the ice cream from the freezer, scooped some into the bowl, and handed it to Cammie.

"None for you?"

Kat shook her head. "As of two minutes ago, I'm in training. My goal is to show Mom that her optimism will pay off. We—*I*—am going to salvage this vineyard if it's the last thing I do."

"That sounds great." Cammie cleared her throat. "But how?"

"I haven't figured that part out yet," Kat admitted. "But my first order of business will be ripping out those dead vines you've been worrying about."

Cammie saluted her with a spoonful of ice cream. "Good luck and godspeed."

"And when I was skateboarding, I wasn't just a person. I was a brand. A product to be marketed. If I did it before with skating, I can do it again with wine." Kat scrolled through her phone's contact list. "I may have been forced to retire, but there are still a few important people out there who owe me favors, and the time has come to collect."

chapter 23

The next morning, Cammie awoke to the murmur of voices in the kitchen and the faint creak of bedsprings as Kat sat down on the edge of her mattress.

"What time is it?" Cammie threw an arm over her eyes as sunlight filtered in through the gauzy white curtains.

"Six thirty." Kat gave her a gentle shake. "Wake up."

"Six thirty?" Cammie shot up into a sitting position. "Gah!"

"I know—daylight's burning," Kat admonished. "Up and at 'em. You've got an interview in a few hours."

Cammie froze, her sheet and blanket a rumpled heap. "A what?"

Kat stood up and motioned for Cammie to do the same. "I'll tell you everything over breakfast. Put some clothes on, and I'll make you some oatmeal."

"No pancakes?"

Kat shook her head. "Sorry, we're in training."

"*You're* in training."

"We're all in training. And you need to eat, shower, do your makeup, and practice your talking points before Reg shows up." Kat started for the stairs, but Cammie called after her.

"Stop. You can't go downstairs right now."

Kat glanced back over her shoulder. "Why not?"

"Because there's some guy in the kitchen." Cammie put a finger to her lips. "Listen. Hear that?"

Kat tilted her head. "Maybe it's the TV?"

"Nope." Cammie shook her head. "I think he's an overnight guest."

"What?" Kat frowned. "Whose guest?"

Cammie gave her a meaningful look and waited for the realization to sink in.

Kat clapped a hand to her mouth. "Oh no."

"It must be that guy she was flirting with at the wine festival," Cammie said. "Can't you hear the giggling?"

"I'm trying not to." Kat jerked her head toward the stairs. "What is going on with this guy? What's the appeal? Did you see his hat?"

"I couldn't *not* see it."

Kat deliberated for a moment, then finally said, "Well, I hope he's a good guy. She's been taking care of so many people for so many years." She rubbed her forehead. "It's still kind of weird though, right?"

"Extremely weird."

More laughter drifted up from the kitchen, along with the smell of fresh coffee.

Kat grabbed one of Cammie's pillows and made herself comfortable on the foot of the bed. "I hope they drink their coffee quickly—I have to pee."

Cammie tried unsuccessfully to shoo her cousin away. "So go pee. Don't tell me about it."

Kat didn't budge. "If they hear the toilet flush, they'll know we're up."

"So?"

"So do you want to go down there and have a pajama meet-and-greet with my mom and the hat dude?"

Cammie rearranged the blanket. "He has a name. I just can't remember what it is right now."

"Girls!" Ginger shouted up the stairs. "Are you up?"

Cammie and Kat both held their breath in an attempt to be completely silent.

"Katherine. Camille." Ginger's voice sharpened. "I know you're awake."

Kat looked at Cammie and mouthed, "How?"

"Stop playing possum and get down here this instant. We have a guest."

"This is your punishment," Cammie grumbled as she got out of bed and pulled on jeans and a T-shirt. "She's getting you back for all the stuff you said last night. I don't see why I have to get dragged into it."

"Go shower." Kat started for the doorway. "Save yourself. I'll tell her you were already in there."

Cammie opened her mouth to protest, but Kat pointed toward the bathroom door and went down the stairs. "Coming, Mother dear."

On a typical morning, Cammie was brisk and efficient in the shower, but today she took her time, lingering until the hot water turned lukewarm, then cool. After she finished toweling off, she took her sweet time drying her hair and then decided to spend a few more minutes applying a full face of makeup. She cracked open the bathroom door and strained to hear what was going on downstairs.

She couldn't detect anything but the birds chirping outside the window. The smell of coffee had faded. She headed down to the kitchen, where she found Ginger and Kat washing breakfast dishes.

"Oh, there you are," Kat said loudly when she noticed Cammie. "You missed a delightful and delicious breakfast."

"Yes, you did." Aunt Ginger was aglow. "We had a little get-to-know-you with Geoffrey."

"And I missed it? Darn." Cammie snapped her fingers in disappointment. "Is Geoffrey your new friend from the wine festival? What was he doing over here so early?"

Aunt Ginger smiled fondly at her. "Aren't you precious. Geoffrey is the man I met at the wine festival, but he's not my friend."

"Mom." Kat's voice had a note of warning.

"He's my lover," Aunt Ginger declared. "As of last night."

"Mother."

"Don't 'Mother' me," Ginger told Kat. "We're all too mature for this 'friend' nonsense."

"No, we're not," Cammie and Kat both insisted.

"You're both old enough to acknowledge that someone else besides you can have a sex life."

"I'm sorry I missed him." Cammie poured herself a huge glass of ice water and looked around for the sunscreen. "Do you think he'll be back again soon?"

"I'm not sure," Ginger mused. "I've got a lot going on for the next few days."

"You had a one-night stand?" Kat looked scandalized.

"You know, you're very puritanical for someone who claims to be a rebel."

"I'm only puritanical when it comes to my mother."

"Well, don't be. I'm allowed to have a one-night stand if I want to." Ginger beamed. "But don't worry; I'll see him again. After all, I'll need him in the fall when it's harvest time."

"You're stringing him along, using him for his wine-making expertise?" Now Cammie was a bit scandalized.

"I'm using him for sex, honey. Keep up."

"We broke her," Kat told Cammie. "Too much time with us has driven her over to the dark side."

"Don't blame me," Cammie said. "She's getting more action than I am right now."

Ginger looked shocked. "You still haven't spent the night with that handsome strawberry farmer?"

"I'm working on it," Cammie muttered.

"All those afternoons in the field together, and you two never finished what you started?" Ginger shook her head. "What have you been doing all summer?"

"Um, trying to figure out how to run a vineyard?"

"Yes, and on that note, I'm glad you took the time to put on mascara today, because there's going to be a reporter and a photographer at our door by lunchtime," Kat said. "I made some calls to people who know people."

"People who know people," Ginger repeated.

"That's right."

"They're coming *today*?" Cammie said.

"My people are good," Kat boasted. "One of the reporters who used to interview me married an editor at one of those lifestyle magazines, and he said he'll write an article on the vineyard for her magazine."

Ginger looked skeptical. "Which reporter?"

"You don't know him. Reg Piltner."

"I remember him." Ginger stage-whispered to Cammie. "He always had a crush on her."

"He did not. And, anyway, he's married now. And his wife agreed to feature our wine in some end-of-summer roundup, but the issue is closing this Friday, so Reg has to get the story done, like, now."

Two hours later, the house was spotless and Kat, Cammie, and Ginger were drinking strawberry wine to calm their nerves.

Between sips of pink booze, Kat doled out her best public relations tips:

"Speak slower than you normally would; otherwise, your sound bite can get garbled.

"If Reg asks a question that you don't want to answer, just answer the question you wished he *would* have asked. You can always bring the conversation back around to the brand message.

"What's a brand message? Pour me another glass of wine and I'll tell you."

By the time the doorbell rang, Cammie was half-excited and half-terrified. Ginger looked wholly terrified.

"Just be cool," Kat advised as she walked to the door. "You're going to be great."

But when Kat opened the door, her confidence evaporated. "Who are you?"

Cammie craned her neck to see a tall, full-figured woman on the porch.

"I'm Wendy Delfino." The woman waved to Cammie over Kat's shoulder. "From *Ladies First* magazine."

"But what happened to Reg?" Kat asked.

"He had a family emergency, so they sent me instead." She cleared her throat and glanced at Kat's hand, which was still gripping the doorknob.

"Katherine, where are your manners?" Ginger practically shoved Kat out of the way. "Come in, come in. I'm Ginger Sheridan, the proprietor of Lost Dog Vineyards."

"Nice to meet you." Wendy held up her camera. "Mind if I take a few pictures?"

"Shouldn't you have a photographer for that?" Kat asked. Cammie shot her a look, and she followed up with, "I mean, Reg gave me the impression that one of the staff photographers would be joining you."

Wendy looked a bit offended. "I do both the writing and photographs for my articles. Double-majored in college."

The reporter started roving around the parlor, sizing up the decor as if she were casing the place for a robbery.

Ginger stepped into Wendy's path, dragging Cammie along with her. "This is my niece, Cammie Breyer. Please sit down and make yourself at home." She pointed to the sofa, giving the reporter no other choice. "I just made some pecan pie—let me get you a slice."

"No, thank you." Wendy perched on the sofa. The journalist's outward demeanor was sunny and sweet, but Cammie saw her gaze taking in every inch of the room, every flicker in their facial expressions.

"Are you sure? I made it myself; it's delicious," Ginger said.

Wendy ignored this. "How did you get into the wine business?"

"Oh, it's a story of serendipity," Ginger began, and all of Kat's talking points went out the window while Ginger regaled the reporter with tales of destiny, delayed dreams, and dramatic near-death experiences.

Wendy had no patience for this homespun charm. After a few minutes, she turned to Cammie asked, "And how did you get involved?"

Cammie decided to stick to the script. "I, um, I have extensive experience in the fine-dining industry." She left out the part where those experiences culminated in financial, emotional, and spiritual ruin. "And the soil and weather here allow for some really rare varietals."

She rattled off the types of wine they planned to make, then segued into the importance of the community and her commitment to local labor and materials.

"Sounds fascinating. Let's go." Wendy gathered up her camera and notepad.

Cammie glanced at Kat. "Go where?"

"Give me a tour." This was a demand rather than a request. "I want to see these legendary Delaware grapes." Wendy paused when she noticed the wineglass on one of the upended barrels near the bar. "That doesn't look like cabernet."

"It's not," Ginger said. "It's our homemade strawberry wine."

"Strawberry wine." Wendy looked supremely skeptical.

"It's fantastic," Ginger said firmly. "Not to mention visionary."

"Visionary." Wendy quirked one eyebrow. "Perhaps you mean 'Victorian'?"

"It's my mother's recipe," Cammie said, hoping to defuse the tension with a poignant human-interest story.

But there was no averting the standoff between her aunt and the reporter. "Victorian?" Ginger let out a scornful little laugh. Kat cringed. "I will have you know that we are on the cutting edge."

"If you say so." Wendy smirked.

"I do say so. Fruit wine is so retro, it's coming back in style." Ginger turned up her nose. "You should know that, being a lifestyle reporter."

Wendy started scribbling notes on her yellow legal pad.

Kat stepped in between them, a huge, desperate smile on her face. "Okay! Enough chitchat! Why don't I—"

A high, indignant bark interrupted Kat's attempt at damage control. Jacques waddled into the room, sniffling and snorting. He made his way over to Cammie, sat down at her feet, and stared up at her with reproach.

"Calm down," she told the dog. "Can't you see I'm in the middle of something here?"

He responded by letting his tongue loll out the side of his mouth. Then he wandered over to Wendy, sniffed her shiny patent shoes, and barked again.

Wendy glanced at Cammie. "What does he want?"

"He wants to go count the rows. We usually do it first thing in the morning, but we missed it today, so he's sulking."

The French bulldog lay down with a phlegmy sigh and stuck his lower lip out even farther.

"Counting the rows?" Wendy started writing again. "What does that mean?"

Cammie explained about walking the fields and checking the crops. "He thinks he's a farm dog."

"He has no idea what he's doing, but he tries. Bless his little heart." Ginger smiled.

"This is his second career," Kat said, rubbing the faded scars on her arm. "He used to be a show dog."

Jacques glared at all of them. He knew when he was being patronized.

"A show dog?" Wendy didn't look up from her legal pad.

"Yeah, he won a bunch of ribbons—best in show and all that jazz—and then he busted his tooth." Kat lifted one of Jacques's jowls, displaying the missing fang. "So he's reinventing himself."

"Interesting." Wendy stopped scrutinizing every detail of the parlor and focused on the dog. "If it's all right with you, I would like to count the rows with— What's his name?"

"Jacques."

"I would like to count the rows with Jacques." She clicked her pen and waited.

Jacques got to his feet and trotted over to the screen door.

"Are you sure we can't tempt you with some strawberry wine?" Ginger got a clean glass out from under the bar. "It's hot out there."

"Well." Cammie could *see* the journalist's resolve crack. "I guess one little glass couldn't hurt."

While Jacques pawed the screen door, Ginger poured four generous servings and distributed the glasses.

"Cheers!"

"Cheers!"

"Cheers!"

Woof!

chapter 24

"That was delightful," Ginger said after she'd sent off the reporter with a hearty hug, a few bottles of strawberry wine, and many admonishments to drive safely and watch out for the broken traffic light at the edge of town. "Kat, you never told me PR work was so much fun."

"I'm glad you had a good time," Kat said. "Jacques is still here, right?"

"Present and accounted for." Cammie nodded toward the corner, where Jacques was zonked out on a little plaid dog bed.

"Good. I think that reporter would have dognapped him if she could."

"But she can't." Cammie gazed at her exhausted canine sidekick. "She sure did like him, though. I think he's going to be the star of the article."

"I can live with that." Kat turned to Ginger. "You guys were huddled up by the barn for a long time. What were you talking about?"

"Oh, this and that." Ginger fluffed her hair. "I told her all about the history of the town, the heartbreak tourists, and the magic dog . . ."

"But the grapes, Mom. You talked about grapes? And wine? Right?"

"Sure, sure." Ginger didn't sound entirely convincing. "Oh, and what's Twitter? It's like Facebook, right?"

"Sort of, but not really," Kat said. "Why do you ask?"

"Wendy said she's going to put up a picture of the vineyard on Twitter."

"Wouldn't that be Instagram?" Cammie wondered.

"You kids and your social media." Ginger threw her hands up.

"Well, let's look up the magazine's social-media accounts." Kat grabbed her tablet from the coffee table. A few moments later, the three of them were looking at *Ladies First*'s newest trending topic.

"'Three chicks and a dog,'" Kat read. "Well. That's . . ."

"Accurate," Ginger concluded.

Cammie exclaimed over the photo of Jacques counting the rows, his snout dusted with dirt. "Look how serious he is." She paused, squinting at the screen. "Look how many likes he's getting."

"Wow."

"Damn."

"He should be the official ambassador for this place," Cammie said.

"Yes," Kat said slowly. "He should. Jacques, buddy, you're the new face of Lost Dog Vineyards."

Jacques snorted in his sleep.

"Wait, wait, there's another picture, too." Cammie clicked on the link. "Of strawberry wine."

"Anything about the grapes?" Kat asked.

"Um, not that I can see."

Kat shrugged and conceded defeat. "All right, here's the deal: We're changing our brand."

"But . . . but talking points."

"We'll come up with new talking points. The reality is that no one cares about our grapes. That's fine; we can't really do anything with the grapes until fall, anyway. Right now, strawberry wine seems to be gaining traction."

"Impressive," Cammie said. "I feel like I'm at a marketing meeting."

"If the powers that be want strawberry wine—and apparently they do—we'll give them strawberry wine. But we need to make it visually appealing. Cammie, you were absolutely right when you said we need a cute bottle and an unusual label. Hell, maybe we should put Jacques on it." Kat drummed her fingers on a wine barrel. "Who do we know that can draw?"

"Not me," Cammie and Ginger said at the same time.

"There must be someone in this town who can. That'll add to the handcrafted, locally sourced aspect. Come on." Kat got to her feet and located her car keys. "Road trip."

The three of them opened the front door to find a group of tourists on the porch.

"Hi!" one of them said. "Do you guys do wine tastings?"

"We do, but not right now," Kat said.

"I'll stay behind," Ginger volunteered. She shooed Cammie and Kat out the door.

As Cammie passed, one of the visitors said, "The land here is so beautiful. We were wondering: Do you let people help pick the grapes at harvest time?"

"Absolutely," Cammie said. "Just leave your name and number, and we'll be in touch."

"Oh, thank you!" the woman gushed. "I've always wanted to work at a vineyard. It sounds so romantic."

"It is," Ginger assured them.

"Every day," Kat added.

"Living the dream," Cammie finished. And with that, she set off in search of someone to help them put a snaggletoothed French bulldog on a bottle of booze.

"You know everyone in this town," Cammie said to Jenna at the Whinery. "Who has graphic-design skills?"

"We need a really cute bottle label," Kat added.

Jenna pressed her lips together for a moment. "No offense, but you might be better off focusing on the wine right now instead of the packaging."

"Oh, it's not for the *wine* wine; it's for the strawberry wine." Kat turned to Cammie. "And I didn't want to say anything in front of my mom, but I have an errand to run before we get serious about label designs."

"Why didn't you want to say that in front of your mom?" Cammie asked.

"Because." Kat examined a loose thread on her sleeve. "I have to go to that little boutique on the other side of the street."

"Which boutique?" Cammie tried to remember the last time Kat had voluntarily gone clothes shopping for anything besides sneakers and skateboard-logo T-shirts.

"Retail Therapy?" Jenna suggested.

"Yeah, that one." Kat looked steely and determined. "Could I get a shot of whiskey, please?"

Cammie glanced at the clock. "It's pretty early for the hard stuff."

Kat straightened her shoulders. "Lingerie shopping requires hard liquor. Fact."

"Hold the whiskey," Cammie told Jenna. "I'll go with her."

"You coming with me will make things even more awkward." Kat shuddered. "I don't need you. I need whiskey."

"Don't worry; Retail Therapy is great," Jenna said. "No awkwardness whatsoever."

"Clearly, you've never been shopping with me," Kat said. "I can make any retail situation awkward. You know all those fun shopping montages in romantic comedies? With the bubbly groups of girls and the cheesy music? Yeah, shopping with me is the opposite of that."

Jenna patted Kat's hand. "Beryl's the owner. Tell her I said she needs to take good care of you."

"Cue the cheesy music." Cammie practically dragged Kat toward the door. "We're off to make a montage."

"Riddle me this." Cammie side-eyed her cousin as they emerged into the afternoon sunlight. "If you hate shopping so much, why are you going shopping?"

"It's part of the rebranding campaign." Kat trudged toward the boutique with all the enthusiasm of a shackled prisoner.

"For the wine?"

"No, for *me*. I'm trying out a new identity. I was Kat the Skater. But now I'm not. Now I'm Kat the Future Vintner . . . and Kat, Josh's Wife. So I'm going to build a new brand."

"A wife brand?" Cammie tried to follow. "That's . . ."

"Brilliant?"

"Um . . ."

"What's my alternative at this point? We've tried everything else." Kat ticked off her efforts on her finger. "We tried ignoring the problems, we tried communicating, we tried taking some time apart . . ."

"You tried building a website for a twenty-year-old male stripper," Cammie added.

"Like I said, we tried everything. And none of it worked. Time for a new approach." Kat picked up her pace as they crossed the street. "Josh and I have established a bunch of patterns over the years. They worked great for us when he was the mild-mannered professor and I was the adrenaline junkie. But now everything's out of whack. I need to restore our equilibrium."

"With lingerie?" Cammie paused to admire the sparkly rings displayed in the window of the Naked Finger, an estate jewelry store. "I don't see how a few frilly nighties are going to pull your marriage back from the brink."

"Me, neither. But I have to do something; he texted me this morning." Kat's expression darkened as she showed Cammie the message on her phone: We need to talk. Call me ASAP.

Cammie's heart sank as she read this.

"The words 'We need to talk' have never led to anything good in the history of mankind," Kat said.

"Well," Cammie said, trying to be optimistic, "maybe he's . . ."

"Finally decided to divorce me because he's so perfect and I'm such a harpy?"

"Don't say that."

"Why not? It's true! He's sweet and steady and dependable, and I'm a walking, talking nervous breakdown."

"Are you going to call him?"

"After I rebrand. Josh is used to seeing me in this." Kat glanced down at her baggy jeans, Chuck Taylors, and T-shirt. "I need to shake things up. Speaking of which . . ." She looked appraisingly at Cammie.

"Rebrand yourself. Leave me out of it."

"I bet Ian would love you in some black lace."

Cammie tried not to think about Ian . . . which meant he was all she could think about. "I'm not buying anything. I'm broke, remember? I didn't even have enough to make rent last month."

"Then you're very lucky to have a generous cousin who wants to finance your dating life." Kat pulled her wallet out of her jeans pocket.

"No," Cammie said firmly as they approached Retail Therapy. "I can take care of my own dating life."

"You sure about that? Because your dating life seems to be a little uneven these days."

Cammie jerked her chin toward the store window, which featured a polka-dot indigo halter dress. "You go pick out whatever it is you want to pick out. I'll be there in a few minutes."

"Ugh." Kat made a face. "You are so boring."

"Because I won't go into debt buying lingerie for a guy I'm not sleeping with?"

"Yes."

"Luckily, you're exciting enough for both of us." Cammie leaned against the warm brick wall and pulled out her phone. "I have some e-mails to answer. Now stop harassing me and go pick out something pretty."

"You're supposed to be helping me. You can't have a shopping montage all by yourself—don't you know anything?"

"I'll help you," Cammie promised. "Soon."

Kat checked her watch. "Give me an exact time."

"Five minutes." She held up her hand before Kat could argue. "Five minutes. I'll meet you in there, I swear."

After Kat finally went into the boutique, Cammie skimmed her e-mails until a shadow fell over her. She glanced up and saw Ian. He must have finished his work in the fields early—he was freshly showered and wearing a clean gray T-shirt and jeans.

"Hey." He smiled when she met his eyes.

"Hi. I—" She put down her phone and tried to look casual. "I'm waiting for Kat. How are you?" She was talking too fast, but she couldn't seem to slow her racing heart, racing thoughts, or racing speech. She was thinking about everything they'd done last time she'd seen him.

Everything they'd done . . . and everything they *hadn't* done.

"I haven't seen you since . . ." She trailed off, blinking against the glare of the sunlight. "Haven't seen you in a while. Not that I'm ignoring you. Or you're ignoring me." *Stop talking, stop talking.*

Ian kept smiling. She couldn't see his eyes clearly under the brim of his ball cap, but his posture was confident and relaxed. "I'm glad you're not ignoring me. I've missed you."

She gave up on pretending to be cool. "I missed you, too."

"Let's go get a drink." He brushed his fingers along her jawline and tilted her chin up.

For a moment, all she could register was the feeling of his skin against hers. "I can't." Her throat felt dry. "I promised Kat I'd help her pick out some underwear."

Ian seemed very, very interested in this topic. "Are you picking out underwear, too?"

"Um, not right now." She didn't know where to look.

"You should." His voice deepened.

She brushed back an errant strand of hair. "I don't have any reason to buy fancy underwear."

His gaze never wavered. "Yes, you do."

She glanced away first, ducking her head and shifting her weight. "Anyway, I should probably get in there."

"Go for it." His voice was positively smoldering now. "And when you're done buying underwear, we're getting a drink. I'll meet you at the Whinery."

"Oh." She wrapped her hand around his wrist. "Okay."

"Fifteen minutes?" he asked.

"Fifteen minutes." She let go of him and took a few steps back. "Oh, and, Ian?"

"Yeah?"

"Do you like leopard print?" She grinned. "'Cause I do." She managed not to look back as she sauntered into the shop.

Her saucy smile faded when Kat approached, brandishing two negligees like they were weapons.

"Black or pink? What do you think?"

Cammie backed away. "I don't have an opinion. You're the one who's going to be wearing it."

"Black is so predictable." Kat fretted. "Badass boarder girls wear black. Always. It's played out."

"Okay, then get the pink one."

Kat frowned, deliberating. "It would be a change, that's for sure. I can't remember the last time I wore pink."

"The dress with the bow that your mom wanted you to wear for senior pictures, so you dyed your hair blue?"

"Oh yeah, that's right." Kat smiled at the memory, then returned her attention to the pink negligee. "I'm not sure I can pull this off. I mean, I'm covered in scar tissue, and I have three piercings in my ear." She held the gauzy material at arm's length. "This is made for someone sweet and shy."

"That's exactly why you could pull it off," Cammie argued. "By itself, it's demure. But if you wore it, it'd be subversive."

Kat brightened. "I like subversive." She must have picked up on Cammie's excitement, because she gave her a knowing smile. "So, have you changed your mind about spending a few bucks on some black lace?"

Cammie struggled to maintain a poker face. "Why do you ask?"

"I saw you talking to Ian out there." Kat led her to the back of the store. "You guys were both undressing each other with your eyes; you might as well be wearing something sexy to take off."

Cammie couldn't deny this. "Be that as it may, I'm not—" She stopped as a bit of red embroidery caught her eye. "Hold on. Are those strawberries?" She picked up what turned out to be a pink balconette bra.

"They're strawberries, all right." Kat ran her fingers over the little red berries dotting the silky fabric. "How fitting."

"Do they have matching panties?" Cammie dug through the pile. "They do. The right size and everything."

She tried to put them back on the shelf, but she couldn't bring herself to actually let go.

"If you don't buy those, I will," Kat threatened. "I don't know why you're torturing yourself. Life is short. Buy the strawberry undies. Sleep with the swarthy farmer."

Cammie stopped trying to resist and headed for the dressing rooms. A few minutes later, she stood at the cash register, strawberry undies in hand. Kat had opted for the pink negligee, but her debit card wouldn't go through.

Kat rubbed the magnetic strip on her shirt and tried again. Still declined. "That's weird."

"I've got it." Cammie charged both purchases on her credit card, figuring that a few more dollars of debt were the least of her problems at this point. "Consider me your relationship rebranding sponsor." Saying the word "sponsor" stirred something in the back of her mind. An idea for promoting the vineyard started to take shape.

Finally out of stalling tactics, Kat dialed her phone and headed for the exit. "Hey, Josh. It's me."

Beryl pulled out a shopping bag and tissue paper to wrap up the strawberry undies.

"Oh, no need for a bag." Cammie grabbed her new purchases and yanked off the tags. "I'm going to wear them."

chapter 25

Cammie sauntered out of Retail Therapy and back into the Whinery. She spotted Ian immediately and slid onto the wrought iron stool next to his.

As soon as he looked her in the eyes, he knew something was different. "What's going on with you?"

She gave him a flirty hair flip and a knowing smile. "You'll find out soon enough."

His interest intensified. "Did you buy anything?"

"Yes."

"Anything leopard?"

"No."

He looked disappointed. Cammie leaned even closer and whispered into his ear, "Strawberries."

"What can I get you two?" Jenna asked. Cammie considered the staggering amount of time Jenna must spend at work—almost every afternoon and evening. No wonder she was burned out.

"Do you still have that peach sangria?" Cammie asked.

"No, but I made a new batch with lemon and blueberries."

"Ooh, yeah, I'll try that." Cammie did a little chair dance of anticipation.

Jenna brought her drink, and Cammie tasted the lemon sangria. "This is good." She offered it to Ian. "Taste."

He shook his head. "I'll wait for beer."

"Taste," she insisted. She handed the cool glass to him, and their hands brushed.

Suddenly, they were all over each other while still seated on their barstools. Their shoulders, arms, and thighs were pressed together. Cammie could feel his body heat through two layers of fabric. She felt buzzed even though she'd had only one sip of sangria.

They kept smiling, they kept touching, and then they were kissing, right in the middle of the bar, right in the middle of the day. Jenna cleared her throat loudly and put down Ian's beer with a clink. Cammie and Ian kept kissing. Her eyes were closed, but she could still see the golden glow of the sun pouring in through the plate-glass windows.

They took a break just long enough to agree that they should get the hell out of the Whinery and find someplace more private.

"You barely touched your drinks," Jenna protested, as Ian threw down some cash and took Cammie's hand.

"Everything was great. Bye." Ian hustled Cammie toward the door. When they reached the sidewalk, she automatically noted that the air was more humid than it had been this morning. *How will that affect the grapes?*

Then Ian was pulling her close and murmuring in her ear. "Where should we go?"

Cammie considered this. If they went to the vineyard, they'd run into Ginger, Jacques, and assorted tourists. If they went to Ian's place, they'd be surrounded by all the land that kept them apart, the land that he'd said he'd never ask her live on again. They needed an emotionally neutral location. Bonus points for romantic ambience and a comfy bed.

She tilted her head in the direction of the beach. "Hotel?"

He looked confused. "The heartbreak-tourist hotel?"

"Is there another hotel nearby?" She pressed her lips against the side of his neck.

"No, but—"

"They're can't turn us away just because we're not breaking up." She slipped her hand into the back pocket of his jeans. "I hope."

Ten minutes later, they were standing in the snickerdoodle-scented lobby of the Better Off Bed and Breakfast, asking for a room with an ocean view.

"And you'll both be staying there?" Marla, the matronly, ruddy-cheeked innkeeper, furrowed her brow. "Together?"

Ian put his arm around Cammie. "Yeah. Is that a problem?"

"No." But Marla kept staring at them. "It's just . . . You know what? Never mind."

She handed them a key and pointed to the staircase. "Second floor, last room on the right. Room number seven. Do you have any bags?"

"Nope."

"So . . . just the one night, then?"

Cammie nodded, even though they wouldn't be staying until tomorrow. With its historical charm, rustic furniture, and resident cat, the Better Off Bed and Breakfast wasn't the kind of establishment that rented rooms by the hour.

"I'm assuming you won't be needing a schedule of our yoga or breakup-support sessions?" Marla pointed out a stack of flyers next to the call bell on the desktop.

"No, thanks."

The innkeeper looked discomfited. "Normally, I take new guests' phones so they can't call their exes. It's our standard policy."

"Here." Ian dug out his phone and handed it over. He looked at Cammie. "Where's yours?"

"Maybe we should drive to Bethany Beach or Rehoboth," Cammie murmured as a trio of female guests entered the lobby and gawked at them.

He kept looking at her. "Right now." The undertone in his voice made her inhale sharply.

She slapped her phone down on top of the flyers. "Here you go."

Ian put his hand on the small of her back, urging her toward the staircase.

"I'll keep them safe for you," Marla called after them.

Cammie and Ian rushed up the stairs, pausing on the landing for a quick kiss. They located door number 7, and she stilled while he fitted the old-fashioned brass key into the lock. Her anticipation was almost painful.

Ian opened the door, revealing a cozy bedroom that was dominated by an antique four-poster bed covered with a patchwork quilt. There were dried flower wreaths adorning the powder-blue walls and lace doilies atop the dresser and nightstand. The air smelled vaguely of fruit and spice, courtesy of a porcelain dish of apple-and-cinnamon potpourri.

They stepped inside and closed the door. The intensity of her desire, the strength of her emotions, overwhelmed her. This wasn't going to end well. They couldn't keep going the way they had been—all or nothing, total deprivation or overindulgence. They couldn't seem to find any moderation.

Which meant that this was going to be really, *really* hot.

As they tumbled down on the bed, Cammie had a fleeting hope that maybe this wouldn't go the way she expected. Maybe all the time apart had warped her memory. Maybe they weren't truly compatible, after all. Maybe the sex would be bad this time.

. . .

The sex was *so* good.

Cammie curled up next to Ian, still atop the soft patchwork blanket, listening to the slowing thud of his pulse. Her skin was bare, her strawberry underwear was on the floor, and her body, mind, and heart were all in agreement for once: This felt right. This was what she wanted.

He was so quiet, she wondered if he was asleep. When she lifted her head to glance up at his face, he was gazing intently at her. She smiled. He smiled. But neither of them spoke. What could they say, after what had just happened? After they'd bared their bodies to each other while keeping their hearts guarded?

Outside the window, she could hear the screech of seagulls and the steady lull of the waves. In the hallway, she overheard snippets of conversation as a pair of female guests loitered outside their rooms:

"It's a good thing Marla took my phone away yesterday. I wanted to call him so bad, but I didn't."

"Good for you," said the woman's companion. "It gets easier, I promise. This is the worst part."

Still flushed and tingly from sex, Cammie reflected that this moment, lying here with Ian, was the best part—which meant the worst part was still to come. She hated thinking this way, but she couldn't see any alternative. Nothing had really changed since they were twenty-two. He was determined to stay in Delaware, stewarding his family's legacy, and she was more certain than ever before that she couldn't devote the rest of her life to farming.

"I knew it," the guest in the hall said loudly. "I knew we were doomed from the first date, but I kept seeing him anyway."

Ian threaded his fingers through Cammie's hair and nudged her head back so he could make eye contact. Then he shifted, turning them both onto their sides and cradling her against him. "I liked the strawberries."

"I noticed." She kissed his wrist. With a soft sigh, she asked, "So, what now?"

"What's your hurry?" He sounded sleepy and satisfied. "We have all day. And all night."

She lifted her head, surprised. "You want to spend the night here?"

"Hell, yeah. And tomorrow night and the next night."

"Oh. Well, then—"

"I want to, but I can't," he concluded. "I have to check the seedlings we put in yesterday."

Cammie went perfectly still. "You're thinking about leaving already?"

"I'm thinking about doing what we just did all over again," he corrected. "But what I'm thinking about doing and what I have to do are different things."

She held her breath for a moment, then released it in a slow, silent exhale. She refused to betray any hint of disappointment or desperation. After all, what had she expected?

He sat up, gazing down at her face. "Or we could just spend the night."

She turned her face away. "No, we can't. You just said the seedlings—"

"They can survive a few more hours without me. I'll call my brother and tell him to hold down the fort."

Cammie thought about everything she was supposed to do today. The walking, the weeding, the soil checks. The promises she'd made and the people depending on her. "The vineyard can survive a few more hours without me."

"Great." He settled back down on the mattress. "I'm starving. Think they have room service?"

"Nope. But I saw a plate of cookies down there. Want me to go grab some?"

"No." He was appalled at the very idea. "Why would I want you to put on clothes?"

Finally, when the moon rose high over the peaceful little bay, they managed to leave the bed long enough to get dinner at the Jilted Café, where everyone noticed their disheveled state but didn't comment. At least not to their faces.

"You realize that we're going to be the talk of the town," Cammie whispered as a Botoxed summer resident gawked at them.

"So?" Ian looked much more concerned with the state of his burger than the possibilities of rumors.

"By tomorrow, people will be saying that I'm just using you for your strawberries."

He looked totally unconcerned.

"Doesn't that bother you?" she pressed.

"I'll take you any way I can get you."

When Cammie arrived back at the vineyard the next morning, sleep deprived but blissful, she saw Ginger pacing in the driveway, talking on her cell phone. Her aunt was wearing a billowy yellow bathrobe and ratty old slippers. Jacques trailed behind her, looking worried in a way only a neurotic French bulldog could.

Ginger hung up when Cammie got out of the car. "Where have you been, young lady?"

Cammie ignored the question. "What are you doing out here?"

"Canceling today's wine-tasting appointments."

"What? Why?" Cammie started for the porch steps.

Ginger threw up both hands and tried to block her path. "You can't go in there."

"Why not?" Cammie raced up the steps and opened the screen door, bracing herself for disaster: Fire. Flood. Flesh-eating zombies.

But the house was still and orderly . . . for about three seconds. Then she heard Kat and Josh yelling at the top of their lungs.

"I can't believe you didn't tell me!" Kat screamed from somewhere on the second floor.

"If I'd told you, you would have left me!" Josh screamed back. They sounded as though they were in Kat's bedroom. Even through the closed door, the length of the upstairs hallway, and the staircase, Cammie could hear every syllable.

"How could you have trusted that shady-ass slickster?"

"My friend from grad school recommended him!"

"Your friend from grad school?" Kat's laugh sounded almost hysterical. "You got a financial referral from a philosopher?"

"At least he was willing to give me advice—you couldn't even be bothered to go to any of the appointments!" Josh's voice, normally so calm and mellow, reverberated off the foyer walls.

"I was on the road!" Kat screamed back.

"Always with the excuses! You never want to take responsibility for your own life."

Cammie retreated to the porch, her eyes huge.

"I told you not to go in there." Ginger stood at the bottom of the porch steps, clutching the lapels of her robe.

"What the hell are they doing?" Cammie asked.

They both cringed at the muffled sound of porcelain smashing against a floorboard.

"Well, it's been hard to piece everything together, what with all the hysterics," Ginger said. "But from what I can gather, the money manager Josh hired lost most of Kat's earnings."

"When?"

"I think he's known for a little while, but Kat just found out."

"Hence the hysterics," Cammie said.

"Precisely." Ginger tsk-tsked. "I had no idea Josh could yell like this."

Cammie eased open the screen door and poked her head back inside for a moment.

"Everyone thinks you're so nice, but you know what? You are *not* nice," Kat hollered. "You are the opposite of nice!"

Josh hollered right back. "At least I didn't run away and cross state lines because I'm afraid of a little conflict!"

"You want conflict? Well, here you go!"

Cammie retreated to the driveway. "How long have they been at this?"

"At least an hour." Ginger leaned down to pet Jacques, who was snorting and whimpering. "Kat came home upset last night, Josh showed up at the crack of dawn, and it's been nonstop ever since."

"Is that why you're still in your jammies?"

"I was trying to enjoy a nice cup of iced coffee," Ginger said, aggrieved. "But I had to flee my own home because those two can't behave like civilized adults."

Cammie glanced at her aunt's empty hands. "What happened to your coffee?"

"I abandoned it on the kitchen counter after World War Three broke out."

"Want me to go get it for you?"

"It's not worth the emotional trauma," Ginger said, but Cammie dashed inside anyway.

On her way to and from the kitchen she heard Kat shout, "How could you let me spend thirty thousand dollars on a tractor when you knew I had no money?"

"Let you?" Josh sounded incredulous. "*Let you?* How was I supposed to know you'd buy a tractor?"

Cammie emerged into the daylight, iced coffee in hand. "Good call on canceling the wine tastings."

Ginger sipped her coffee. "I'd just like to go in and get dressed sometime before noon."

"Well . . ." Cammie sat down next to Jacques and gave the worried pup a little kiss. "Don't worry—your mom and dad won't fight forever."

"I don't know," Ginger fretted. "They certainly seem to have a lot of stamina."

At various intervals over the next hour, Ginger and Cammie scurried into the house and tried to avoid getting caught in the cross fire. When Cammie ducked into the kitchen to grab a snack, she heard:

"I trusted you to take care of my money!"

"You made me do it by refusing to do it yourself!"

When she darted in to grab a book for Ginger:

"What am I supposed to do now? Sponge off you until I line up some judging gigs?"

"It's not sponging when we're married, Kat. We're supposed to be a team—you never got that!"

When she had to use the bathroom:

"So you're telling me that that ancient, rusty tractor—the tractor I can't even drive—is the sum total of my assets right now?"

"That's right! I hope you enjoy it!"

After she was safely back outside, Cammie reported, "They're not making any progress. We could be out here all day."

Ginger glanced at the sun, high in the sky. "Should we go get some lunch?"

"We might as well." Cammie escorted her aunt into the house. "Hurry up and get dressed. I'll cover you."

As they tiptoed up the stairs toward the master bedroom, Ginger murmured, "Should we call the police on them?"

"For what?" Cammie asked.

"For disturbing the peace."

Cammie froze on the landing as she realized that the yelling had ceased.

They heard Josh's voice, deep and clear: "We're not disturbing the peace."

"We're *communicating*," Kat clarified.

"Okay, well, we're grabbing a quick change of clothes," Cammie called back. "Don't mind us. Carry on."

Kat and Josh did exactly that.

"You don't love me!" Josh said.

"Of course I love you." Kat sounded thoroughly exasperated. "Just because I want to kill you doesn't mean I don't love you! *You're* the one who doesn't love *me*!"

"I do love you! I've told you that a million times! Why are you so stubborn?"

"I'm not! FYI, while you were busy hiding all my financial losses from me, I was buying pink lingerie to seduce you!"

Another long pause ensued. "You were?" Josh asked.

"Yes! Trying to prove what a great wife I am. Like an idiot!"

Josh's tone changed. "Can I see it?"

Ginger turned to Cammie. "Let's go. I'll just wear my pajamas to lunch. It's fine."

"Go outside. Save yourself," Cammie instructed. "I'll find something in your closet and meet you at the car in two minutes."

After a leisurely lunch at the Jilted Café, Cammie and Ginger wandered over to the Whinery for a glass of iced tea. While they snacked on miniature candy bars, Cammie checked the vineyard's brand-new social media accounts.

"Jacques is going to be a superstar." She showed the most recent posts to Ginger. "Look, Kat gave him his own Twitter and Instagram accounts, and he's getting a ton of followers, thanks to the *Ladies First* posts. Our little snaggletooth is Internet famous."

"I don't know about all this social media," Ginger tutted. "It seems like it's never enough."

"Well, it's definitely not enough yet." Cammie hesitated, then shared the idea she'd been mulling over for a few days. "How would you feel about giving away a weekend trip to the vineyard?"

"To whom?" Ginger asked.

"To some random person who follows Jacques on Twitter."

Ginger looked scandalized. "You're suggesting we let a random stranger stay at our house?"

"I'm suggesting we put a random stranger up in a swanky hotel," Cammie corrected.

"But how?"

"What we need is a corporate sponsor," Cammie said. "Like Kat used to have in skateboarding."

"Well, before we can put this random stranger up in a hotel, we'll have to get them to Delaware. How are we going to do that?" Ginger challenged.

"I'm still thinking through all the details."

"Maybe Kat could use some of her frequent-flier miles," Ginger said. "Or, ooh, maybe we could find a sponsor with a private jet!"

"Let's try to keep this in the realm of reality," Cammie said.

"What do you need a private jet for?" Jenna placed a stack of pink napkins next to the candy dish.

"Oh, we're just daydreaming." Cammie explained her sweepstakes idea. "We want the winner to have an experience we can showcase on social media."

Jenna gazed up at the crystal chandelier, thinking. "Well . . ."

Cammie thought about the night she'd just spent at the inn by the sea. "I'll talk to the owner of the Better Off Bed-and-Breakfast. Maybe she'd be willing to comp us a room for a night or two."

"We could give her some wine," Ginger suggested.

"Marla doesn't drink." Jenna shook her head. "But if you're serious about wanting a private jet, I could make a few phone calls."

"You know someone who has a private jet?" Cammie unwrapped a tiny Twix and popped it into her mouth.

"I sure do. And he's really nice. Really nice and ridiculously good-looking."

Cammie and Ginger exchanged glances. "I take it you and this jet guy have a history?"

"No." Jenna's eyes were wistful. "But he used to hang out here all the time. He doesn't come here much anymore. Not since he got married."

"That's too bad."

"It's fine." Jenna started to slice up some lemons. "His wife still comes here all the time, and she's even nicer than he is." She picked up the phone. "I'll give her a call right now." A few seconds passed; then Jenna pressed the receiver to her ear. "Hey, Brighton, it's Jenna. Remember how I was telling you that the vineyard just outside town has new owners? Well, they're sitting at my bar, and we have a question for you."

chapter 26

"Brighton!" Jenna rushed out from behind the bar as a cute, curvy brunette strolled in. "I haven't seen you in forever! Have you guys been in Montana?"

"We got back last week." Brighton's cheeks flushed. "We've just been, um, busy."

"I'll bet. How's Rory?"

"Sweet and clueless, as always." Brighton addressed Ginger and Cammie. "Hi, I'm Brighton Sorensen." She offered a handshake to Cammie, who noticed her engagement ring was a bright orange gemstone instead of a traditional diamond. With her windblown hair, unmanicured nails, and casual cotton sundress, Brighton didn't look the way Cammie imagined someone with a private jet would look. Her hazel eyes were warm and friendly.

"I like your ring," Cammie said.

Brighton's eyes got even warmer. "Thanks."

"Brighton is a genius with jewelry," Jenna said. "She—"

"Let's not get sidetracked with all that," Brighton said. "Jenna says you ladies need help, and if Jenna is willing to help you, I am, too."

"Like I said, she's awesome," Jenna told Cammie. "Brighton, what can I get you to drink?"

"Just water, thanks." Brighton turned to Cammie and confided, "I have a bad track record with booze here."

"What are you talking about?" Jenna cried. "You have a great track record! The first time you got drunk in here, you married the man of your dreams."

Brighton laughed. "It sounds so simple and romantic when you put it that way."

"You met your husband here?" Ginger beamed. "That's lovely."

"Sort of. I was in a white-hot rage at the time and I married him for spite, but it all turned out great." Brighton thanked Jenna as the bartender handed her a glass of water. "Anyway, enough about my sordid past. Jenna says you need a jet. You're welcome to use ours."

"We haven't worked out all the details yet," Cammie said. "So we can't give you dates or locations."

Brighton shrugged. "Just shoot me a text when you do." She pulled out a business card and wrote down her cell number.

Ginger frowned. "Don't you have to ask your husband?"

"He'll say yes." Brighton winked. "Trust me."

That was way easier than Cammie had imagined. "Thank you. That's incredibly generous. We'd be delighted to give you some wine, even though you don't drink."

"Ask for the strawberry wine," Jenna advised.

Brighton finally got around to asking what they needed the jet for.

"We're trying to get some publicity for our wine," Cammie explained. "Right now, it's a very small brand. To the point of being nonexistent. I thought we could launch a contest on social media. You know, win a weekend at a vineyard."

"Fun," Brighton said.

"The problem is, now that I'm thinking about all the details, I'm not sure we have the budget. Even if we get the jet taken care of, we'll still need to provide lodging—"

"We really should give the winner some kind of entertainment, too," Ginger chimed in.

"And meals. And maybe some shopping," Cammie added.

"It's going to be a huge project," Ginger concluded. "A huge expense."

"And a huge opportunity," Cammie said. "We need to think bigger. Black Dog Bay has everything you need to survive a breakup, right?"

"Right." Jenna said. "It's not just a town; it's an experience."

"You're right," Cammie mused. "It's an *experience*." She turned to Ginger. "We should put together a whole Breakup Bonanza."

Ginger brightened. "Ooh, that's better than a boring, luck-of-the-draw sweepstakes."

"People can send in their bad breakup stories," Cammie continued. "Best—by which I mean worst—story wins."

Brighton sipped her water. "Well, it's a good thing I won't be entering, because you'd have to close the contest down. No one could beat my breakup story."

Jenna considered this. "That's probably true."

Cammie lifted her chin. "I bet I could beat it."

"I doubt that." Brighton looked cheerful about this.

"Try me."

"Ooh, this is great." Jenna rubbed her palms together. "Breakup showdown."

"We could make brackets, like they do for March Madness," Ginger suggested.

"My fiancé dumped me over a stupid fight about traffic, and married a stranger that same night," Brighton said.

Jenna smiled fondly. "I remember it like it was yesterday."

"My boyfriend was the chef in my restaurant and deserted me for another kitchen while I went bankrupt," Cammie countered.

Jenna sucked in her breath. "A worthy opponent."

Brighton and Cammie appealed to Jenna. "Well? Which is worse?"

Jenna drummed her fingers on the bar top. "That's a tough call."

"We *will* do brackets like March Madness." Cammie started scribbling ideas down on a napkin. "We'll choose semifinalists and let people vote online."

"I love it," Ginger declared. "As long as a stranger isn't staying in my house."

"Now we just have to hit up all the local businesses and plead our case. We'll come back tomorrow and let you know how it goes." Cammie hopped off her barstool and prepared to pound the pavement. "Shall we?"

"We shall," Ginger said. "Right after we run home and make sure the house is still standing."

The house was still standing, but it was eerily silent, as though it were holding its breath.

Cammie climbed the stairs and tiptoed down the hall. She hesitated for a moment in the low-ceilinged hallway, then knocked lightly on Kat's door. "Kat?"

On the other side of the door, she heard rustling and a low, masculine murmur.

"Just a sec," Kat called.

Cammie took a step back. "Oh. Never mind, I'll come back later."

But the door opened and Kat poked her head out. Her cheeks were flushed and her hair looked as messy as Cammie's had last night. She was wearing Josh's university T-shirt and no pants. "Hi."

"Oh, good, you're alive."

Kat stretched her arms over her head, lazy and languorous. "I'm great. We're great."

"So Josh is alive, too?"

His voice drifted out. "Hi, Cammie."

"The pink negligee was a hit." Kat combed her fingers through her hair.

Cammie took another step back. "Great. Fantastic."

"Yeah, Josh and I have never gotten quite so—"

"Keep the details to yourself." Cammie hastened to change the subject. "So, no pressure, but later on, after you've, uh, collected yourself, I want to bounce a new marketing idea off you."

"Okay." Kat adjusted the neckline of her T-shirt, inadvertently exposing a fresh hicky. Cammie looked away, stifling a smile. "It can wait?"

"For a little while."

"Good. Right now, Josh and I are going down to the barn."

"Do I need to hide all the sharp implements?" Cammie was only half kidding.

Kat laughed as if this were the most absurd thing she'd ever heard. "Of course not. We're just going to work on the tractor."

"You are?"

"Yes." Kat's afterglow dimmed for a moment. "Apparently, that tractor is all I have left to show for fifteen years of professional skateboarding."

Josh spoke up from inside the room: "I told you I was sorry about that."

"I know you are, honey." Kat squared her shoulders. "Since the tractor's what we have, that's what we'll focus on."

"We're going to get it up and running," Josh confirmed. "It's going to be great."

Cammie tried to figure out what had changed. "Okay, but you

were screaming like banshees about that tractor a little while ago. I couldn't help overhearing."

"Mistakes were made," Kat conceded. "By everyone. And we'll be pursuing every legal option to try to get my money back. But in the meantime, we have dead vines to pull."

"The here and now," Josh intoned.

"Sounds like you've got it all figured out." Cammie started back down the stairs to let Ginger know it was safe to return.

"Yeah," Kat called after her, "I think we do."

chapter 27

The next morning, while she fended off a flock of starlings that were eating the unripe grapes, Cammie heard the distant rumble of an engine.

It sounded like a tractor. A fully functional tractor.

She shook her hat to scatter the birds and warned them, "You're going to be sorry you were ever hatched!"

Then she walked along the row of vines until she could see the barn. Josh and Kat were standing next to the rusty red tractor, which was shuddering as the engine roared.

"You guys!" Cammie yelled. They couldn't hear her. The two of them were so absorbed with their project that they didn't notice her until she was practically on top of them.

"Hey!" She waved her arms until Josh saw her and turned off the engine.

"You did it." Cammie tried to keep the shock and disbelief out of her voice.

"Of course we did it!" Kat, drenched in sweat, looked ready to run a victory lap around the vineyard. "Well, Josh did it. The engine wouldn't start, so I thought the battery was dead, and I was like, how the hell are we going to replace a tractor battery?"

"Luckily, we don't need to." Josh puffed out his chest beneath his sweat- and oil-stained shirt.

"Yeah. He said that before we spent money on a new battery, we should check all the . . ." Kat turned to consult her husband. "What are they called again?"

"Terminals," Josh supplied.

"Yeah, you know, where the wires connect to the battery."

"Okay," Cammie said.

"So we did, and it turns out that there was a bunch of dirt and grease caked on one of the cables. Josh cleaned it off, and voila! We're in business."

"Nice," Cammie said.

"He teaches philosophy *and* fixes tractors." Kat gazed adoringly at Josh. "Such a Renaissance man."

Josh feigned modesty. "I had the idea, but you did all the dirty work."

"I live for dirty work." Kat breathed in the exhaust fumes as if relishing the freshest mountain air.

Cammie sneezed as a dust mote swirled up from the dirt beneath the tractor. "How did you know to check the terminals?"

"I had a crappy old car in grad school that used to do this all the time," Josh said.

"We already had everything we needed. All we had to do was clear out the connection," Kat marveled. "So simple."

"You guys are the best. I can't wait to get rid of the dead vines." Cammie hugged them both, giddy with relief. "Kat, if you're interested, we're having a marketing summit meeting at the Whinery in half an hour."

"I'll make the next one," Kat promised. "Right now, we're bonding and figuring out how to work the clutch."

"At the same time?" Cammie asked.

Kat and Josh looked at each other, both of them brimming with excitement. "We're nothing if not multitaskers."

"Here's what we've got so far." Cammie slapped a yellow legal pad on the glossy black bar top. "Wine, spa treatments, the best room at the bed-and-breakfast, a gift certificate to the Naked Finger, and the private jet. Oh, and a skateboarding lesson, if they want it."

"People were surprisingly helpful," Ginger reported. "Once we showed them Jacques's Instagram account."

"Who doesn't love an Internet-famous dog? This is brilliant." Summer Benson inspected the notes Cammie had jotted. "I love everything about this."

"It was Cammie's idea." Ginger smiled at her niece. "My little marketing genius."

Jenna had mentioned that Summer was the head of the Black Dog Bay Historical Society, although the bright-eyed blonde with a platinum pixie cut and moxie to burn didn't look like the type to hang out with dusty books and board members all day. But Cammie had started to accept that nothing in this town was as it first appeared.

"It sounds like you're doing just fine without my help, but I'll make Hattie Huntington throw in some goodies, too," Summer said.

"Who's Hattie Huntington?" Cammie asked.

"She owns that hideous purple eyesore on the far end of the bay." Summer pointed out the bar's front window.

"Ah. I was wondering about that." The eyesore, as Summer put it, was a sprawling purple mansion complete with a private beach and a pool.

"Hattie Huntington is the meanest, pettiest woman since . . ." Jenna trailed off. "Ever."

"That's why we love her." Summer snagged a clean wineglass and poured her own drink, to Jenna's evident dismay. "I'll make her cough up some of those fancy truffles she imports from France. Or, ooh, she can have her private chef prep a fancy picnic on the beach to go with the wine."

"That sounds amazing." Cammie was writing madly.

"I know." Summer brushed back her hair. "Which is great, because I'm totally going to win the contest. I don't mean to brag, but my breakup story can beat all y'all's breakup stories."

"My fiancé married a stranger," Brighton reminded them.

"My boyfriend left my restaurant for a hotter kitchen," Cammie said.

"Amateurs." Summer rolled her eyes. "My boyfriend dumped me after I almost died in a plane crash."

Ginger seemed suitably impressed.

"And he was the pilot." Summer seemed perversely smug about all this. "He dumped me while I was still hospitalized with a head injury. I win."

"You can't win." Cammie shook her head. "No one here can win. This is for random strangers only."

"Boo." Summer stuck out her tongue.

"We're wasting some top-tier tales of woe!" Brighton said.

"You can be judges," Cammie decided. "Someone needs to pick the finalists that people will vote on. Jenna, you can be a judge, too. You must have heard every breakup story under the sun in here."

"Pretty much." Jenna nodded.

"We'll get Kat to call up every journalist and publicist she's ever met," Cammie said. "I'll take point on the grassroots marketing campaign. Jenna, do you have a mailing list? Some way to contact your customers?"

"No, but Marla does. She sends a holiday card to every guest who's ever stayed at the bed-and-breakfast."

"The historical society has a pretty sizable mailing list," Summer offered.

"So does the Naked Finger," Brighton added. "And we've had some customers that could definitely medal in the Bad-Breakup Olympics."

"Okay, so we'll send out postcards and e-mail to everyone we can," Cammie said.

"What about me?" Ginger cried. "What can I do?"

"Make more strawberry wine," Cammie ordered. "Vats of it. Stockpile like the apocalypse is coming."

"Consider it done."

Cammie had vowed not to get emotionally involved in another food-and-beverage venture. She knew better than to go down this road again, and yet, here she was, envisioning grand plans and opening up her heart. With Ian and with the vineyard. But whatever. She'd worry about that later. Right now, she had an empire to build.

chapter 28

By Friday, the contest was basically good to go. Kat and Cammie secured air travel, lodging, meals, spa services, a shopping spree that included both clothing and accessories, and a VIP wine tasting.

"What's VIP about it?" Kat asked when Cammie announced it.

"Our charm and hospitality?" Cammie raised a glass of strawberry wine to their future. "All we have to do now is send the e-mails, plaster our message all over Twitter and Instagram, and wait for the breakup horror stories to roll in."

"Damn, dude. Listen to *this* one." Summer whistled as she scanned an e-mailed entry. "This woman was dating a guy and they were talking about moving in together, but he kept leaving the lids of metal cat food cans right at the top of the recycling bin. She kept asking him to wrap them in newspapers or bury them under a cereal box or something, but he kept forgetting."

Cammie looked up from her iPad, where she was perusing her share of the entries. "Eh, that's not so bad."

"Hold on. I'm not done yet." Summer cleared her throat. "So finally, one Sunday morning, this chick cuts her finger so bad on the metal edge that she has to go to urgent care. Blood was spurting everywhere. That's a direct quote: 'Blood was spurting everywhere.'"

"Gross." Across the bar, Jenna wrinkled her nose.

"But her boyfriend kept insisting it was just a little cut and she was being dramatic, so she had to drive herself to the ER. Then it turned out she had to get surgery."

"Well, that's bad," Jenna allowed. "But it's not the worst thing I've heard today. Or even this afternoon."

"Still not done." Summer held up her hand. "Then the whole thing got infected and she lost her fingernail. She says it took months to heal and she had to quit her job because she couldn't type, and now she has to think about him every time she gets a manicure."

"From a cat-food can lid?" Cammie was horrified. "Can that actually happen?"

Summer lifted up her laptop to display the screen. "She attached a photo."

Everyone recoiled in horror.

"I give it an A-minus," Kat said. "Would've been a run-of-the-mill B, but the photo puts it over the edge."

"B-plus," Brighton said.

"You give everything a B-plus," Summer said.

Brighton shrugged. "When I hear an A story, I'll give it A."

"Well, I give it an A," Summer said. "The woman has to live the rest of her life with nine fingernails because some dumbass couldn't figure out that sharp edges are sharp."

"Yeah, all right." Jenna glanced at the chalkboard over the bar and handed a piece of pink chalk to Kat. "Put her on the short list."

Kat added "cat-food chick" to the short list, which was rapidly turning into a long list. When she'd brainstormed this idea, Cammie had thought it would be fun. But after days of skimming increasingly horrifying tales of heartbreak, Cammie no longer considered this entertaining in any way. "Guys, we need to stop."

"We can't stop." Kat didn't even look up from her screen. "These entries aren't going to read themselves. Look, here's one from a woman who had her breakup live-tweeted by a famous blogger who was sitting at the table next to her at a restaurant."

"But think about what this is doing to our hearts. To our souls! Think about what this is doing to our dating expectations."

"Well, you don't have to worry about me and Brighton," Summer said. "We don't have dating expectations. Although I feel like I lived half these stories before I met Dutch."

A male voice interrupted all the laughing and chattering. "Cammie?"

Cammie whirled around to find Ian just inside the bar's front door. "Oh! Hey! We were just . . ."

She glanced around at the short list and the photos of cat-food-lid injuries and the onlookers watching them with rapt attention. "Let's step outside," she suggested.

He walked with her to the little white gazebo in the town square. "You look busy," he said.

"We've spent all day reading breakup stories." She filled him in on the details. "It's just one romantic disaster after another."

He sat down on the shaded steps of the gazebo. She sat next to him. They watched the tourists strolling on their way to the boardwalk. The weathered bronze dog statue stood watch over the proceedings.

"It makes me think about how important perception is," Cammie said. "Like, two people can go through the same breakup and have completely different takes on it."

"Like what happened with us," he said quietly.

She tried to figure out how to respond to this. They hadn't talked about it yet, not in any depth or detail. No matter how much time they spent together or how close they felt, this was the one thing that she hadn't been able to bring up.

"Yes." She inclined her head. "I'm sure that you and I have very different versions of what happened and why."

He put his hand on her shoulder. "How does your story go?"

Her first impulse was to protect herself—and him—by being vague and circumspect. But she couldn't shake the stories she'd spent the day reading—all the pain, the hilarity, the bravery of people who'd fallen in love and then fallen apart and pulled themselves back together. So she told the truth—her version of it, anyway. "In my story, I was the bad guy. I'm the one who left." She settled back against the wooden slats and stared out at the ocean. "I was the villain because I had a choice to stay or go, but you didn't. You had to stay, but I chose to go. So I'm selfish by default."

"That's the end of the story," he pointed out. "What's the beginning?"

"Oh, well, the beginning is all empty gas tanks and strawberry patches and hormones." She tried to sound detached. "Remember all the hormones?"

He smiled. "I remember."

"The beginning was so sweet and the middle was so good that it made the end so bitter." She took a breath. "But I also know that the story couldn't have ended any other way. I couldn't be the girl you wanted me to be."

He absorbed this, quiet and still. Cammie stared at the whitecaps cresting on the horizon. Finally, she asked, "What's your version?"

"In my story, you were the girl who was too good to settle down with a twenty-two-year-old farmer in a tiny town in Delaware. You were meant for bigger and better things."

"I assume you're being ironic."

He shook his head.

She kept looking at the water. "You're the one who predicted—correctly, I might add—that my restaurant would fail."

"I should never have said that. You dreamed bigger than I could. It's one of the things I love about you."

And there it was. The *L* word. In present tense, too. This was her chance to ask all kinds of questions, open all kinds of doors.

She remained silent.

"In my story," he continued, "I'm the guy who didn't do anything. That's worse than being the villain. I just stood there and let things happen."

"I had no idea you felt that way." How could she? They'd never talked after she'd left.

"Revise your story," he urged her. "You weren't the bad guy. You had a choice, but so did I."

"Not really," Cammie said. "Family legacy and all that."

"I had options, but I didn't see that until after you'd left."

"And you'd sworn you'd never ask me to come back."

"But you came back, anyway. I'm glad you did." He leaned over and pressed a soft kiss against her temple. "Even though you're not staying."

She didn't realize she'd expected him to ask her to stay until now. No matter how many times she left, he would let her go. No matter how many different ways they spun their stories, he would never change that part. He'd asked her to stay once, and he'd never ask again.

He had his sticking points, and she had hers.

"I thought about you," she confessed. "After I left."

"I thought about you, too."

They watched the waves for a few more minutes, and then her phone's alarm beeped.

"I have to go." Cammie got to her feet. "The grapes call, and I must answer."

He stood up, too. "You're doing a great job."

"I'm trying." She reached out to touch his arm. "I'm trying to love farming. Truly. I'm trying."

"But you don't."

She shook her head. "It's just not who I am." Part of her wanted to apologize, but she stopped herself.

He walked her back to her car. "Hey."

"Yeah?" She matched his pace and stride.

"We still have options."

"You think so?"

He took her hand in his. "Always."

chapter 29

The next morning, Kat was wrapping up a phone call in the parlor when Cammie came in from the vineyard. "Want the latest grape report?"

Kat clicked off the phone with a big smile. "Who cares about grapes?"

"Uh, I do." Cammie glanced at her aunt, who was polishing wineglasses by the tasting bar. "We all do, don't we?"

"Right now, we're focusing on strawberries." Kat put the phone down on an upended wine barrel. "That was the guy who owns the snooty little grocery store down by the boardwalk."

"The one we never shop at because it makes Whole Foods look like a bargain?" Cammie asked.

Kat nodded. "That's the one. Mom, did you talk to him about donating some stuff for our breakup contest?"

Ginger sniffed. "I tried, but he said no."

"Well, he may have said no, but he said you were very charming."

"Well." Ginger adjusted her necklace, slightly mollified. "Obviously."

"Did he change his mind about donating?" Cammie asked.

"No, but he said he might want to stock the strawberry wine." Kat paused to wave through the window to Josh, who was lovingly detailing the tractor by the barn. "He said he's been hearing rumors about it all over town."

Ginger's hands flew to her cheeks. "He did? My basement wine might find a home in a real brick-and-mortar store?"

"Yep. And they'll probably charge a ton of money for it, too."

"This is fantastic!" Ginger stepped back from the bar and did a little jig. "Our money problems will be solved!"

"Not quite." Kat held up her palm. "It's one tiny shop that might go through a case or two per month."

"Buzzkill," Cammie muttered.

"Truth teller," Kat corrected.

"But it's a start," Cammie insisted. "If we keep hustling and building our brand, eventually we'll turn a profit."

"Define 'eventually,'" Ginger pressed.

Kat ignored this and started barking out orders. "Everyone go get dressed. Our goal is to have the display up and running before lunch."

Cammie blinked. "We're going right now?"

"Yes! No time like the present! Time is money!" Kat clapped her hands to spur them to action. "We'll have to stop and pick up a white tablecloth and those little paper cups, maybe some food to pair with the wine." She looked at Cammie. "What goes with strawberry wine?"

"I have no idea."

"Guess. Pretend you're back in your restaurant, bullshitting to a bunch of snobs in suits."

Cammie closed her eyes and envisioned exactly that. A wistful smile spread across her face. "Maybe a rich dessert? Like pound cake or cheesecake?"

Kat started making a shopping list. "Okay, so tablecloth, cups, napkins, toothpicks, cheesecake, pound cake . . ."

"Wait a minute," Ginger said. "Are we just allowed to hand out wine to random people in a store?"

"Why not?" Kat shrugged. "As long as they're over twenty-one."

"That doesn't sound legal."

"Does to me." Kat grinned. "And we're going by the motto that it's easier to ask for forgiveness than permission."

"Good luck with that. Call me when you get arrested."

"I won't have to call you; you'll be right there with me." Kat slung her arm around Cammie's shoulders, then beckoned for Ginger to join them. "The family that goes to jail together, stays together."

"*I'm* not going to get arrested." Ginger batted her eyelashes. "Just look at me. Who would arrest such a sweet, helpless old lady?"

"Spoken like a true grifter." Kat looked proud. "All right, go get yourselves cleaned up. And don't be afraid to show a little skin. Sex sells, you know."

"Then take your own advice and wear that lovely blue dress I got you for Christmas," Ginger said. "It shows off your cleavage and it covers your scars. And your tattoos."

"I'll let you pick my outfit if you'll let me pick yours," Kat retorted.

Cammie left them to bicker, and hurried to shower and change. A familiar, almost pleasurable tension was starting in her shoulders and back. She couldn't farm worth a damn, but she could present food and beverage like nobody's business. By the time she headed back downstairs, she had her game face on and the address of the nearest restaurant-supply store mapped out on her phone.

Jacques was waiting for her at the bottom of the staircase, and she bade him good-bye with a kiss on his wrinkly forehead. "Wish us luck, buddy."

. . .

"Excuse me, ma'am, would you like to try some organic, locally sourced strawberry wine?" Cammie held out a white paper cup. "Handcrafted right here in Black Dog Bay."

The woman in the grocery store aisle was wearing a preppy pair of pink capris, about fifty thousand dollars' worth of diamond jewelry, and a tight, sour expression.

"Strawberry wine?" She lifted the cup to her nose and took a suspicious sniff. "Isn't that something that hillbillies make in a bathtub?"

"You're thinking of moonshine," Kat said helpfully. "Which is actually making a comeback among the Brooklyn elite."

Ginger gave Kat a death glare and stepped in to save the conversation. "This was handcrafted from heirloom strawberries with the very latest in small-batch wine-making technology."

Kat and Cammie both gaped at Ginger. Apparently, the ability to bullshit about wine ran in the family.

The customer looked intrigued. "Really?"

"Yes." Ginger managed to appear entirely earnest. "It's a secret family recipe with a modern twist."

"I suppose I'll risk it." The woman barely wetted her lips with wine. Then she took another, bigger sip. "That's delicious."

"In season and on point," Cammie said. "Sweet, but not too sweet."

"Hmmm." The woman took another sip. "And how much is it?"

Everyone looked at one another, panicked.

"Thirt— *Forty* dollars," Cammie blurted out. Ginger gasped. Kat cringed.

"Forty dollars?" The woman blinked. "Per bottle?"

"Yep. We're running a sale."

Ginger let out a little moan of despair.

But the woman regarded them with newfound respect. "I had no idea fruit wines cost so much."

"Mass-produced fruit wines probably don't." Cammie kept her tone and posture aloof. "But this is unique. Locally sourced." She paused, eyeing her potential customer. "Limited edition."

Ding, ding, ding.

The blinged-out blonde cocked her head. "Limited edition?"

Cammie nodded, her eyes earnest. "When it's gone, it's gone." She neglected to mention that Ginger would just whip up another "limited-edition" batch.

"I'll take six." The woman piled bottles into her European-style grocery trolley. "I'm having a dinner party this weekend, and I've invited the mayor. I want to serve something besides the same old crab cakes and sweet corn."

"The mayor?" Cammie tried to remember if she'd met him. "You mean Summer's husband?"

When the woman finally smiled, she bore an uncanny resemblance to the Grinch. "Yes, I suppose that is how Dutch is described these days. You know Summer?"

Cammie nodded. "She's great."

"And she loves this wine," Kat threw in. "She was an early adopter of the brand."

At this, the customer seemed a bit panicked. "I'll take it all. All the stock you have on hand."

While Ginger started to protest, Cammie loaded up the lady's trolley and helped her over to the cashier. A few minutes later, she be-bopped back to the wine display, whistling a merry tune.

"Let's pack it up. Our work here is done."

"What was *that*?" Ginger demanded, her cheeks pink.

"That was us selling your strawberry wine to the highest bidder and adding a ton of cachet to our brand." Cammie paused, waiting for the gratitude and accolades to start rolling in.

"But it's all gone!" Ginger threw up her hands. "The whole point of this was to get the word out!"

"Trust me: I know what I'm doing," Cammie assured her. "That lady is going to blab about her exclusive, limited-edition wine *all* over town. By the time your next batch is ready, we'll have a waiting list."

"About that waiting list . . ." an unfamiliar male voice interrupted.

The women all startled. Cammie turned around to find a tall, balding man wearing baggy cargo shorts and a threadbare Yale T-shirt.

"Couldn't help overhearing," he said with a smile.

"Yeah," Kat murmured. "'Cause you're eavesdropping."

The man pretended not to hear this. "I'm Darryl Kilgore. I have a house on the beach over in Bethany."

Cammie and Kat exchanged glances. "Okay."

"Are you really using organic strawberries in your wine?" he asked.

"Yeah, they're from a farm right down the road."

"The McKinlays' farm?"

"How do you know the McKinlays?" Cammie asked.

"Be right back." Kat rushed to help the woman who'd bought all the wine carry the bottles out to the parking lot. "Don't say anything juicy without me."

Darryl fixed his attention on Ginger. "You must be the new owner of the vineyard."

"Wait." Cammie frowned. "Who are you again?"

"I'm a summer resident who owns a number of businesses—including a wine club."

"A wine club?" Ginger looked intrigued. "People get together and drink wine? We want in."

Darryl chuckled. "The wine club sends monthly selections to its members, who live all over the country. We have the largest subscriber list of any club east of Napa." He moved in on the sole remaining bottle of strawberry wine, the one Cammie had poured samples from. "May I?"

He proceeded to taste the wine in almost a parody of pretension—swirling the liquid in the paper cup, looking down at the color of the wine, smacking his tongue as he assessed the effect on his palate.

"I like what you've done here," he finally said. "Elegant but whimsical. Very summery." He focused all his attention on Ginger. "You're the vintner?"

"Well. I use the stove in my kitchen and the shelves in the basement."

"We're looking for commercial production space," Cammie said quickly. "To comply with health and safety codes."

Ginger turned to her and whispered, "We are?"

"Starting tomorrow," Cammie murmured back.

"How soon can you make another batch of this?" Darryl asked.

Cammie waved as Summer Benson wandered into the shop.

"Hey, guys!" Summer's eyes lit up when she saw the samples. "Ooh, cake. And is that wine?"

"Not just wine—*free* wine. Cheers." Cammie stepped away from her aunt's side and filled a paper cup to the brim. "You should've been here a few minutes ago—we just sold a bunch of this to some woman who knows you."

Summer drank deeply, relishing every drop. "Who?"

"I didn't catch her name." Cammie tried to come up with a good description. "She was blond, tiny, head-to-toe Lily Pulitzer."

"That was probably Mimi Sinclair." Summer tilted her head. "Was she mean?"

"I was scared of her."

Summer nodded. "Mimi Sinclair."

"I'm kind of surprised that you two are friends," Cammie said.

Summer scoffed. "Oh, we're not."

"But you're going to her dinner party this weekend."

"That's what she thinks." Summer held out her cup for a refill.

Kat returned from the parking lot, visibly limping from pain but trying to hide it. "Oh, hey. Fancy meeting you here."

Summer put down her cup, concerned. "What's wrong?"

"Just a little twinge from an old injury." Kat sucked in her breath and pressed both hands on her back. "Ow. Sorry. Ow."

"You need to slow down," Cammie admonished her cousin. "You're going to hurt yourself. Correction—you're going to hurt yourself worse than you're already hurt."

"I'm *fine*," Kat insisted, though she was wincing.

"You don't look fine," Cammie said.

"You look like I did when I woke up in the hospital after an emergency plane landing," Summer chimed in.

Kat gritted her teeth. "Totally. Fine."

"Do I need to call Josh?" Cammie threatened.

"No. Please, no. I'll be good." Kat swore. "He'll make me lie on the couch all afternoon with a heating pad and a bottle of Advil."

"A fate worse than death," Summer said dramatically.

"Inertia *is* death," Kat informed her. "I have plans for this afternoon. They involve a tractor, not the couch."

"Listen, I'll deal with the heavy lifting. Could you stay with her?" Cammie nodded at Aunt Ginger, who was deep in conversation with the guy in the ratty T-shirt.

Kat shook her head. "That's dude's still yammering on about what a big deal he is?"

"Yeah. I don't want to leave her alone to deal with him."

"No problem. See you at home. Oh, and, Cammie?" Kat showed them the screen of her cell phone, which featured Jacques's latest glamour shot. "Our boy's practically a Kardashian."

chapter 30

The next morning, Cammie got up at four thirty, headed out to the grapevines with Jacques, and stumbled back to bed at nine a.m. She was drifting off to sleep when she heard Aunt Ginger calling her from the kitchen. "Cammie! Rise and shine!"

Cammie burrowed under her covers.

"Cammie!" The voice was closer this time. Ginger was climbing the stairs.

Cammie groaned into her pillow as the bedroom door opened.

"Camille Breyer!" Ginger whapped Cammie's feet with a rolled-up magazine. "Get yourself out of that bed this instant. I've been calling you for five minutes straight."

"You have?" Cammie lifted her head off the pillow, trying to look groggy and innocent.

"Knock it off. You're much too smart to play dumb." Ginger whacked her with the magazine again. "Now hop to. I have something to discuss with you."

"What now?" Cammie sat up, trying to steel herself for the latest fiasco.

Ginger gave Cammie's feet another smack. "Move over and I'll tell you." She sat down at the foot of the bed, her expression bemused. "You know, I always tried to do my best by you girls . . ."

Cammie's hands flew to her mouth. "Oh my God, the cancer's back."

"What? No, don't be silly."

"But you just said—"

"Let me finish." Ginger used her sternest school-secretary voice. "It's rude to interrupt."

Cammie hung her head, chastened.

"When I bought this winery, I thought it would be a good bonding experience. I thought we could have one last summer out here as a family." Ginger cleared her throat. "I also thought you and Kat needed some direction in your life, after everything that's happened this year." She smiled ruefully. "I was so busy thinking about hopes and dreams and missed opportunities that I didn't really think about the grapes."

Cammie smiled, too. "Ah yes. The grapes."

"The grapes and the roses and the fungus and the bugs and the pesticides and the weather."

"And the weeds," Cammie added. "Don't forget the weeds. And the birds."

"Ugh." Ginger made a face. "Farming is the worst."

"But we've made it this far," Cammie pointed out. "If the rain holds off, we might actually have something to harvest in the fall."

"Here's hoping." Ginger reclined and settled her head onto the pillow next to Cammie's. The two of them stared up at the shadows on the ceiling. "But while we're waiting—all three of us—for the grapes to grow, something else is happening."

Cammie thought about the kitschy wooden magnet on the refrigerator. "We're blooming where we're planted?"

"That's right." Ginger chuckled. "Well, some of us more than others."

"Listen, I'm trying. I downloaded a weather app, okay? I'm practically *American Gothic* over here."

"You're doing great, Cam. We all are. Kat bought the tractor, I fermented the strawberries, and you masterminded a marketing plan starring a toothless show dog."

"You also found a boyfriend," Cammie reminded her.

"Slow down." Ginger held up one hand. "Geoffrey and I are just dating. There's no need to label everything."

"But you like him." Cammie paused. "Hats and all."

She expected Ginger to start raving and ranting about not being so superficial, but Ginger surprised her by laughing. "He does have unusual fashion sense."

"That's an understatement."

"There was a time," Ginger conceded, "when I was, oh, about your age, when that would have put me off. I would have been too self-conscious to go out with someone who wears what he wears. But now? It's very freeing. He's confident in who he is. And that leaves me free to be who I am."

Cammie patted her aunt's arm. "I never thought of it that way."

"Well, honey, one day you'll learn: There's more to life than looking cool."

"I'm glad that you're happy and I'm glad you're confident, but are you sure he's qualified to make the wine in the fall?"

"I'm sure." Ginger sounded completely at peace with the decision.

"Then I'm on board. And I'll help with the strawberry wine, now that we're increasing production," Cammie volunteered. "As long as we're waiting for the harvest, we might as well make ourselves useful."

"Well, yesterday we did more than make ourselves useful. We made money." The mattress shifted as Ginger pulled a folded piece of paper out of her bathrobe pocket and handed it to Cammie.

Cammie unfolded the pages, then sat up and stared at her aunt. "What is this?"

"Turns out locally sourced strawberry wine has a niche market. That man at the grocery store—"

"The self-important blowhard in the Yale T-shirt?"

"That's the one. He's made a provisional offer to buy the North American distribution rights for the strawberry wine."

Cammie started scanning the documents as fast as she could.

"He said he was interested; he said he was going to write up an offer." Ginger rolled her eyes. "I thought he was blowing smoke. But five hours later, that showed up in my e-mail."

"Damn." Cammie located the financial-terms clause. "That's a lot of money."

"I know."

"You're going to get a lawyer to look this over, right?" Cammie squinted at the small typeface. "I mean, this is just an opening offer; you can probably negotiate for more."

"That's why I'm coming to you with this. You have experience in this industry. What should I be thinking about? What else do I need to know?"

Cammie started to reread the written offer from the beginning. "Well, you'll have to spell out that you'll retain the rights to the recipe, the brand name, and licensing. All he's getting is distribution rights."

"Could you write that down?"

"Sure. Let me maybe put on pants first, though."

"No hurry," Ginger assured her. "And a third of it will be yours, of course."

Cammie froze. "A third of what?"

"The distribution money." Ginger got out of bed and headed for the door. "See you at breakfast."

"No." Cammie double-checked the amount specified in the offer letter. "I can't take this."

"It's yours, honey. You earned it."

"*You* earned it," Cammie countered.

"We earned it together, so we profit together."

Cammie tried to figure out a way around this. "Then I'm going to reinvest my profit back into the vineyard."

"Nope. Sorry." Ginger turned up her nose. "It's yours. End of discussion."

"But I didn't even kick in to buy this place," Cammie protested. "I know you're still in the hole."

Ginger tightened the sash on her yellow robe. "But I love it here. As I said, this is my dream. You have other dreams."

"But—"

"Stop arguing. You're taking the money and that's final, young lady." Ginger closed the door behind her, leaving Cammie alone in her room.

"This isn't over," Cammie called after her aunt.

"Yes, it is," Ginger yelled back through the door.

Cammie felt paralyzed with conflicting emotions for a minute or two. Then she opened her closet and pulled out her running shoes. Those seemed like the right thing to wear when chasing down a dream.

The Whinery was locked and dark when Cammie arrived. She hesitated by the front door, debating her next move. It made perfect sense that a wine bar would be closed on a Saturday morning—after all, Jenna had to sleep sometime.

She slipped her fingers into her pocket and touched the smooth, folded papers that Ginger had given her. Until that morning, she'd thought that money was the only thing stopping her from trying to buy this bar. She'd convinced herself that if only funds weren't an issue, she would be brave enough to try again, despite her previous failures.

But now, looking through the plate-glass window at the empty barroom, she wasn't so sure. The Whinery was an institution in Black Dog Bay. If she ran it into the ground, the community would suffer.

Now that the biggest obstacle was out of the way, she had to admit the truth: She didn't trust herself. She knew what she wanted, but she wasn't brave enough to reach for it. She took her hand out of her pocket and turned away from the glass door. She would go back to the vineyard and keep the grapes alive until fall. That was more than enough of a challenge.

Cammie started back to her car, but before she'd taken ten steps, she heard Jenna's voice from across the street. "Hey!"

Cammie turned and raised one hand in a halfhearted wave.

"Are you looking for me?" Jenna looked rumpled in flannel pajama pants and an oversize hockey jersey.

"No, I just . . ." Cammie glanced at the Whinery, conflicted. "No."

"Come on." Jenna pointed to the Jilted Café. "Let's get coffee."

"But I—"

"Coffee."

Cammie gave in and dashed across the street. She and Jenna were lucky—a padded booth by the café's brick wall opened up as they entered.

Jenna placed her order with the nearest server: "Two huge mugs of black coffee. No, wait. Bring three, just to be safe. And maybe throw a shot of espresso in them for good measure."

Cammie stared at the curly-haired brunette. "Should we just hook you up to an IV full of caffeine and adrenaline?"

"God, I wish you could." Jenna stifled a huge yawn. "I'm exhausted. Friday nights at the bar are like a frat party."

Cammie nodded and picked up the menu, feigning interest in the omelet descriptions. "Mmm."

Jenna practically started salivating when she saw the waitress approaching with three mugs of coffee. "So, what'd you need?"

"Nothing." Cammie stared at the menu text.

"Come on, tell Auntie Jenna. Are you having another wine emergency?"

"No." Cammie finally glanced up. "The vineyard is actually under control. For once."

"That's all you can ask for." Jenna closed her eyes and savored her first sip of coffee. "If the building's still standing, I'm winning. That's what I say."

Jenna looked at Cammie.

Cammie looked at Jenna.

"Make me an offer," Jenna said. It was an order, not a request.

Cammie thought about the contract draft in her pocket.

"I'm a very reasonable woman," Jenna assured her, "who wants to move back to Boston."

"I'm about to come into some money," Cammie hedged. "But not enough to secure a business loan. I'll need a huge down payment because my last restaurant went bankrupt."

"What about finding a business partner?" Jenna pressed.

"Kat might've been willing to go in with me, but she just lost a bunch of investments. All she has in her portfolio now is a tractor."

Jenna held her mug in both hands and leveled her gaze. "I'm selling it, whether you buy it or not."

"I know." Cammie ran her fingernail along the chipped laminate tabletop. "I just don't want to screw it up."

Jenna shrugged and moved on to weighing the merits of waffles versus crepes. "Then I'm going to tell my broker to get serious about looking for other bids."

Cammie dug her phone out of her pocket as a text came in. She scanned the message, then pushed her mug away. "I have to run. Kat says a bunch of people just showed up at the vineyard. We need all hands on deck."

"Isn't it kind of early for a wine tasting?" Jenna asked.

"Oh, they're not there for the wine. They want to meet Jacques. We charge them the tasting fee as the price of admission."

"Jacques?" Jenna took another huge gulp of coffee. "The dog?"

"The patron saint of Lost Dog Vineyards." Cammie tossed down some cash. "Coffee's on me."

chapter 31

The bride showed up unannounced on a sweltering afternoon in late July.

Cammie and Ginger were sitting on the front porch, watching Josh and Kat trundle along in the rusty red tractor.

"They look so happy," Ginger said. "That tractor has really brought them together."

"And, bonus, the dead vines are gone," Cammie added.

Ginger's phone chirped, and she glanced at the screen with annoyance. "Hold on, I have to get this. It's the distributor—*again*."

"It ain't easy being a strawberry-wine mogul."

"No, it is not," Ginger agreed. "I told them twice already, the next batch won't be ready until next week." She made a noise of impatience as she put the phone to her ear and stepped inside the house. "Darryl, for the last time, you need to be patient. Good wine is like alchemy. My process is sacred."

As the screen door slammed behind Ginger, a battered old Jeep drove up the narrow gravel road. Cammie got to her feet, preparing to welcome a new group of impromptu wine tasters. But when the Jeep stopped, she recognized the couple in the front seat. She shaded her eyes with one hand. "Hey, aren't you supposed to be in South America?"

"Tomorrow." Bronwyn climbed out of the passenger's side, careful not to step on the hem of her long, gauzy white sundress. "My flight leaves at six a.m."

James came around from the driver's side, looking dapper but casual in a crisp white shirt and khakis. "I head to Oklahoma on Wednesday."

Cammie frowned, confused. "Well, then, why . . . ?"

Bronwyn took her beloved's hand and beamed. "Today's our wedding day."

"I thought you decided to postpone."

James gazed at Bronwyn with sheer adoration. "We decided to postpone the wedding, not the marriage." He reached into the Jeep's backseat and pulled out a small bouquet of daisies, which he handed to Bronwyn. The young couple looked expectantly at Cammie.

"Um . . ." was all she could manage. "Do your mothers know about this?"

"God, no." Bronwyn looked horrified at the very idea. "And no one's ever going to tell them."

"They can still have their big wedding," James chimed in. "Today is just for us."

"Is Ginger here?" Bronwyn asked. "She's the one I spoke to on the phone."

Cammie bounded up the porch steps and called through the screen door, "Aunt Ginger? Did you talk to—"

"Bronwyn! James!" Ginger bustled back to the porch. "Sorry, Cam, I forgot to tell you. I've been so busy with the strawberry wine."

Cammie looked around at all the happy, hopeful expressions. "Forgot to tell me what?"

"We're having a tiny little wedding and you're going to be a witness." Ginger made a shooing motion. "Go put on something pretty and tell Kat and Josh to come in."

The wedding was small, simple, and surreptitious.

In her casual white dress, Bronwyn no longer looked like a diffident daughter. She looked strong and confident, a woman coming into her own. "We're ready," she announced, taking James's hand.

Cammie looked around. "But who's going to marry you?"

"I am." Ginger strolled over. "Basic vows, right? Nothing fancy?"

"No frills," Bronwyn said. "We're keeping it old school."

Cammie stared at her aunt. "Since when are you allowed to officiate wedding ceremonies?"

"Since I got ordained on the Internet." Ginger beamed. "I figured if we're going to be having a lot of weddings here, I need to be prepared. So I went online, a few clicks, done. Easy peasy."

Bronwyn surveyed the barn and the vines and the house. "Let's do it by that tree over there." She strode briskly across the lawn. "Now, what about witnesses?"

"We'll be your witnesses." Kat and Josh joined them under the shade of the huge old tree.

Bronwyn and James looked into each other's eyes. Kat and Josh were gazing at each other, too.

All of them had come together in this moment because of failure. Ginger had failed to accept her limitations. Kat had failed to appreciate her husband and her marriage. Cammie had failed at her dream of owning a restaurant. They had all failed spectacularly.

And it was beautiful. Failure had set them free to find new dreams, to rebuild relationships, to discover who they really were.

"I guess we can get started."

Everyone turned to Ginger, who produced a few printed sheets of paper and began reading from them. "Dearly beloved, we are gathered here today . . ."

After the ceremony, while James and Bronwyn were setting a world record for Longest Kiss in History under a loblolly pine tree, Ginger pulled Cammie aside.

"Cammie, hon, remember those papers I gave you to look at?"

"How could I forget?"

"I want to sit down with you tonight and go over your notes. I set up an appointment with a business attorney in Rehoboth tomorrow. We're going to go forward with the distribution deal."

"How'd you find the lawyer?" Cammie asked. "A bad lawyer is worse than no lawyer, you know."

"I know. Geoffrey recommended him." Ginger reached up to cup Cammie's face in her hands. "I'm so proud of you, sweetheart."

"I'm so proud of *you*." Cammie hugged her aunt and closed her eyes. For a moment, she allowed herself to pretend that she was embracing her mother, that her mother could still see and hear and share her life. After years of trying so hard to be stern and unsentimental about this, Cammie softened and let herself feel. She expected a rush of unbearable grief—she had felt certain she'd be swamped with sorrow—but instead she felt lighter. Hopeful.

For the first time in recent memory, she was sure that her mother would be proud of her. She allowed herself, in that moment, with her face pressed to her aunt's shoulder, to remember what it felt like to be loved unconditionally.

Ginger let Cammie hold on as long as she needed to, then let her go when she was ready. And bonus: She pretended not to notice that Cammie was a teary-eyed mess.

"Good?" Ginger asked.

Cammie nodded. "Good."

Ginger looked at her expectantly. "Well, then. Don't you have places to go and people to see?"

"Only one place and one person."

chapter 32

The Whinery was gearing up for yet another jam-packed evening.

"I have good news and bad news," Cammie announced as she took a seat at the bar.

"Bad news first," Jenna said. "Always."

"The bad news is, you can't carry my aunt's strawberry wine here because she's selling exclusive distribution rights to some guy she met at the grocery store."

"What?" Jenna put down the glass she was checking for hard-water stains. "A guy at the grocery store?"

"Some fast-talking entrepreneur in a T-shirt and flip-flops." Cammie recounted the conversation. "Kat and I thought he was all talk and no action, but we were wrong. Oh, so wrong."

"Some of these summer residents are serious business," Jenna said. "They're so successful, they don't need the fancy suits and ties anymore."

"I guess you know you've arrived when you can get a deal done in shorts and sandals."

"Well, I'm happy for her." Jena paused. "You'll still sneak me bootleg bottles when no one's looking?"

"Obviously."

"All right, then. What's the good news?"

"The good news is, I'm hoping that your broker hasn't found a buyer for this place yet."

Jenna put down her dishtowel. "We haven't, actually."

"I'm ready to make you an offer." Cammie looked around, taking in the candy and the chandeliers and the cocktails. A bar by the beach, full of charm and character. Just what she'd always wanted.

"Finally." Jenna rested her elbows on the bar. "What're you thinking?"

Cammie threw out a number. The maximum she could possibly afford.

As soon as the words left her lips, she knew the answer was no. Jenna regarded her with a mixture of pity and disappointment.

"I'm sorry." Cammie wanted to shrivel up with shame. "That's the best I can do right now."

"I'm sorry, too," Jenna said. "I'd love to sell this place to you, but I need at least twice as much."

Cammie had known that buying the bar was a long shot, so she decided to settle for the next-best thing. "Even if I can't buy it right now, maybe I could work some shifts on weekends? I'm sure you could use a break sometimes."

"I could use a break right now." Jenna pulled a keyring from her pocket, slipped off a tarnished brass key, and pressed it into Cammie's palm.

"Wait, what?"

"You've run a bar before, right?"

"Yeah, I've run a whole restaurant."

"Then this should be easy." Jenna untied her black apron and draped it across the bar. "Lock up when you're done for the night."

Cammie stared down at the key. "But how do you know you can trust me?"

"It's a small town. I know where you live." Jenna lunged for the door. "You're officially hired as bartender. I'm paying you minimum wage. Congratulations, and I hope you get some big tips."

"But—"

Jenna looked back over her shoulder, her eyebrows lifting. "Think you can handle the weeknight crowd?"

Cammie picked up the apron, her fingers trembling with nerves and excitement. "I guess we'll find out."

"Call if you need anything." Jenna pushed open the swinging metal door to the back room. She raised one fist in the air. "Parole starts now. I just got out of prison, baby."

"But—"

"Oh, and, Cammie? Good luck with the health inspector."

As the door closed behind Jenna, Cammie surveyed the pink and toile walls of what the bartender described as prison. But she didn't see obligation; she saw opportunity. She tied the apron on, washed her hands, and got to work.

"It's avant-garde and a little bit boisterous. Some people might even go so far as to call it obstreperous," Cammie told the trio of women poring over the wine list.

The three heartbreak tourists oohed and aahed over Cammie's wine expertise, then asked one another what they should order.

"It's all good," Cammie assured them. "But you need to choose now, because it's last call."

"Already?" The tourists looked crestfallen. "Can't you stay open for another hour?"

"Not tonight." Cammie smiled inwardly and wondered whether Kat, Ginger, and Jacques were entertaining late-night wine tasters at the vineyard right now. "But we'll be open later on Friday and Saturday."

Fifteen minutes after she'd poured the last few drinks, she turned down the music, turned up the lights, and began ousting the late-night stragglers with a combination of finesse and firmness. Finally, twenty minutes after the official closing time, she had the bar to herself—and glasses to wash, a floor to mop, and receipts to tally. She'd been on her feet working nonstop since Jenna waltzed out the door, but she didn't feel fatigued. On the contrary, she felt energized, triumphant, abuzz with adrenaline.

This was what she was meant to do. And this tiny, unlikely bar in this tiny, unlikely town was where she was meant to do it.

If only she had more time and money to make it happen.

She crossed her arms and surveyed the black and pink barroom. She wanted this so badly, but she couldn't have it—not yet, anyway. Maybe later, next season, next year. Maybe it was for the best that she couldn't squander her new windfall the way she'd squandered the inheritance from her mother.

Maybe and maybe not. Only one thing was certain—she needed to take out the trash. She tied up two bulging black plastic bags and wrestled them out the back door and into the Dumpster in the alley. She wiped her brow as the Dumpster's lid clanged closed.

While the sound still echoed against the tall brick walls on either side of the alley, Cammie heard a low, booming bark. She glanced over her shoulder to see a huge, shaggy black dog standing at the far end of the alley, wagging his tail and watching her with dark eyes that glinted in the moonlight.

Cammie and the dog regarded each other for a long moment, both of them waiting, though she wasn't sure for what. Finally, she stepped forward and extended her hand.

"Hey, buddy. You want a treat? A bowl of water? Come here!"

The dog took a single step toward her, his tail wagging faster. Then he turned around and trotted off into the mist blowing in from the ocean.

She stared at the pavement where the dog had been standing, and was puzzled, but positive that she'd just witnessed a good omen. Rubbing the back of her neck, she headed inside. While she was rummaging through the supply closet in search of clean dish towels, she heard the front door open. The front door she was certain she'd locked.

She hurried out of the closet, calling, "Sorry, we're closed."

"My timing is perfect."

She recognized Ian's voice but was still shocked to see him when she pushed through the swinging metal door. He stood under the crystal chandelier, totally out of place in his worn jeans and dusty work boots, amid all the pink and toile. She braced both hands on the bar. "What are you doing here?"

"Finding out if the rumors are true." He took in the black apron and the stack of towels in her hand.

She put down the towels and ducked out of her apron. "What've you heard?"

"I heard you want to buy this bar."

"Oh." She forced a big, brave smile. "Well, you heard wrong, I'm afraid."

"You don't want to buy this bar?"

Cammie grabbed a glass and poured the last splashes of a bottle of tempranillo into it. "Oh, I do. But I can't." She took a sip of wine, then offered it to him. "This is all I've got left. We'll have to share it."

He accepted the glass. "What if you had a partner?"

"A wine-drinking partner? Yes, please."

He smiled and handed the glass back. "A business partner."

She stilled, watching his face.

"Could you swing it if you had someone to go in on the sale with you? Fifty-fifty?"

She kept staring at him, overwhelmed but afraid to speak. Afraid to hope.

He started to look concerned. "You okay over there? Blink twice if you can hear me."

"I . . . " She coughed, then managed to rasp, "Are you serious?"

"I'm serious. We can write up a letter of intent tomorrow."

Cammie tried to envision how this could work. "So you'll be . . . what? Like my silent partner?"

"Oh, no, I'll be right here. In your face and in your ear."

"But we close after midnight. How are you going to get up at four in the morning?"

"I'm not. I'll let my brother handle early mornings." As soon as Ian said the words, he started backpedaling. "Some of them. Maybe four a week. Maybe three."

"But you don't know anything about running a bar," she pointed out.

"You'll teach me."

She leveled her gaze at him. "Ninety percent of restaurants fail in the first year."

He smiled again, slow and warm. "Odds don't apply to us. You're going to make it work."

"*We're* going to make it work. If we do this."

He stepped closer and took her hand. They stood in the cool silence, holding on to each other with the glossy bar top between them.

"Cammie Breyer, will you be my business partner?"

"I will."

He leaned over, closed the distance, and kissed her. When he finally pulled back, he didn't ask her to stay. He didn't tell her he loved her. He didn't say they'd be partners forever.

He didn't have to.

One look and they both knew.

chapter 33

Six weeks later

The dawn broke crisp and clear on the day of the grape harvest. Cammie had set an alarm but didn't need it—she woke up at four thirty a.m., wired and jittery.

She lay perfectly still in bed, but her energy must have been contagious. Ian stirred and threw one arm around her.

"You okay?" His voice was thick and heavy with sleep.

"I'm great." Cammie felt like a child on Christmas morning. "It's harvest day! Finally!"

"It's the middle of the night," Ian protested.

"And you call yourself a farmer? Shame on you." Cammie started to get up, but Ian held her close.

"We have at least half an hour to sleep," he mumbled.

She rested her cheek against his, then kissed him. "This is a big day. I kept the grapes alive."

"Let's celebrate." He kissed her again, and she felt herself melting against him. "With sleep."

"I love you," she said against his lips. "But I have to go."

He reluctantly let her pull away. "Love you, too."

She forced herself to stand up and start getting dressed. "I gave it my all this summer, but I still hate farming."

He stood up, too, and reached for a shirt. Neither one of them turned on the light. "Then it's lucky you're not a farmer."

"Yeah, but I'm surrounded. You, my aunt, Kat—it's grapes and strawberries and tractors everywhere I turn."

"It's not too late." She could hear the smile in his voice. "You can still give in and be assimilated. Apple season is coming up."

"Never," she vowed. "I love the Whinery, and my people need me."

"They do," he agreed.

"My people, who would rather sip champagne at midnight than wake up at dawn." Cammie wrapped her arms around herself rapturously. "My people, who would rather scrub a bar top than walk the field and count the rows."

"Your people, who send back every mixed drink I make," Ian added.

"Mixed drinks are hard," she said sympathetically.

"There's so many of them!" His voice grated with frustration. "Mojitos and mimosas and Manhattans. Some woman asked for a horsefeather the other night. What the hell is a horsefeather?"

"Whiskey, ginger beer, lemon juice, and bitters," Cammie rattled off.

"How do you know that?"

"It's my life's work. Don't worry; you'll get the hang of it." She raised his hand to her lips and kissed his scratched, sunburned wrist. "If you ask nicely, I'll give you a tutorial later."

He moved his hand to cradle the nape of her neck. "Give me a tutorial now."

She pressed her half-dressed body against his. "I can't. I promised my cousin I'd help her—ooh. *Ooh*."

"Ten minutes," he murmured into her ear.

"I can't. Help me find my shoes."

"I'll help you find your shoes, your shirt, and your underwear. In ten minutes."

Twenty minutes later . . .

Cammie snapped out of her postcoital stupor long enough to glance at the clock on the nightstand. "Crap. I am so late."

"Worth it." Ian sat up next to her.

She sat up, too, and gave him a quick kiss. "And that's why we're together. Also why I'm late."

Ian watched her pull on underwear, jeans, and a sweatshirt. "I'm going to do a quick check-in with my brother about the fields, and then I'll come help you with the harvest." He handed her the shoe she was searching for. "See you soon?"

"If my family doesn't kill me." She dashed into the bathroom.

"I'm going to kill you," Aunt Ginger declared when Cammie dashed out into the vineyard. "We've been standing around waiting for you."

Cammie nodded at the line of unfamiliar cars in the driveway. "Who's 'we'?"

Kat emerged from the house, carrying a stack of plastic laundry baskets. "Everyone."

And, indeed, it did seem as though half the populace of Black Dog Bay was lining up to take a basket from Kat. Cammie recognized

Summer, Jenna, Brighton, and lots of the regulars from the Whinery, but there were several unfamiliar faces.

"I set up a mailing list," Kat said by way of explanation.

"You're so clever!" Ginger exclaimed.

Kat shrugged. "Everyone kept saying they wanted to help with harvest, so I figured, *Free labor. Why not?*"

"Always so enterprising." Josh put his arm around Kat.

"You know it. Now let's get this show on the road." Kat glanced at her watch. "We've got to get this done in the next two days, because our flight leaves Wednesday night."

Josh had decided to spend his upcoming sabbatical in France and Italy. While he reviewed literature from the Age of Enlightenment, Kat would be apprenticing at vineyards, learning about soil, sunlight, and moisture. Her goal was to be prepared to take over as chief grape grower by next spring. Jacques would be staying with Ginger and Cammie in Black Dog Bay, so his adoring fans could make pilgrimages to take selfies with him.

After all the locals and tourists had equipped themselves with baskets, pails, or boxes, Aunt Ginger climbed the porch steps and held up her hand for silence. She addressed her attentive audience as if she were winning an Oscar.

"First of all, I'd like to thank my niece, Cammie Breyer, for keeping the grapes alive."

Applause all around. Cammie curtsied, almost stumbling over Jacques, who was stationed at her side.

"And my daughter, Kat, and my son-in-law, Josh, for working mechanical miracles with our tractor."

More clapping and cheering.

"Before we begin, we have to make sure that the grapes are ready." Ginger turned toward Cammie.

"Oh, they're ready," Cammie assured her. "I would never have gotten up this early if they weren't."

Ginger lowered her voice. "I know that, honey. But all these people showed up. Give them a show."

"Um . . ." Cammie was relieved to see Geoffrey approaching with a cluster of grapes and some technical-looking equipment.

"Taste these." Geoffrey made a big show of presenting her with the grapes.

"Okay." Cammie bit into the purple grape, noting the rich, deep color. When her teeth broke the skin, the grape popped, releasing sweet, crisp juice.

"Not too acidic?" Geoffrey prompted. "Not sour?"

"It's perfect," Cammie declared loudly. "Nice and . . . grapey."

"All right, then. Let's check the Brix degrees on the refractometer." Geoffrey produced a small red plastic box and started squeezing a grape.

"Yes." Cammie tried to look knowledgeable. "Let's."

Eventually, Geoffrey decreed that the grapes were ready, and everyone raced to the vineyard, exclaiming as they went:

"This is so romantic!"

"It's like that one *I Love Lucy* episode."

"Wait until I tell everyone at home that I worked in a vineyard—they'll be so jealous."

They donned gloves and set to work, and it was fulfilling and exciting and almost magical. For about twenty minutes. Then the sweating commenced, the bugs came out, and they all started to notice the ache in their shoulders and the parched feelings in their throats.

"Hey." A Whinery regular wandered over from the next row of vines and handed her basket to Cammie. "I just remembered, I have an appointment this morning."

Cammie glanced at the few grapes that had made it into the basket. "An appointment?"

"Yeah. Gotta run."

Ten minutes later, Summer's sister-in-law, Ingrid, announced that she had a term paper to write.

Two minutes after that, a pair of tourists experienced the shocking realization that they needed to dial in to a work conference call immediately.

And then the floodgates were open:

"Ooh, look at this cut, I should go to urgent care."

"I have to, um, get a cavity filled. I better get to the dentist."

"Have I told you I'm trying to break into acting? Yeah. I just took new head shots last week, and my agent might be calling. My cell has no bars out here. I'm going to head back into town."

Cammie collected their grapes and thanked them for coming. As the morning wore on, the harvesting group dwindled until only she, Ginger, Geoffrey, Kat, and Josh remained.

But that was fine; her family was all she needed. She took a moment to stretch and assess the progress they'd made. This vineyard—this entire summer—hadn't been what she'd expected. But it'd been exactly what she needed.

As she stooped down to resume picking, she heard the rumble of tires on the gravel driveway.

"Hey, Cammie!" Kat yelled from a few rows away. "Your boyfriend-slash–business partner's here!"

Ian got out of the truck and strode across the dirt to offer Cammie gifts more precious than diamonds or pearls.

"Here." He handed her a bottle of ibuprofen and a bottle of cold water.

"Have I told you lately that I love you?" She wrapped her arms around him. "How did you know I'd need this?"

He kissed the top of her head. "I'm a farmer."

"Oh, that's right." She closed her eyes as he rubbed her lower back. "Ow. My back. My neck. My arms. Ow. My whole body hurts."

"I was wondering why you were so excited to get up this morning."

"Because I thought grape harvesting would be spiritual and satisfying." She gave him a little swat. "Stop laughing."

"Why the hell did you think picking grapes would be spiritual?"

"Because the movies. *Stop laughing.* In the movies, it's all Tuscan landscapes and canoodling under the vines and, like, Russell Crowe and Keanu Reeves." She took her ibuprofen, swigged the water, and tried to look on the bright side. "At least we had help. For a while." She told him about the mass exodus of volunteers. "It was kind of entertaining, though. All the excuses."

"So now it's just you and the grapes?" He grabbed a discarded pair of leather work gloves and picked up one of the empty pails.

Cammie smiled. "It's me, the grapes, and my family." She kissed him. "And you."

"And the bar." He kissed her back. "You've got a lot going on."

"Stop talking and get back to work!" Kat yelled from two rows away. "These grapes aren't going to pick themselves!"

"Leave her alone!" Ginger cried from somewhere off to the left. "She's been working nonstop all summer!"

Cammie rested her chin on Ian's shoulder. Her gaze skimmed over the rosebushes and that's when she saw it.

"Hey." She pulled away and turned him around so he could see the red blooms on the young green climbing rose. "Look at that."

He followed her gaze, resting his hand on her back. "I see it."

"That's not supposed to happen." She glanced up at him. "You said that wouldn't bloom for another two years."

"It shouldn't."

"It's too early. And summer is over."

He nodded in agreement.

"This is the wrong time." She could smell subtle notes of the roses' fragrance on the breeze. "It's totally out of season."

"It sure is." Ian looked unperturbed.

"Then how . . . ?"

"Nature doesn't care what's 'supposed' to happen. Things bloom when they're ready to bloom."

The scarlet blossoms provided a vivid contrast to the field of green and gold. What had originally been a mistake had turned into something bright and beautiful and completely unexpected.

"It's official," Cammie decreed. "These are the days of wine and roses."

"And tractors and French bulldogs," Ian added.

"And you and me." Cammie put her scraped, dirt-smudged hand on Ian's, and together they reached for the vines. "Living the dream."

READERS GUIDE

once upon a wine

BETH KENDRICK

READERS GUIDE

QUESTIONS FOR DISCUSSION

1. At various points in this story, Cammie is urged to "bloom where you're planted." How does this theme recur, both literally and figuratively, as Ginger, Kat, and Cammie struggle to adapt to life at the vineyard?

2. Ginger decides to pursue her wildest dream only after she believes she has terminal cancer. If you received a similar diagnosis, what would you regret not having done?

3. Cammie inherits money and the recipe for strawberry wine from her mother, and in the end, both of these shape her future. What are the most important legacies (material and emotional) you've gotten from your parents and grandparents?

4. In the throes of an identity crisis, Kat puts her relationship in crisis. Do you have any empathy for the way she behaved at the beginning of the story? What relationship advice would you have given Kat if she had come to you?

5. Bronwyn finished school before planning her wedding, but was initially willing to forgo a once-in-a-lifetime educational opportunity to be with her husband. In your opinion, are there certain items you should check off your "life list" before getting married? If so, what?

6. Ian and Cammie started a habit of walking the fields and "counting the rows," which Jacques the French bulldog eagerly joins in on. What do you think might be calming about this ritual, and do you have any similar rituals in your own life?

7. Cammie and Ian parted ways at age twenty-two because they were drastically different people who wanted drastically different things. Years later, they reunite and agree to compromise, but they're still very different. How did each one change to make compromise possible?

8. Every year, Ian buys a copy of the *Farmers' Almanac*, which he says is unreliable . . . "but it might be." What does this superstition say about him and the farming life?

9. Ginger spent most of her life trying to compensate for Kat's lack of a father and Cammie's lack of a mother. To what extent is she "owed" their support in her vineyard venture? At what point in a child's life should parents be able to return their focus to their own goals and personal relationships?

Read on for an excerpt from

cure for the common *breakup*

Available now from New American Library

chapter 1

"Good evening, ladies and gentlemen. This is your captain speaking."

"He's so hot." Summer Benson nudged her fellow flight attendant Kim. "Even his voice is hot."

"Welcome to our flight from New York to Paris." Aaron's voice sounded deep and rich, despite the plane's staticky loudspeaker. "Flying time tonight should be about seven hours and twenty-six minutes. We're anticipating an on-time departure, so we're going to ask you to move out of the aisles and take your seats as quickly as possible."

Summer leaned back against the drink cart in the tiny first-class galley. "Ooh, I love it when he tells me what to do."

Kim, a petite Texan with a sleek blond bob, rolled her eyes and started checking the meals that had arrived from catering. "Get a room."

"As soon as we get to Paris, we will," Summer assured her. "And then we're going to walk by the Seine and go to the Eiffel Tower and eat croissants. If it's cheesy and touristy, we're doing it. I actually packed a beret."

"I was wondering why you had two gigantic carry-ons," Kim said. "That's a lot of luggage for a three-day layover."

"One bag's half full of scandalous lingerie," Summer replied. "I left the other half empty so I can buy more scandalous lingerie." She frowned at a snag in her silky black nylons. "These eight-hour flights are hell on my stockings. This pair was my favorite, too. They're all lacy at the top. Hand-embroidered."

Kim's jaw dropped. "You're wearing thigh-highs? All the way to Paris? Do you hate yourself? Do you hate your veins?"

"When I'm on a flight to Paris with my boyfriend, I don't wear support hose. Not now, not ever."

"And do you hate your feet?" Kim glanced down at Summer's patent leather stilettos. "I don't have a ruler with me, but I'm guessing those heels are higher than two and a half inches." She shook her index finger. "Airline regulations."

"Airline regulations also state that we have to wear black shoes and black tights with a navy uniform," Summer said. "That doesn't make it right. Besides, France has laws against ugly shoes. You can look it up."

"You're going to be begging for flats by the time you're through with the salad service," Kim predicted.

Summer had to admit that her coworker had a point—international first-class service didn't offer a lot of downtime. Between distributing hot towels, drinks, place settings and linens, appetizers, salads, entrées, fruit and cheese, dessert, coffee, cordials, warm cookies, and finally breakfast, a sensible flight attendant would wear comfortable footwear.

Summer had never been accused of being sensible.

"The only thing more high-maintenance than the meal service is me," she said. "I refuse to be hobbled by a few plates of lettuce."

Kim ducked out of the galley with a pair of plastic water bottles.

"Hang on. I'm going to go check if the pilots want anything before takeoff. Want me to say hi to your boyfriend?"

"Sure, and ask if he has any M&M's. I forgot to bring a fresh supply, and he knows I'm an addict."

Two minutes later, Kim returned from the flight deck, walking as fast as her polyester pencil skirt permitted. "I just saw Aaron!"

"Score." Summer held out her palm as Kim handed over a bag of candy. "He truly is the best boyfriend ever. I'll have to keep him around for a while."

"For a while? How about forever?" Kim clutched Summer's forearm and gave her a little shake. "He has a diamond ring for you!"

Summer pulled away and braced both hands on the narrow, metal-edged countertop.

"It's gorgeous!" Kim squealed. "He was showing it to the first officer when I opened the door."

Where was an oxygen mask when you needed one? Summer inhaled deeply, smelling stale coffee grounds and the plummy red wine Kim had just uncorked for a passenger.

"I . . ." She waited for her emotions to kick in. She should laugh. Cry. Faint dead away. *Something.*

"He's going to propose in Paris! How romantic." Kim looked as though *she* might faint dead away. "A guy like him, with a ring like that . . . God, you're so lucky."

All at once the emotions kicked in. Complete, overwhelming terror, served up with a side of denial. "Slow down—slow down." Summer sagged back against the counter. "This is crazy. I mean, Aaron and I have a great time together, but we've certainly never talked about marriage."

"Well, why else would he buy a diamond ring?"

"Maybe it's for his mom. Or his sister." Summer scrambled for any plausible explanation. "Maybe he's carrying it for a friend, like a drug mule for Cartier. He's not proposing—he's just smuggling!"

"No way. You should have seen his face." Kimberly clasped her hands beside her cheek. "He looked so nervous. It was adorable." Her rapturous expression flickered for just a moment. "He made me promise not to tell you. Oops."

"Oh my God," Summer rasped.

"I know!"

"Oh my God." She grabbed the nearest bottle of wine and took a swig. "Don't serve that."

"You know where you should go?" Kim's eyes sparkled. "There's a great little boutique hotel right off rue du Faubourg Saint-Honoré. Hotel de la something. I'll Google it. Super-swanky, super-secluded." She shook her head. "I guess wearing thigh-highs and four-inch heels was a good call, after all."

Summer took another bracing sip of wine and wiped her lips on the back of her hand. "I can't believe this."

"Me, neither!" Kim planted her hands on her hips. "We've all been drooling over Aaron Marchand for years, and you get to spend the rest of your life with him? Not fair. You've landed the unlandable bachelor."

"Well . . ." Summer realized, as she forced herself to release her death grip on the wine bottle, that her hands were shaking. "I haven't landed him yet. I mean, this ring is still speculation and hearsay at this point."

"*Pfft.* I know an engagement ring when I see one." Kim pursed her lips in a little pout. "One less tall, dark, and handsome man for the rest of us." She sighed, then frowned at Summer. "Wait. Why are you freaking out?"

"I'm not freaking out." Summer straightened up and cleared her throat. "But, you know, let's not get ahead of ourselves. He hasn't actually asked. I haven't said yes."

Kim laughed. "Come on. You wouldn't say no to Aaron Marchand." Her eyes widened. "Would you?"

Summer ducked her head and let her hair fall over her eyes. "Well . . ."

Kim wrapped her fingers around Summer's arm again and demanded, "How old are you?"

"Um. Thirty-two."

"Thirty-two," Kim repeated. "And you've done your share of partying, yes?"

Summer nodded. "I'm sure you've heard the rumors. They're all true."

"Okay, so you've had your fun. But, let's face it, you're not twenty-five anymore."

"Twenty-five is a state of mind." Summer tried and failed to free herself from Kim's grasp.

"You're never going to do better than Aaron Marchand. You know that, right?"

Summer stared down at her shiny patent shoes.

"What are you waiting for? Why on earth would you say no?" Kim threw up both hands in exasperation.

Summer darted around her fellow flight attendant and escaped into the first-class cabin. "Hold that thought. I have to go do the dog and pony show." She took her place beneath the TV monitor while the safety demonstration video played. While she pointed out the emergency exits, she scanned the sea of faces, looking for any sign of potential troublemakers.

But tonight the passengers looked docile and weary, most of them ignoring her as the video droned on about inflatable slides and oxygen masks. An elderly couple was already sleeping in the third row, the wife resting her head on her husband's shoulder.

Summer found a thin navy blanket and draped it across the couple's armrests. Then, she dashed to the bulkhead and dialed her best friend, Emily's, number.

When Emily's voice mail picked up, Summer started raving

into the receiver: "Hey, I know you're in Vancouver and you probably have thirty thousand things going on right now, but I need a consult. I'm about to take off for Paris with Aaron. The pilot, remember? The one who's all perfect and dreamy and nice? Well, he's about to ask me to marry him. *Marry him.* Out of nowhere! Like an ambush! What should I say? What should I do? Call me back, Em. I'm scared."

She hung up, rested her forehead against the cool, curved plastic walls of the cabin, and forced herself to arrange a smile on her lips before she turned back to the passengers. As she walked through the cabin to do her final safety compliance check ("Fasten your seat belt, please. . . . Here, let me help you with that tray table"), she was waylaid by a passenger with an English accent and a red soccer jersey. He exuded entitlement and the smell of stale beer, and she guessed he was either a professional athlete or a professional musician.

"Could you take this, doll?" He handed her a magazine that had been left in his seat pocket.

"Of course." When Summer took the magazine from him, he brushed his fingers against hers.

"You're gorgeous. Has anyone ever written a song about you?" He met her gaze, then gave her a thorough once-over. Charming, cocky, and incorrigible. A year ago, she would have been all over him.

But she had finally outgrown bad boys. She had finally moved on to a good man. The kind of man she should marry.

"Twice, actually." Summer laughed at the passenger's expression. "What, you think you're the only musician to ever fly commercial?"

"Anyone written a song about you that people have actually heard?" He grinned gamely. "Won Grammys? Gone platinum?"

"Sounds like someone could use a big glass of ice water."

He leaned into the aisle until the side of his head grazed her hip. "What's your name?"

She gave his perfectly coiffed hair a pat. "I'll be right back."

"What's that?" Kim asked when Summer squeezed into the galley to dispose of the magazine.

"Oh, 4C found it in his seat pocket." Summer glanced at the photo on the cover: a quaint seaside village featuring golden sand dunes and gray cedar-shingled houses. The headline read: *The Best Place in America to Bounce Back from Your Breakup.*

"Black Dog Bay, Delaware." Kim peered over her shoulder. "Never heard of it."

"Me, neither. I don't think they even have an airport in Delaware."

"Black Dog Bay. Where all the stores sell Ben & Jerry's and Kleenex."

Summer laughed. "And multiple cats are mandatory."

"And the official uniform is sweatpants and a ratty old bathrobe."

"And *Steel Magnolias* is on TV twenty-four/seven."

Kim tossed the periodical in the trash. "What you need is a magazine all about awesome honeymoon destinations. Because when Aaron Marchand says, 'Will you marry me?,' you say, 'Yes.'"

"We're number two for takeoff," Aaron's voice intoned. "Flight attendants, please be seated."

Summer buckled herself into the jump seat by the bulkhead, facing the passengers in coach. As the plane began to taxi, she automatically "bowed to the cockpit," tilting her head in the direction of the flight deck as a precaution against whiplash.

As always, she devoted the last moments before takeoff to conducting a mental inventory of the emergency medical equipment and glancing around the cabin for ABAs—able-bodied assistants—who could potentially help out in a crisis.

Then they were lifting off and she was thinking about Aaron. Visualizing a diamond ring and fighting back the sour taste of bile in her throat.

It wasn't that she didn't love him. She did love him, more than she'd meant to.

But could she keep his heart without wearing his ring?

Thump.

She heard a loud bang and felt the plane shudder.

"What was that?" A woman gasped. Passengers started murmuring in both English and French.

Summer put on her best flight attendant face, striving to convey both competence and nonchalance as the passengers looked to her for guidance. Her job was to keep everyone calm and safe. And to figure out what the hell was going on.

The plane continued to gain altitude, but something about the alignment was off. Her stomach lurched as the cabin tilted suddenly.

"Oh my God!" someone screamed. "Fire!"

Summer saw the bright streak of flames out the window and knew, with sickening certainty, that an engine was on fire.

We're going to die.

Every muscle in her body locked up, and for a long moment, she was frozen. Her mind went blank.

And then years of training overrode her panic. She grabbed the gray plastic interphone next to her seat and dialed the code for the flight deck.

She pressed the receiver to her ear and waited to hear Aaron's voice, telling her that everything would be fine.

The pilots didn't pick up.

As soon as she hung up, Kim rang from the galley: "Did you feel that? What's going on?"

"I'm not sure." Summer was acutely aware of the panicked gazes of the passengers. "It's possible one of the engines is damaged." She lowered her voice. "Fire."

Kim sucked in her breath. "What did the pilots say?"

"Nothing yet. I tried to reach them, and they're not picking up."

Kim didn't respond to that; she didn't have to. They both knew what it meant.

Summer put down the phone and concentrated on calming the passengers in coach. "Yes, I felt that, too. Yes, I see the flames. But don't worry, the pilots have this under control. We're all trained for this sort of thing and, you know, the plane can fly perfectly well with only one engine."

We're going to die.

She kept her hand clamped on the interphone, waiting to hear from the flight deck. But there was nothing.

The plane stopped climbing.

Halfway through her breezy explanation of aerospace engineering, the plane tilted sharply and plummeted downward. People started screaming again.

After what seemed like an eternity but was probably only a second or two, the plane leveled off again, and Summer started breathing.

Still no word from the flight deck.

The cabin lights blinked off and the screams faded into tense silence. Her memory summoned snapshots of her past, the proverbial life flashing before her eyes.

She'd seen the northern lights in Sweden and fed baby elephants in Thailand. She'd danced at Carnival in Brazil and gone snorkeling on the Great Barrier Reef. She'd traveled all over the world having once-in-a-lifetime experiences.

But she'd never had a garden.

She'd never learned to play the piano.

She'd never let herself fall completely in love.

This is the worst bucket list ever.

If she weren't so petrified, she'd laugh. Pianos were for singing along to and draping oneself across while wearing a sequined gown.

And a garden? Really? That was crazy talk. She'd never even *wanted* a garden.

As for love, well, she could try, right? She could open up and let herself be vulnerable. She could accept Aaron's marriage proposal and settle down and live happily ever after.

I can't.

She white-knuckled the vinyl seat cushion and tried to keep a smile on her face. Tried to slow her heartbeat and catch her breath and say something comforting and authoritative.

The plane pitched sideways again and plummeted down through the darkness. The thick shoulder straps of her seat belt bit into her flesh despite the sensation of weightlessness. She heard the rush of her pulse in her ears. She felt a flood of adrenaline coursing through her limbs.

She forced herself to keep her eyes open as she braced her body for the impact she knew was coming.

chapter 2

Two days later

Before she even opened her eyes, Summer could smell roses. The floral perfume was stale and cloying, almost nauseating, in the warm, dry hospital air.

She lay motionless while she regained her bearings, mentally reviewing the few facts she'd been able to retain over the past forty-eight hours:

My head is concussed.

My back is burned.

My ribs and spleen are tore up from the floor up.

Walk it off.

She was safe. No matter how many times she repeated that to herself, she still couldn't quite believe it. Even though she could feel the tissue-thin cotton of the hospital gown on her shoulders and the starched bedsheets against her calves, even though the confusion of the last few days was punctuated with flashbulb memories of doctors and nurses changing her bandages and asking her questions ("Can you tell me your name?" "Can you tell me what year it is?"), she couldn't recall anything about how she'd gotten from the plane to the hospital.

She remembered prepping for takeoff to Paris. She remembered the bag of M&M's and Kim teasing her about her shoes and the British passenger who smelled like a distillery. She remembered the plane's sudden lurch and the screams in the darkness and the acrid smell of smoke. But then there was a gap, a thick and impenetrable mist clouding her memory. All she knew for sure was that she'd been in a New Jersey medical center for two days now, and a dozen red roses had arrived with Aaron's signature on the card.

So she understood, on a detached, intellectual level, that she was safe. Her body would mend.

Aaron was safe, too. He'd been busy with debriefings and corporate damage control, but he'd be here as soon as he could. In the meantime, he'd sent flowers she could smell even in her sleep.

So now she had to open her eyes, start patching reality back together, and figure out what to do next.

Or at least try to get her hands on some good drugs.

She took a deep breath, wincing as sharp pain shot through her rib cage, and surveyed the tiny private room. Her lips were chapped, her throat parched. There was a plastic tan water pitcher just out of arm's reach—*so close, yet so far*—on a low metal table. Various electronic monitors hummed and beeped, and a flimsy shade covered the steel-framed window.

She startled as she heard a soft rustling from across the room. Her neck ached as she turned her head to glimpse a shadowed figure seated in the vinyl recliner next to the door.

"You're awake," Aaron's voice said.

She could hear him, but she couldn't see him. Just like the moments before takeoff. Overwhelmed by emotions she couldn't even name, she had to try three times before her dry throat would swallow.

"You're here." Her voice came out thin and hoarse.

"I've been here all afternoon." He got to his feet, cutting a striking silhouette in the late afternoon shadows. The handsome hero, straight out of central casting.

She had dated handsome men before. Fascinating, witty men who were long on charisma and short on integrity. They wined and dined her. They enthralled her. They left her at the first sign of trouble.

Until Aaron.

He was so much more than handsome; he was honest and hardworking and respectful and loyal. The kind of man that every woman hoped for.

Summer had never seen herself as the marrying type, and in fact had strict rules in place: *Never stay in one place too long. Never stay with one man too long.* She knew what would happen if she broke these rules. If she needed a man more than he needed her. She had experienced the fallout firsthand.

Kim was right. Summer should be able to do this—to grow up and settle down and form lasting attachments. Her friends were all getting married, having babies, buying houses. Being adults. Being normal. They made it look so effortless, this transition from reckless youth into stable families. As if the whole thing couldn't unravel at any second.

She loved Aaron; he loved her. He had literally saved her life. She should marry him.

I can't.

"Why didn't you wake me up?" She struggled to sit up straighter, wincing and reaching for the water pitcher.

"You need your rest." He intercepted the pitcher and poured lukewarm water into a clear plastic cup. "Ice?"

She shook her head again, heedless of the pain, and gulped the water. Despite the steady drip from the saline IV, her body craved fluid. She felt empty inside, almost hollow.

He adjusted the window shade, and as golden sunlight streamed in, she saw worry and fatigue etched in the lines of his face. The sparkle in his blue eyes had gone flat, and his devil-may-care grin had given way to an expression of grim resolve. He still wore a crisp navy pilot's blazer, but he'd unfastened the buttons of his white shirt, and she could see a patch of gauze taped to his collarbone.

And, in that moment, both of them half-hidden and half-revealed in the shadows and sunlight, she sensed something different about him, a subtle shift in the way he looked at and spoke to her.

"Come here." She put down the cup and stretched out her hand to him. "Are you okay? What happened to your shoulder?"

He took a single step in her direction. "Nothing, just a scratch."

"That's a pretty impressive bandage for 'just a scratch.'"

"It's nothing," he repeated. "You got banged up pretty good, though. I've been calling two or three times a day for updates." He came closer and smiled down at her. "You look great."

She tried to laugh, but it came out as a cough. "You lie."

"It's the truth." He brushed a strand of hair back from her cheek. "Not a scratch on that perfect face."

"Tell that to my spleen." As she gazed up at him, she felt the same hot rush of attraction she'd experienced the first time she'd met him.

His right hand patted his blazer pocket, then fell away. Reached again and fell away. And then she remembered: the ring.

She picked up her cup as her throat went dry again.

"I'm sorry I couldn't be here with you the whole time," Aaron said. "But legal had to interrogate me. And then the public relations team had their turn."

"Public relations?"

"Oh, yeah. They want to make sure they spin this as a victory against all odds rather than an equipment failure that justifies a lawsuit. I had to go on one of those morning shows yesterday, and tonight I'm booked for some cable news interviews. Hence, the uniform."

"I bet you did great. You're very photogenic, and—" She broke off as his hand drifted back to his pocket.

He rocked back on his heels. "That's what the public relations team said. They had the first officer go on air with me. Kim, too. Said her Southern accent was good for the company image. They wanted you, too, but . . ."

Summer let her head settle back against the pillow. "I'm an unreliable witness whacked out on pain pills and prone to passing out."

"They didn't use those exact words." He finally came close enough to kiss her, pressing his lips against the top of her head. "Does that hurt?"

"No." She tilted her face up so he could kiss her on the mouth. "Thank you for the flowers." She nodded at the bouquet. The rose petals had gone dark and crisp around the edges.

His hand went all the way into the pocket this time, and he started to extract something before he changed his mind and put it back. "Summer. You know I love you." He sat down next to her on the bed.

"I love you, too," she forced out.

"How much do you remember about the landing?" he asked.

She finally drew a breath. "What?"

"The doctors won't tell me much since I'm just your boyfriend and not your husband."

She stilled. "Uh-huh."

"And your family isn't . . . They're not returning my calls." He shifted his weight. "I looked up your dad's office number on the university Web site. His department secretary said he's out of town. And your mother . . ."

He gazed at her, a glimmer of pity in his eyes.

Summer lifted her chin and stared at the roses.

He waited for her to respond for another long minute, then gave up. "Anyway, from what I've managed to get out of the nurses, you don't remember much."

"Yeah." She laced her fingers together and squeezed, wondering where he was going with this. "Everything after takeoff's a little hazy. They told me one of the engines blew out?"

He nodded. "I had to make an emergency landing. We didn't have time to circle and dump the fuel, so things got pretty exciting for a minute, but we made it."

"Is that why I have burns on my back?"

"Like I said, things got a little exciting."

"But you saved us," she said. "You're a hero."

"*You're* the hero," he corrected. "Once we got back on the ground, people were trying to get out the emergency doors, and a little boy fell in the aisle. You managed to push back the crowd and pull him up."

Summer suddenly wanted an extra dose of morphine. "I let go of the door handle?"

Aaron nodded. "That's how you got hurt. You fell onto the tarmac."

"Which is why we're not supposed to let go of the door handle." Summer shook her head. "That's like, flight attendant 101." She closed her eyes and concentrated, sifting through her consciousness for any recollection. "I really . . . I can't remember any of that."

"The whole thing was over in less than five minutes," Aaron said. "But those five minutes changed everything." He reached into his pocket.

She held her breath and waited for him to produce the ring.

And waited. And waited.

He continued to look at her with that wistful expression. "I do love you, Summer."

"I love you, too." She smiled. "We're even."

He stood up and turned his back to her. "There's so many things I want to say to you, and I don't know where to begin."

She couldn't stand this any longer. "I know about the ring, Aaron."

He froze, then turned to face her. "You do?"

"Kim told me everything." She waited for him to look up.

"Okay, then." His hand moved back to his pocket. "Kim was right. There was a ring."

"'Was'? Past tense?"

He caught her gaze and held it. "When I said I love you, I meant it. I've loved every minute we've spent together. You're fun. You're spontaneous. You make me laugh."

"Okay," she said faintly. "But . . . ?"

"I love you. But I don't love you enough."

She went perfectly still.

He watched her face. "Say something."

She took a moment, cleared her throat. "You're breaking up with me?"

He lifted his shoulders and blew out a breath. "I've been carrying that ring around for months."

Her stomach clenched. "Months?"

"I wanted to ask you to marry me. I really did. But it never seemed to be the right time. And after a while . . ."

"You were going to propose in Paris," she insisted. "It would have been perfect."

"It would've been," he agreed. "But we didn't make it to Paris. And maybe that's a sign." He turned his face away. "Please don't take this personally. My whole life has changed in the last few days. I've realized that all the clichés are true. Life is short. We can't do things halfway. And you and I, we had fun, but we're not marriage material. There's something missing. I wish I could explain it better, but I can't."

She took her time sipping the lukewarm water.

"You'll be fine." He couldn't even look at her. "You're the strongest woman I know."

Walk it off.

At this, Summer finally regained her voice.

"Go." Her voice came out flat and low. "Just go."

"I'm sorry." He reached for her, but she flinched away.

"Don't apologize," she said. "I don't want apologies. I don't want explanations. I just want you to go."

Still, he hesitated.

Her voice got louder, sharper. "Please."

As the door closed behind him, she felt the prickle of tears in her eyes, but she managed to compose herself. Aaron was right about her strength—she had always been resourceful and resilient. When life got hard, she didn't stop—she put one foot in front of the other, moving faster and farther until she pushed through the pain.

She would survive this, she knew. She always did.

And in the end, Aaron wasn't the one who got away. He was the one who reminded her of everything she'd been trying to get away from.

The room seemed to close in on her. She couldn't bear to stay here, confined, inhaling the scent of dying roses with every breath. So she did the only thing she could under the circumstances: She hit the call button, and when the nurse arrived, she announced, "Bring the consent forms or whatever I need to sign. I'm discharging myself, effective immediately."

Before the nurse could start arguing, the door swung wide again and a firm, feminine voice rang through the room: "Simmer down, crazycakes. No one's going anywhere."

This time, Summer couldn't hold back her tears. "Emily?"

Photo by Anna Peña

Beth Kendrick is the author of twelve women's fiction novels, including *Put a Ring On It*, *New Uses for Old Boyfriends*, *Cure for the Common Breakup*, *The Week before the Wedding*, *The Lucky Dog Matchmaking Service*, and *Nearlyweds*, which was turned into a Hallmark Channel original movie. Although she lives in Arizona, she loves to vacation on the Delaware shore, where she brakes for turtles, eats boardwalk fries, and wishes that the Whinery really existed.

CONNECT ONLINE

bethkendrick.com
facebook.com/bethkendrickbooks
twitter.com/bkendrickbooks